CHAPTER ONE

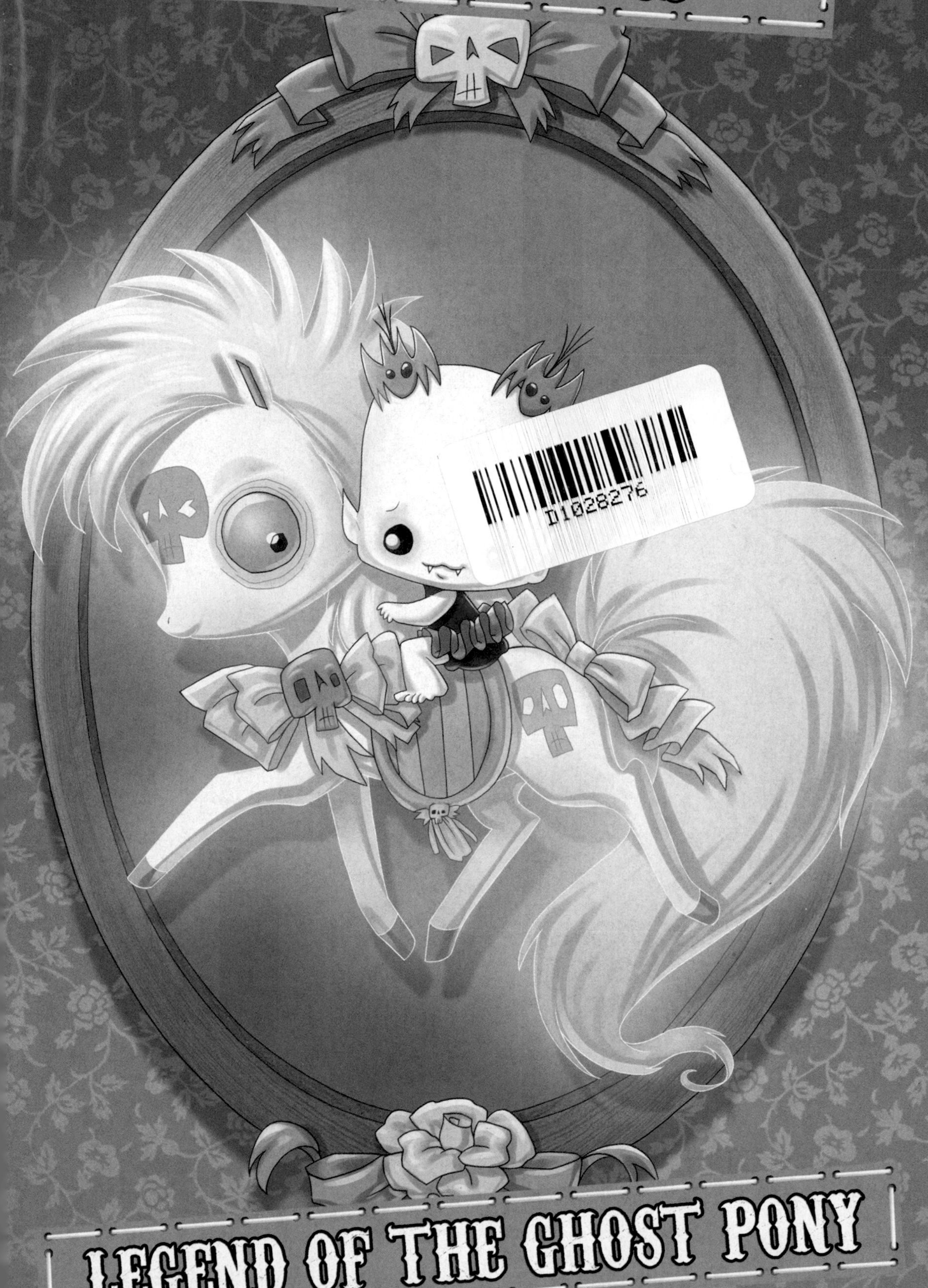

LEGEND OF THE GHOST PONY

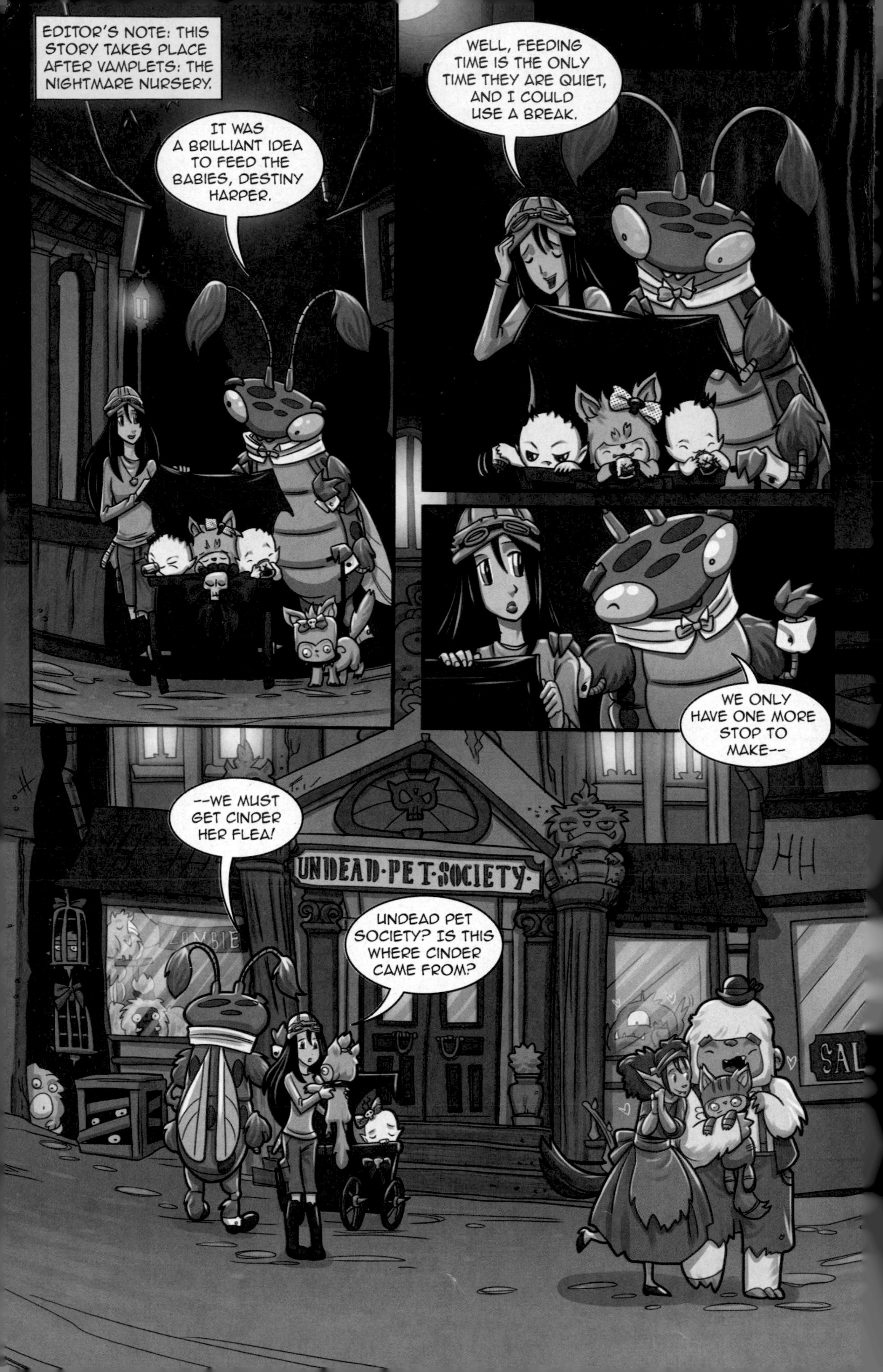
EDITOR'S NOTE: THIS STORY TAKES PLACE AFTER VAMPLETS: THE NIGHTMARE NURSERY.
IT WAS A BRILLIANT IDEA TO FEED THE BABIES, DESTINY HARPER.
WELL, FEEDING TIME IS THE ONLY TIME THEY ARE QUIET, AND I COULD USE A BREAK.
WE ONLY HAVE ONE MORE STOP TO MAKE--
--WE MUST GET CINDER HER FLEA!
UNDEAD·PET·SOCIETY
UNDEAD PET SOCIETY? IS THIS WHERE CINDER CAME FROM?

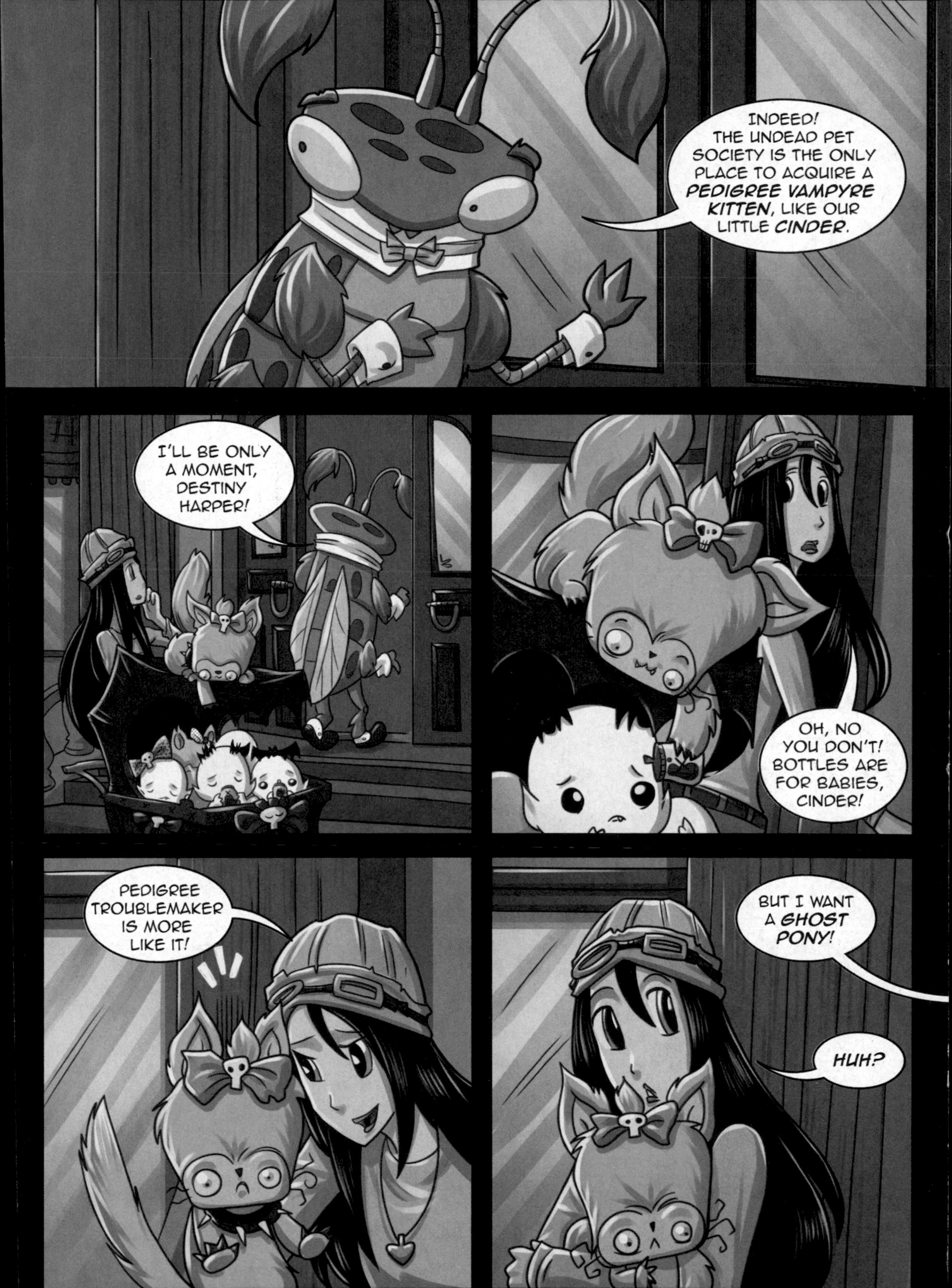
INDEED! THE UNDEAD PET SOCIETY IS THE ONLY PLACE TO ACQUIRE A *PEDIGREE VAMPYRE KITTEN*, LIKE OUR LITTLE *CINDER*.
I'LL BE ONLY A MOMENT, DESTINY HARPER!
OH, NO YOU DON'T! BOTTLES ARE FOR BABIES, CINDER!
PEDIGREE TROUBLEMAKER IS MORE LIKE IT!
BUT I WANT A *GHOST PONY*!
HUH?

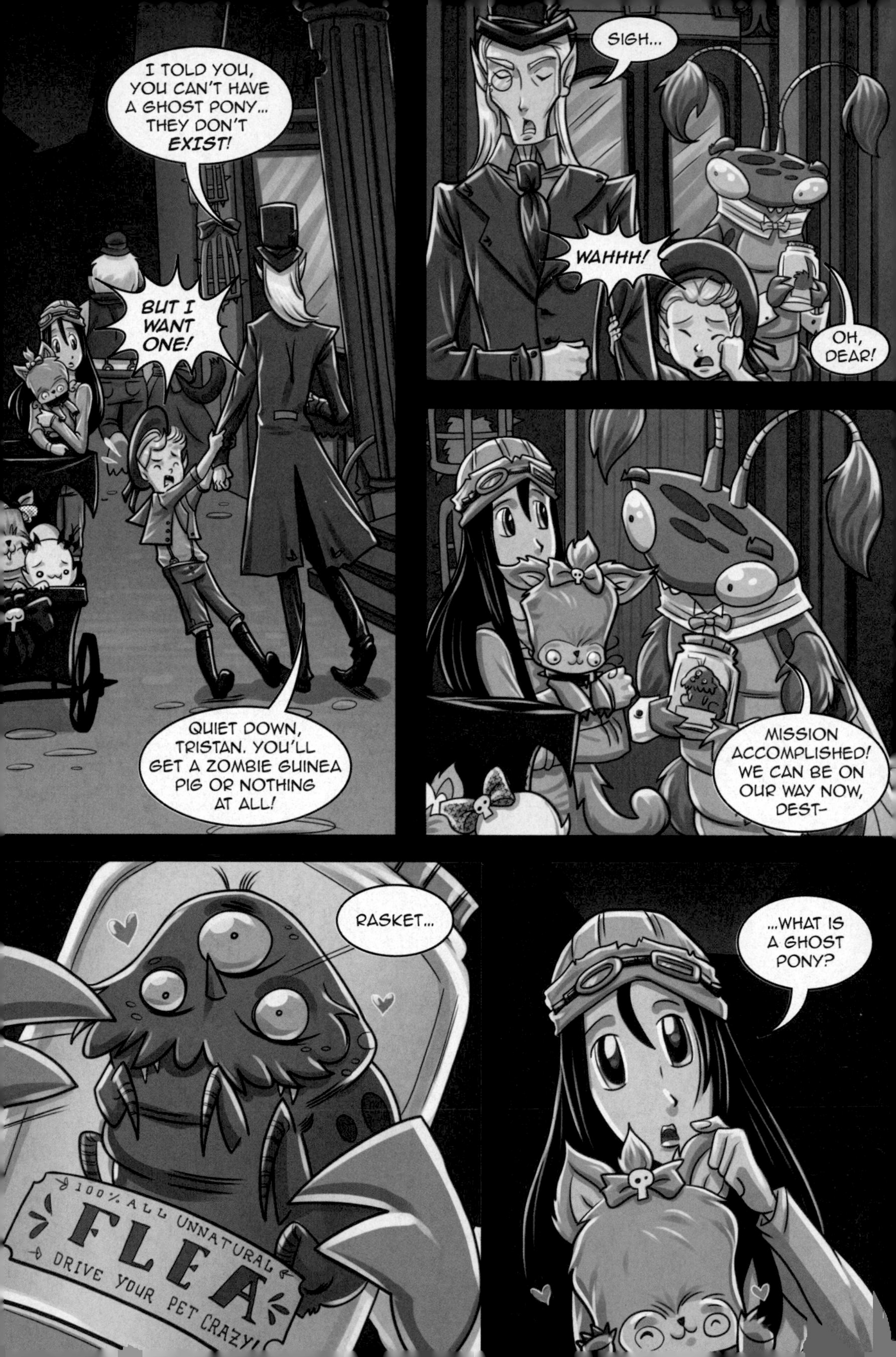
I TOLD YOU, YOU CAN'T HAVE A GHOST PONY... THEY DON'T EXIST!
BUT I WANT ONE!
QUIET DOWN, TRISTAN. YOU'LL GET A ZOMBIE GUINEA PIG OR NOTHING AT ALL!
SIGH...
WAHHH!
OH, DEAR!
MISSION ACCOMPLISHED! WE CAN BE ON OUR WAY NOW, DEST-
RASKET...
100% ALL UNNATURAL
FLEA
DRIVE YOUR PET CRAZY!
...WHAT IS A GHOST PONY?

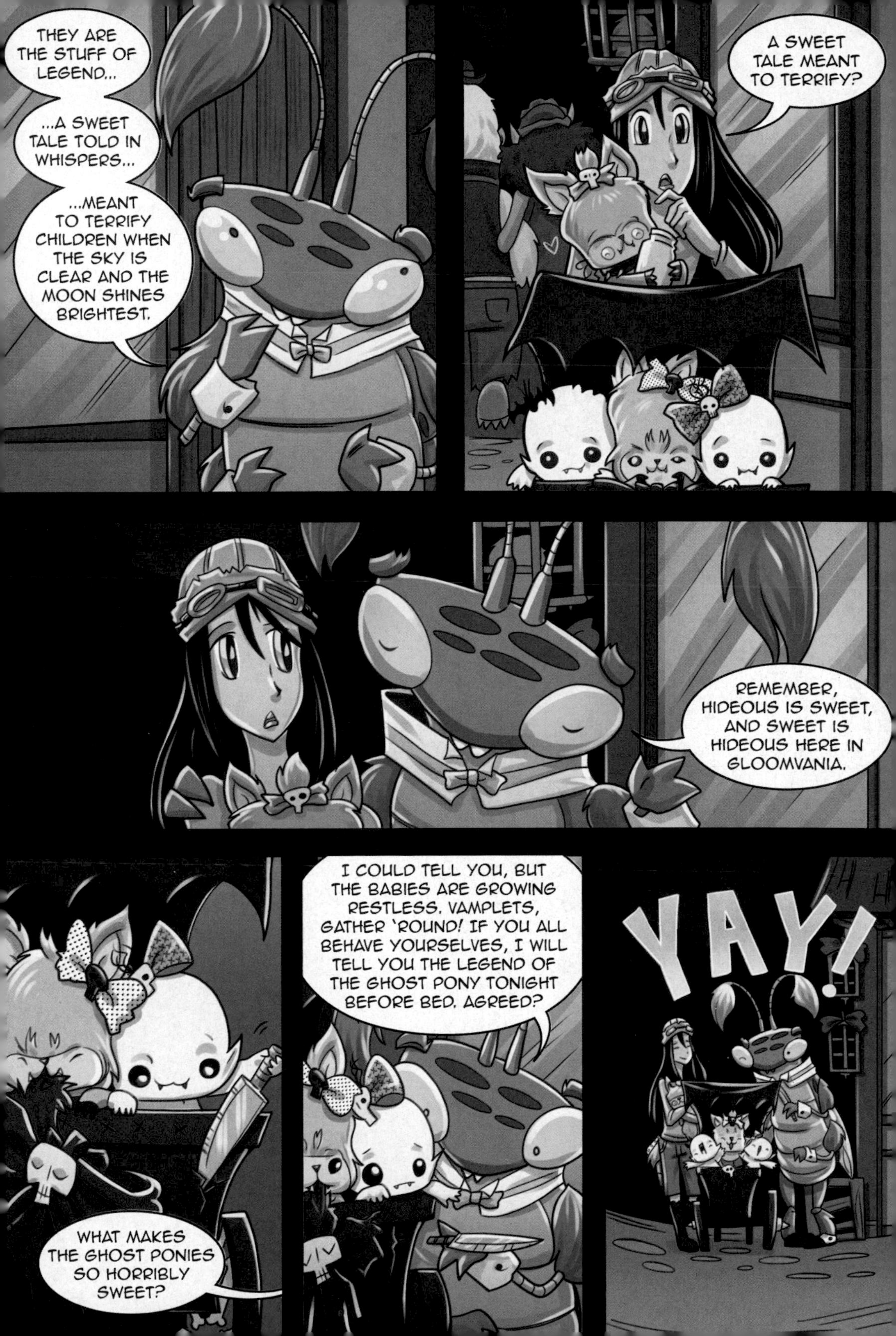
THEY ARE THE STUFF OF LEGEND...
...A SWEET TALE TOLD IN WHISPERS...
...MEANT TO TERRIFY CHILDREN WHEN THE SKY IS CLEAR AND THE MOON SHINES BRIGHTEST.
A SWEET TALE MEANT TO TERRIFY?
REMEMBER, HIDEOUS IS SWEET, AND SWEET IS HIDEOUS HERE IN GLOOMVANIA.
WHAT MAKES THE GHOST PONIES SO HORRIBLY SWEET?
I COULD TELL YOU, BUT THE BABIES ARE GROWING RESTLESS. VAMPLETS, GATHER 'ROUND! IF YOU ALL BEHAVE YOURSELVES, I WILL TELL YOU THE LEGEND OF THE GHOST PONY TONIGHT BEFORE BED. AGREED?
YAY!

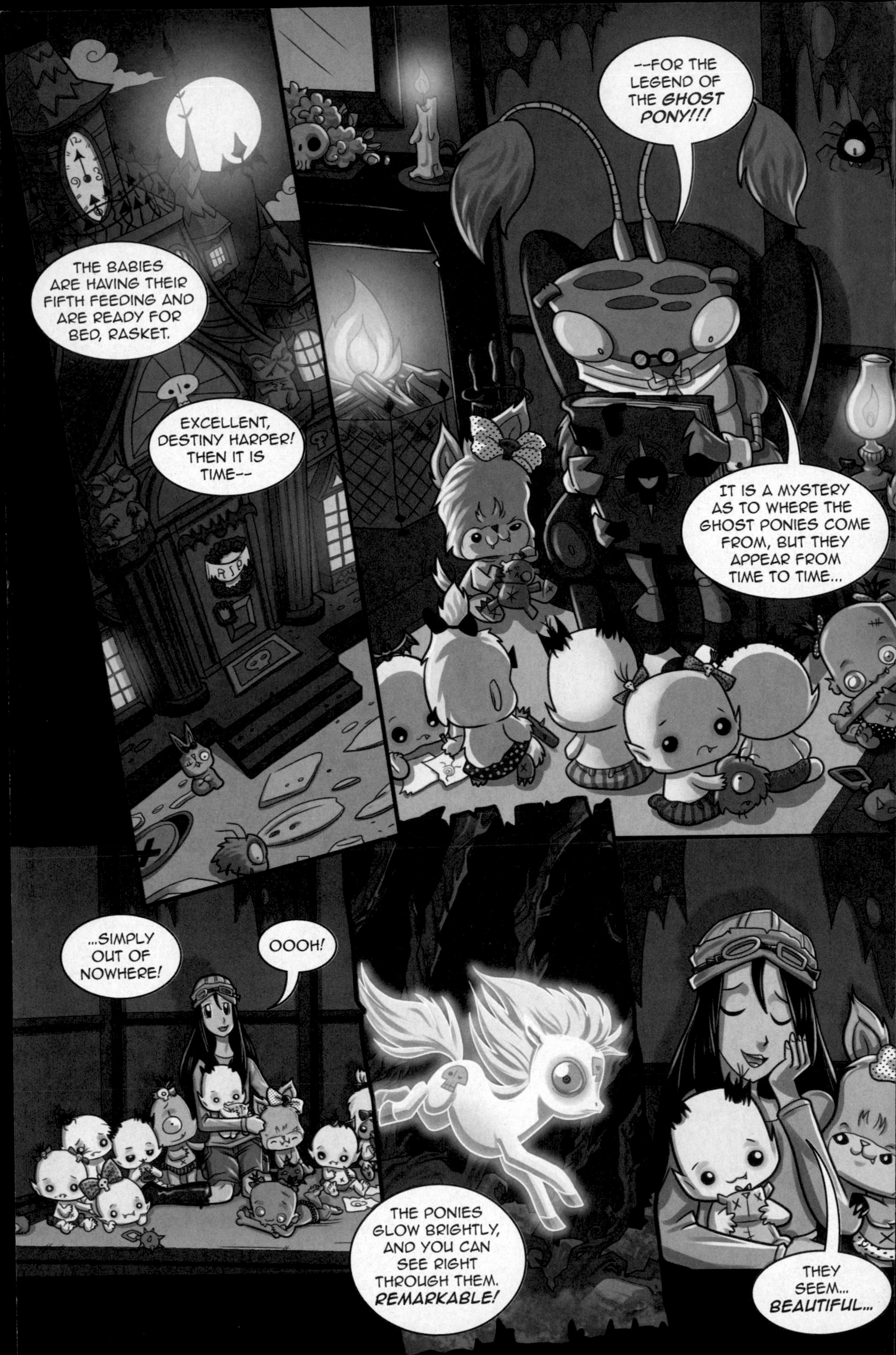
THE BABIES ARE HAVING THEIR FIFTH FEEDING AND ARE READY FOR BED, RASKET.
EXCELLENT, DESTINY HARPER! THEN IT IS TIME--
--FOR THE LEGEND OF THE GHOST PONY!!!
IT IS A MYSTERY AS TO WHERE THE GHOST PONIES COME FROM, BUT THEY APPEAR FROM TIME TO TIME...
...SIMPLY OUT OF NOWHERE!
OOOH!
THE PONIES GLOW BRIGHTLY, AND YOU CAN SEE RIGHT THROUGH THEM. REMARKABLE!
THEY SEEM... BEAUTIFUL...

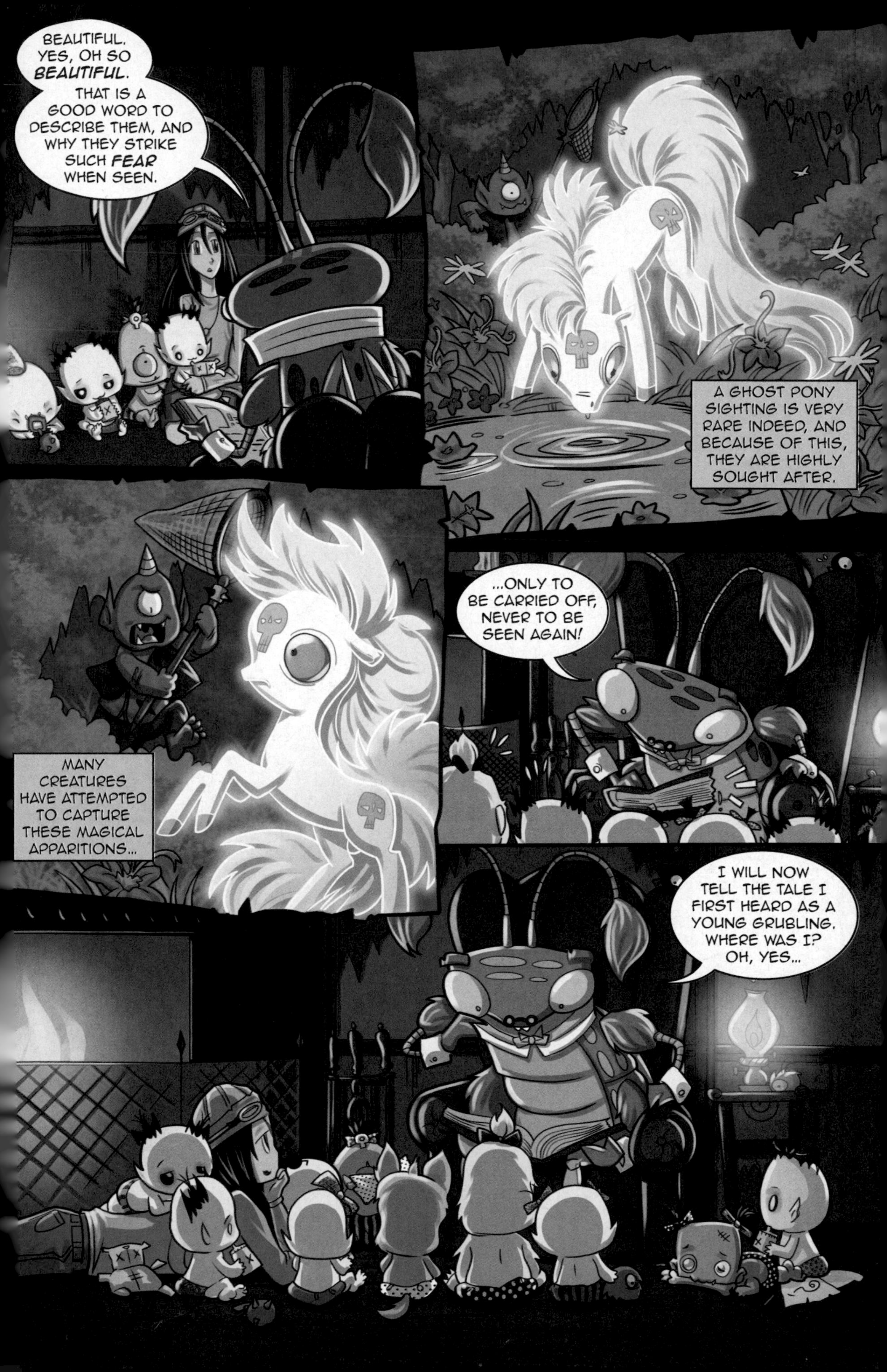
BEAUTIFUL. YES, OH SO BEAUTIFUL.
THAT IS A GOOD WORD TO DESCRIBE THEM, AND WHY THEY STRIKE SUCH FEAR WHEN SEEN.
A GHOST PONY SIGHTING IS VERY RARE INDEED, AND BECAUSE OF THIS, THEY ARE HIGHLY SOUGHT AFTER.
MANY CREATURES HAVE ATTEMPTED TO CAPTURE THESE MAGICAL APPARITIONS...
...ONLY TO BE CARRIED OFF, NEVER TO BE SEEN AGAIN!
I WILL NOW TELL THE TALE I FIRST HEARD AS A YOUNG GRUBLING. WHERE WAS I? OH, YES...

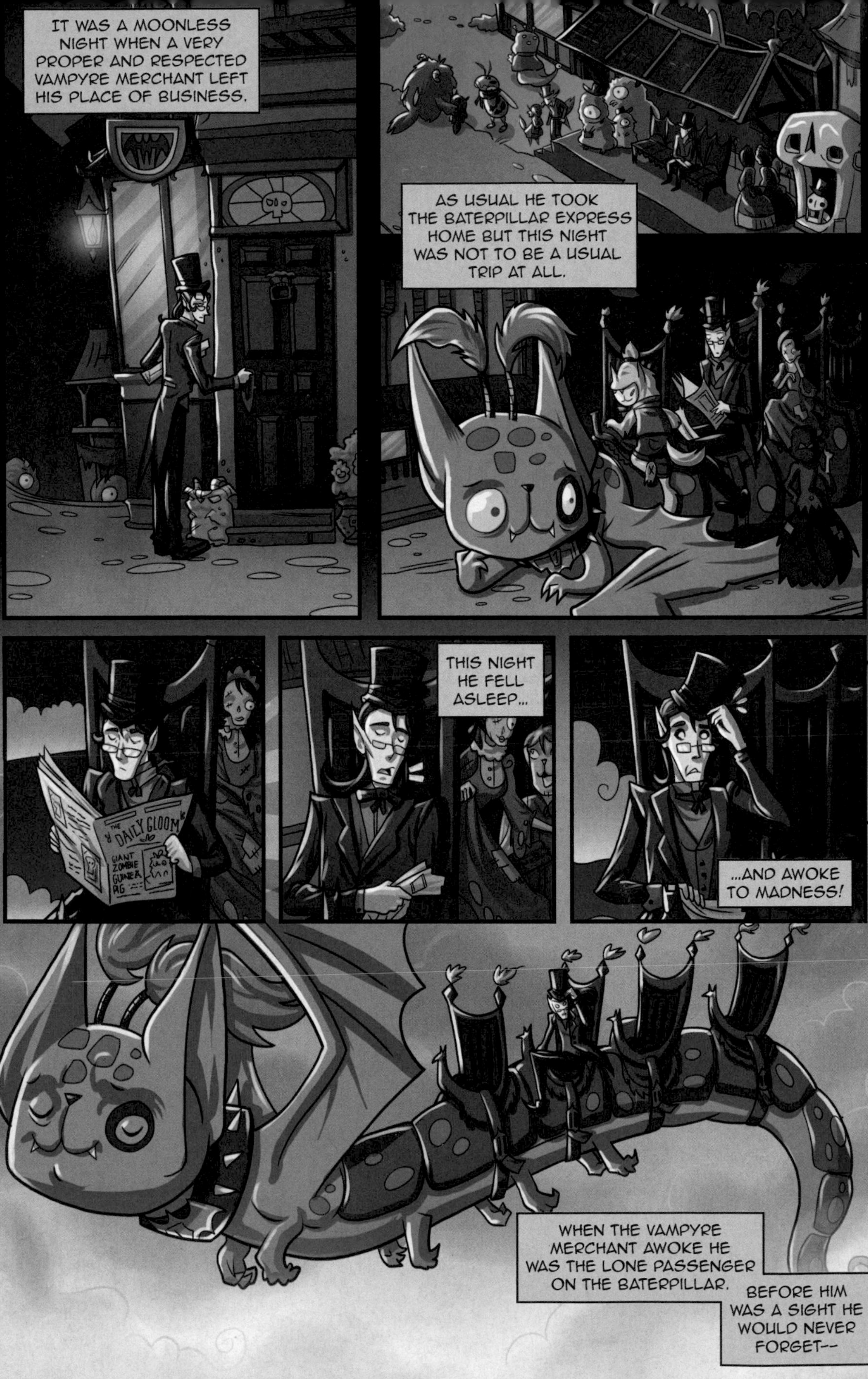
IT WAS A MOONLESS NIGHT WHEN A VERY PROPER AND RESPECTED VAMPYRE MERCHANT LEFT HIS PLACE OF BUSINESS.
AS USUAL HE TOOK THE BATERPILLAR EXPRESS HOME BUT THIS NIGHT WAS NOT TO BE A USUAL TRIP AT ALL.
THE DAILY GLOOM
GIANT ZOMBIE GUINEA PIG
THIS NIGHT HE FELL ASLEEP...
...AND AWOKE TO MADNESS!
WHEN THE VAMPYRE MERCHANT AWOKE HE WAS THE LONE PASSENGER ON THE BATERPILLAR.
BEFORE HIM WAS A SIGHT HE WOULD NEVER FORGET--

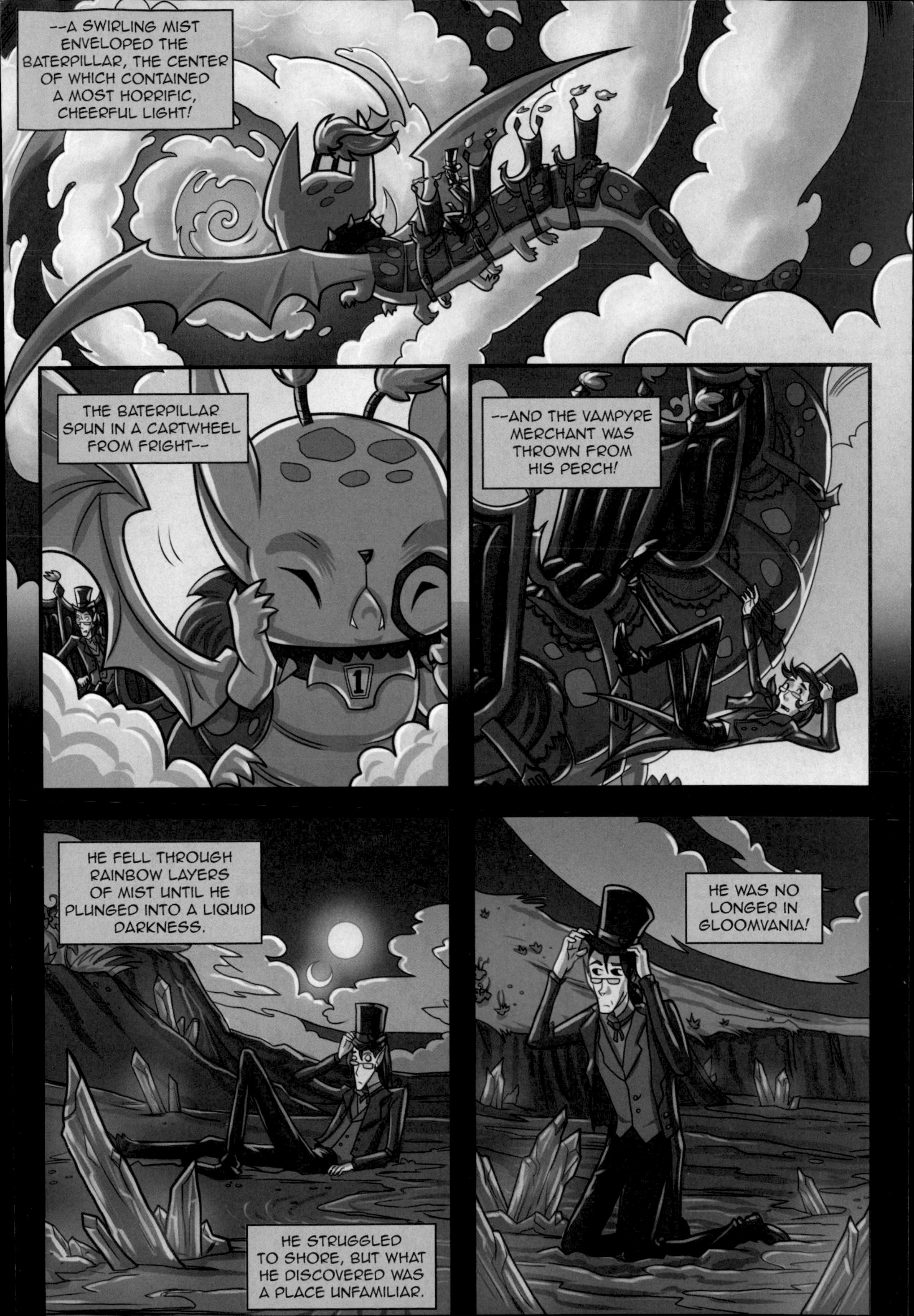
--A SWIRLING MIST ENVELOPED THE BATERPILLAR, THE CENTER OF WHICH CONTAINED A MOST HORRIFIC, CHEERFUL LIGHT!
THE BATERPILLAR SPUN IN A CARTWHEEL FROM FRIGHT--
1
--AND THE VAMPYRE MERCHANT WAS THROWN FROM HIS PERCH!
HE FELL THROUGH RAINBOW LAYERS OF MIST UNTIL HE PLUNGED INTO A LIQUID DARKNESS.
HE STRUGGLED TO SHORE, BUT WHAT HE DISCOVERED WAS A PLACE UNFAMILIAR.
HE WAS NO LONGER IN GLOOMVANIA!

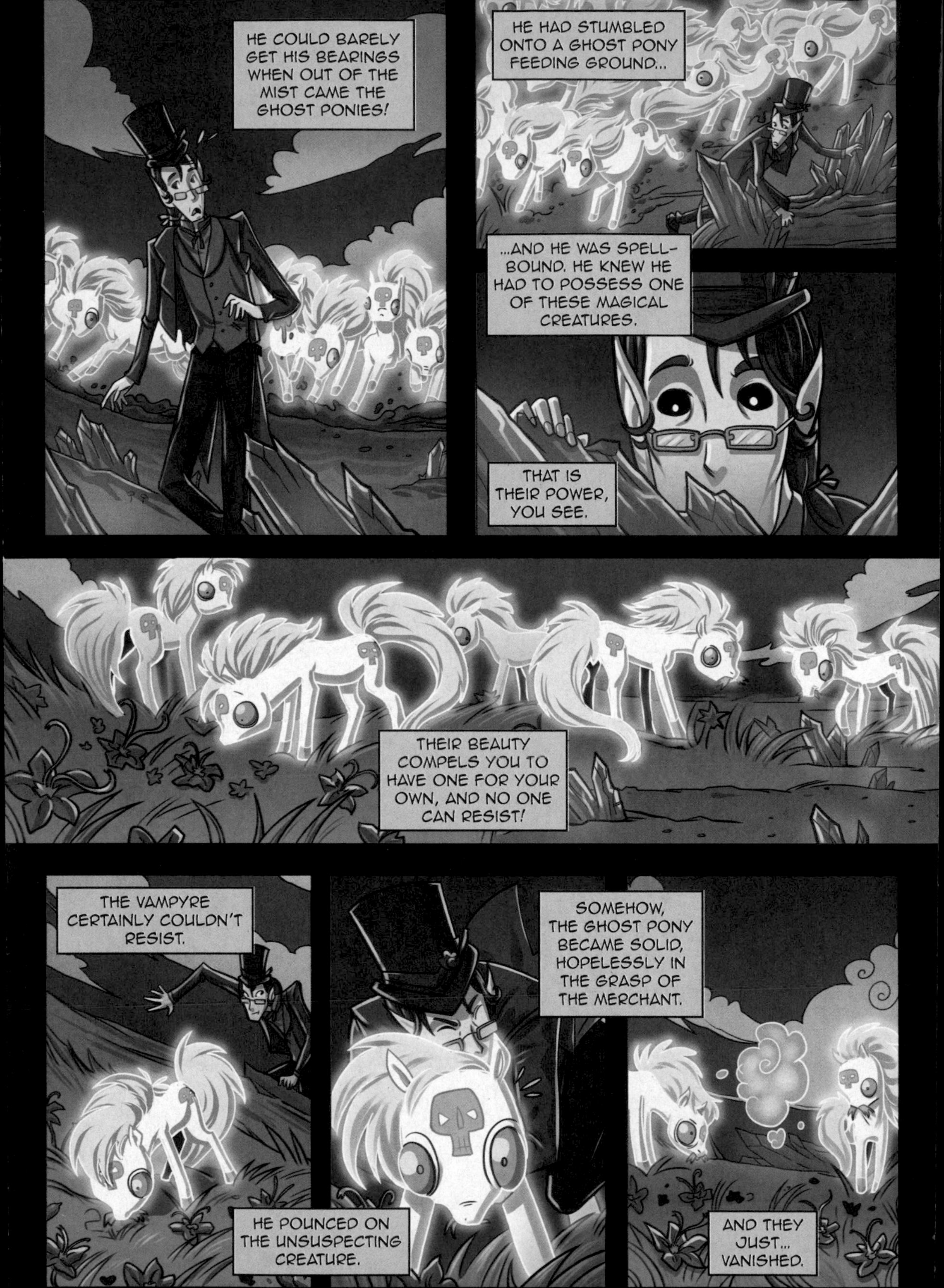

HE COULD BARELY GET HIS BEARINGS WHEN OUT OF THE MIST CAME THE GHOST PONIES!
HE HAD STUMBLED ONTO A GHOST PONY FEEDING GROUND...
...AND HE WAS SPELL-BOUND. HE KNEW HE HAD TO POSSESS ONE OF THESE MAGICAL CREATURES.
THAT IS THEIR POWER, YOU SEE.
THEIR BEAUTY COMPELS YOU TO HAVE ONE FOR YOUR OWN, AND NO ONE CAN RESIST!
THE VAMPYRE CERTAINLY COULDN'T RESIST.
HE POUNCED ON THE UNSUSPECTING CREATURE.
SOMEHOW, THE GHOST PONY BECAME SOLID, HOPELESSLY IN THE GRASP OF THE MERCHANT.
AND THEY JUST... VANISHED.

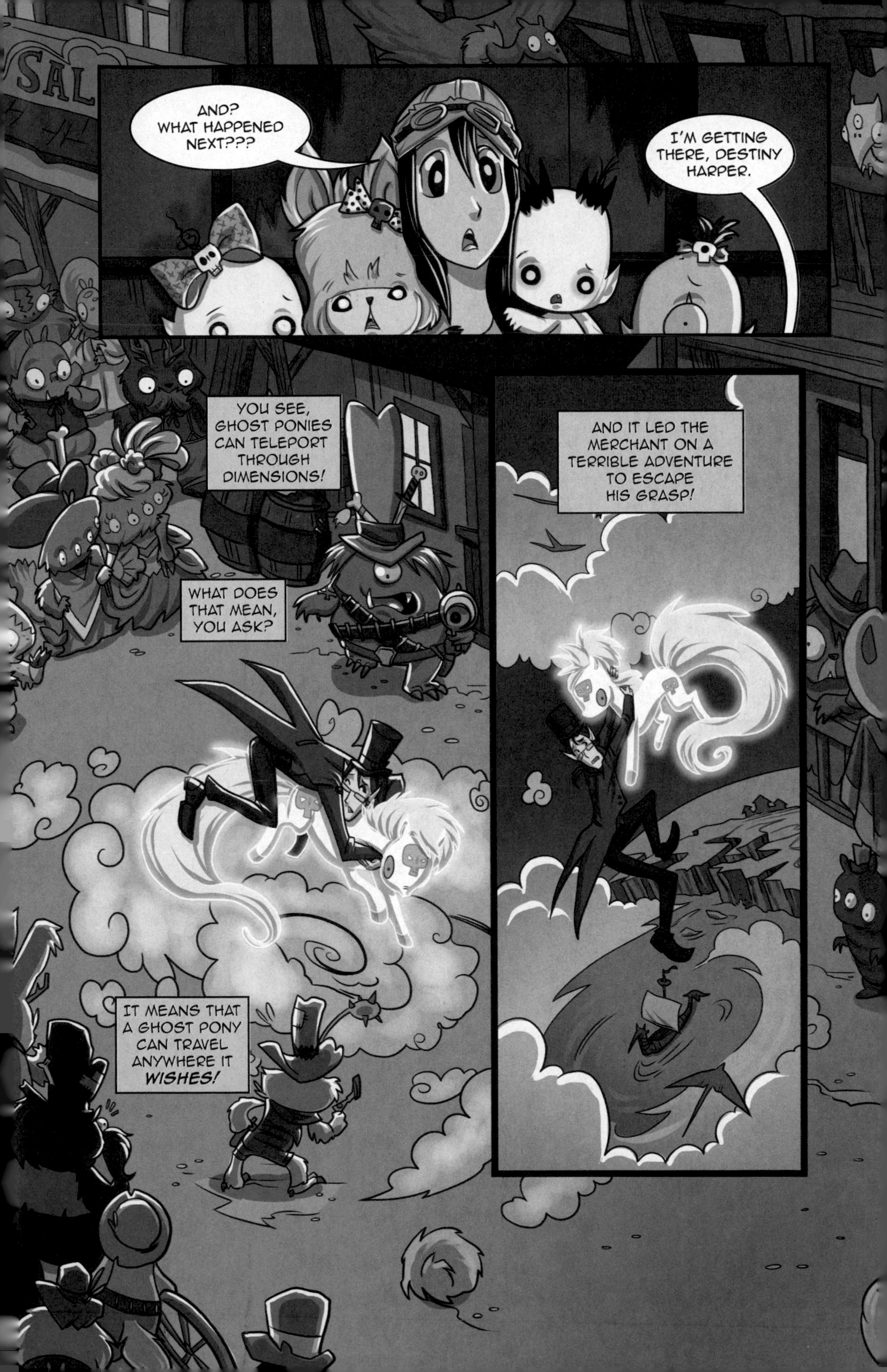

AND? WHAT HAPPENED NEXT???
I'M GETTING THERE, DESTINY HARPER.
YOU SEE, GHOST PONIES CAN TELEPORT THROUGH DIMENSIONS!
WHAT DOES THAT MEAN, YOU ASK?
IT MEANS THAT A GHOST PONY CAN TRAVEL ANYWHERE IT *WISHES!*
AND IT LED THE MERCHANT ON A TERRIBLE ADVENTURE TO ESCAPE HIS GRASP!

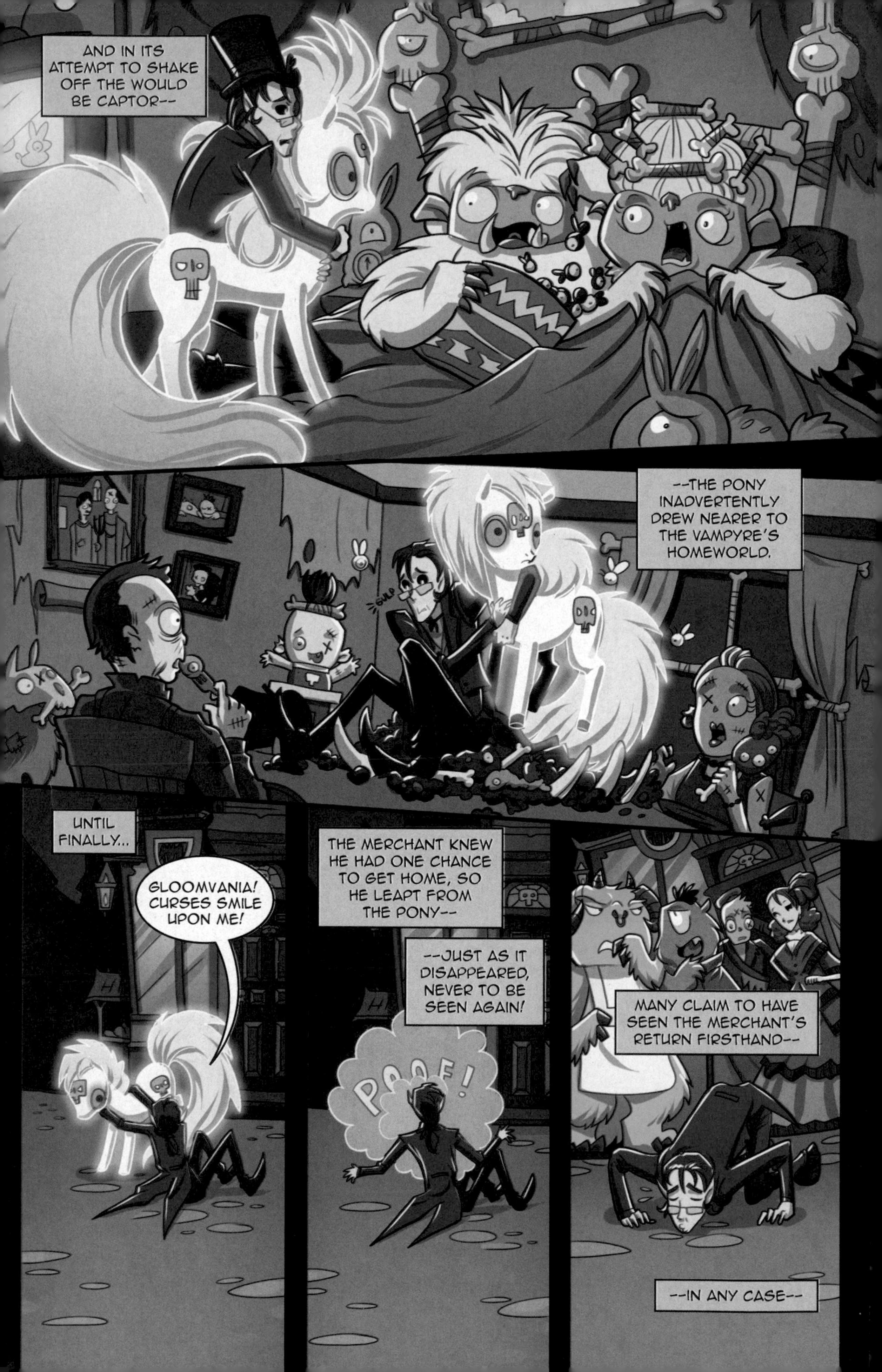
AND IN ITS ATTEMPT TO SHAKE OFF THE WOULD BE CAPTOR--
--THE PONY INADVERTENTLY DREW NEARER TO THE VAMPYRE'S HOMEWORLD.
GULP
UNTIL FINALLY...
GLOOMVANIA! CURSES SMILE UPON ME!
THE MERCHANT KNEW HE HAD ONE CHANCE TO GET HOME, SO HE LEAPT FROM THE PONY--
--JUST AS IT DISAPPEARED, NEVER TO BE SEEN AGAIN!
POOF!
MANY CLAIM TO HAVE SEEN THE MERCHANT'S RETURN FIRSTHAND--
--IN ANY CASE--

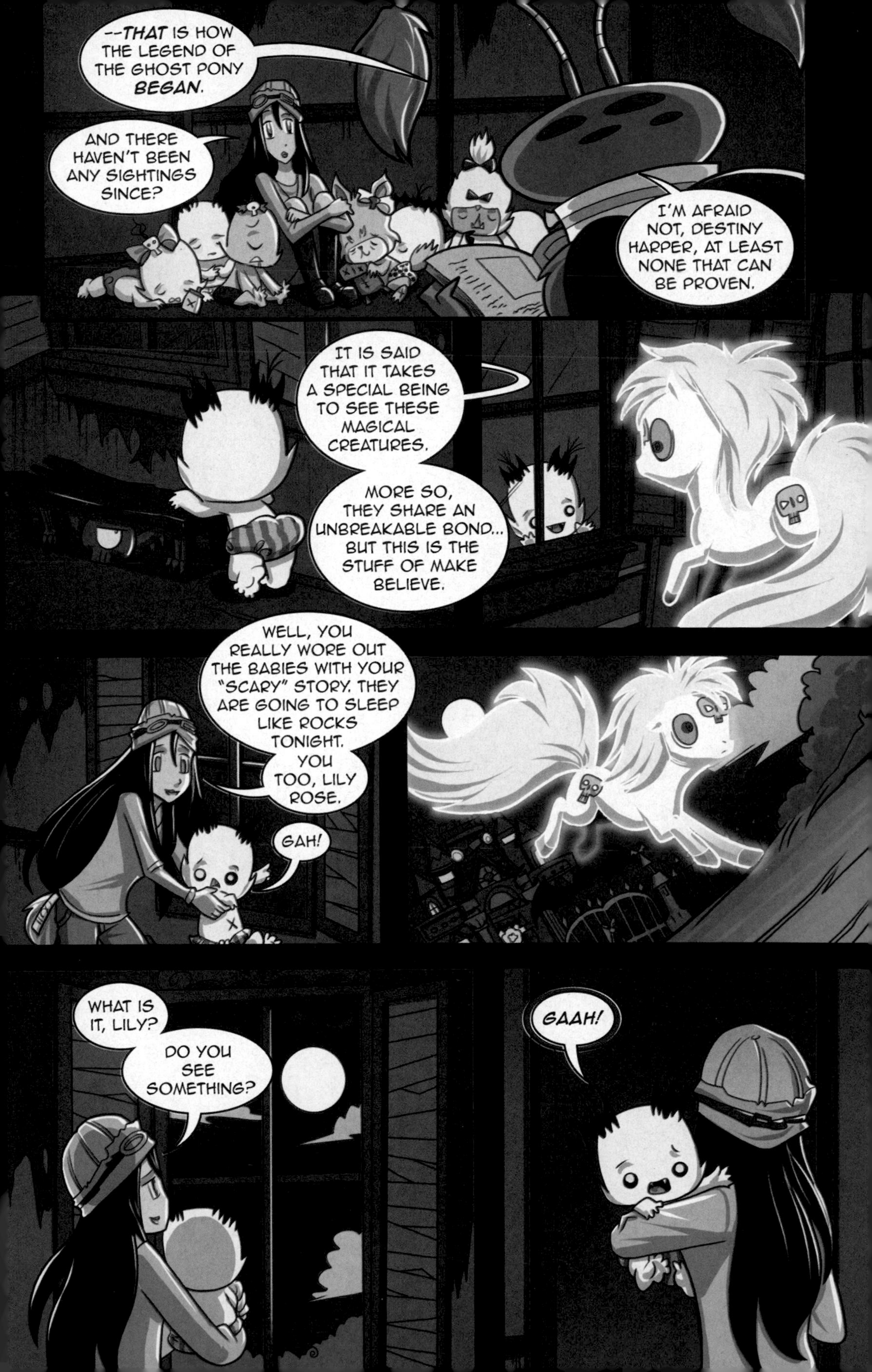
--THAT IS HOW THE LEGEND OF THE GHOST PONY BEGAN.
AND THERE HAVEN'T BEEN ANY SIGHTINGS SINCE?
I'M AFRAID NOT, DESTINY HARPER, AT LEAST NONE THAT CAN BE PROVEN.
IT IS SAID THAT IT TAKES A SPECIAL BEING TO SEE THESE MAGICAL CREATURES.
MORE SO, THEY SHARE AN UNBREAKABLE BOND... BUT THIS IS THE STUFF OF MAKE BELIEVE.
WELL, YOU REALLY WORE OUT THE BABIES WITH YOUR "SCARY" STORY. THEY ARE GOING TO SLEEP LIKE ROCKS TONIGHT.
YOU TOO, LILY ROSE.
GAH!
WHAT IS IT, LILY?
DO YOU SEE SOMETHING?
GAAH!

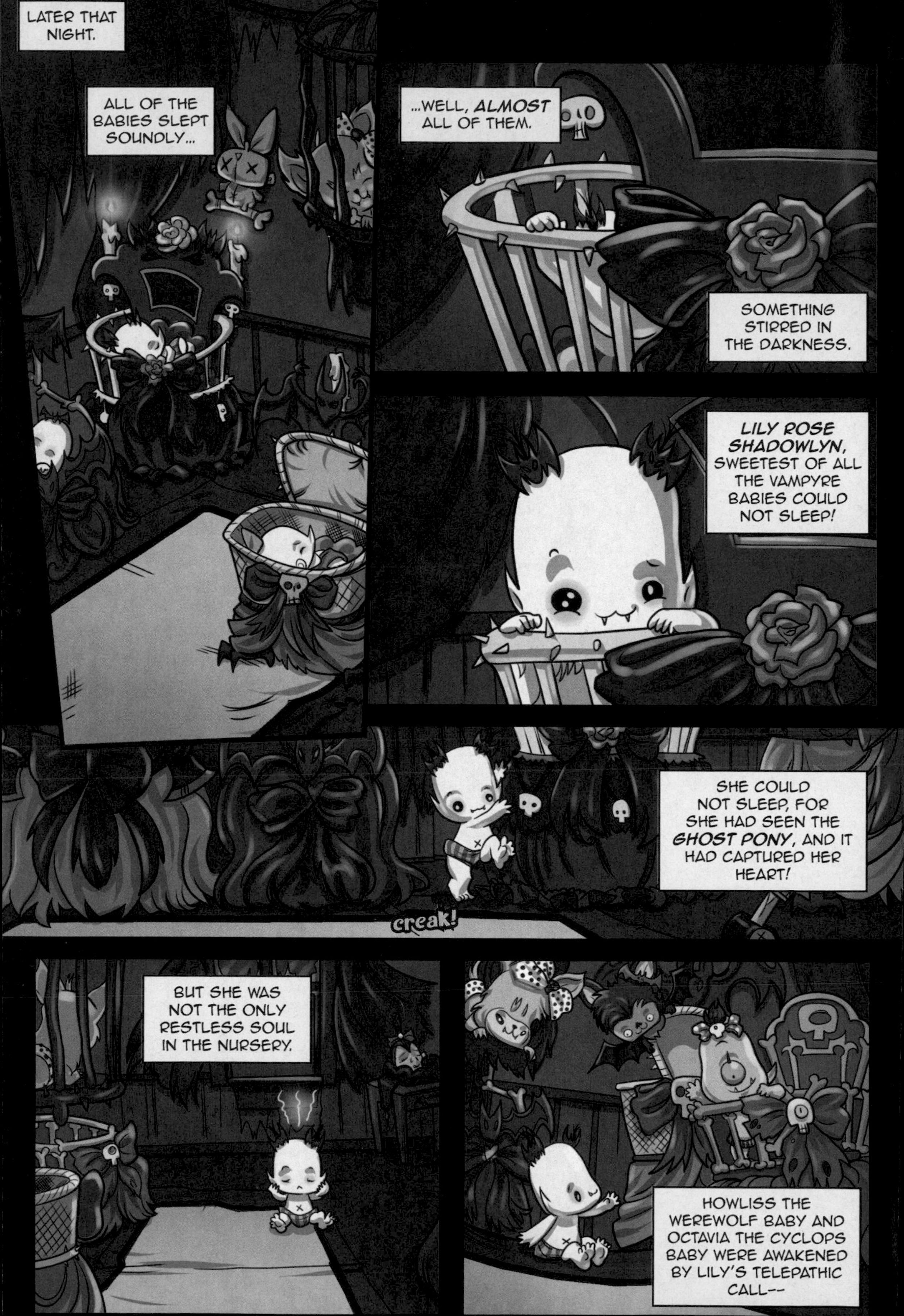

LATER THAT NIGHT.
ALL OF THE BABIES SLEPT SOUNDLY...
...WELL, *ALMOST* ALL OF THEM.
SOMETHING STIRRED IN THE DARKNESS.
LILY ROSE SHADOWLYN, SWEETEST OF ALL THE VAMPYRE BABIES COULD NOT SLEEP!
SHE COULD NOT SLEEP, FOR SHE HAD SEEN THE *GHOST PONY,* AND IT HAD CAPTURED HER HEART!
creak!
BUT SHE WAS NOT THE ONLY RESTLESS SOUL IN THE NURSERY.
HOWLISS THE WEREWOLF BABY AND OCTAVIA THE CYCLOPS BABY WERE AWAKENED BY LILY'S TELEPATHIC CALL--

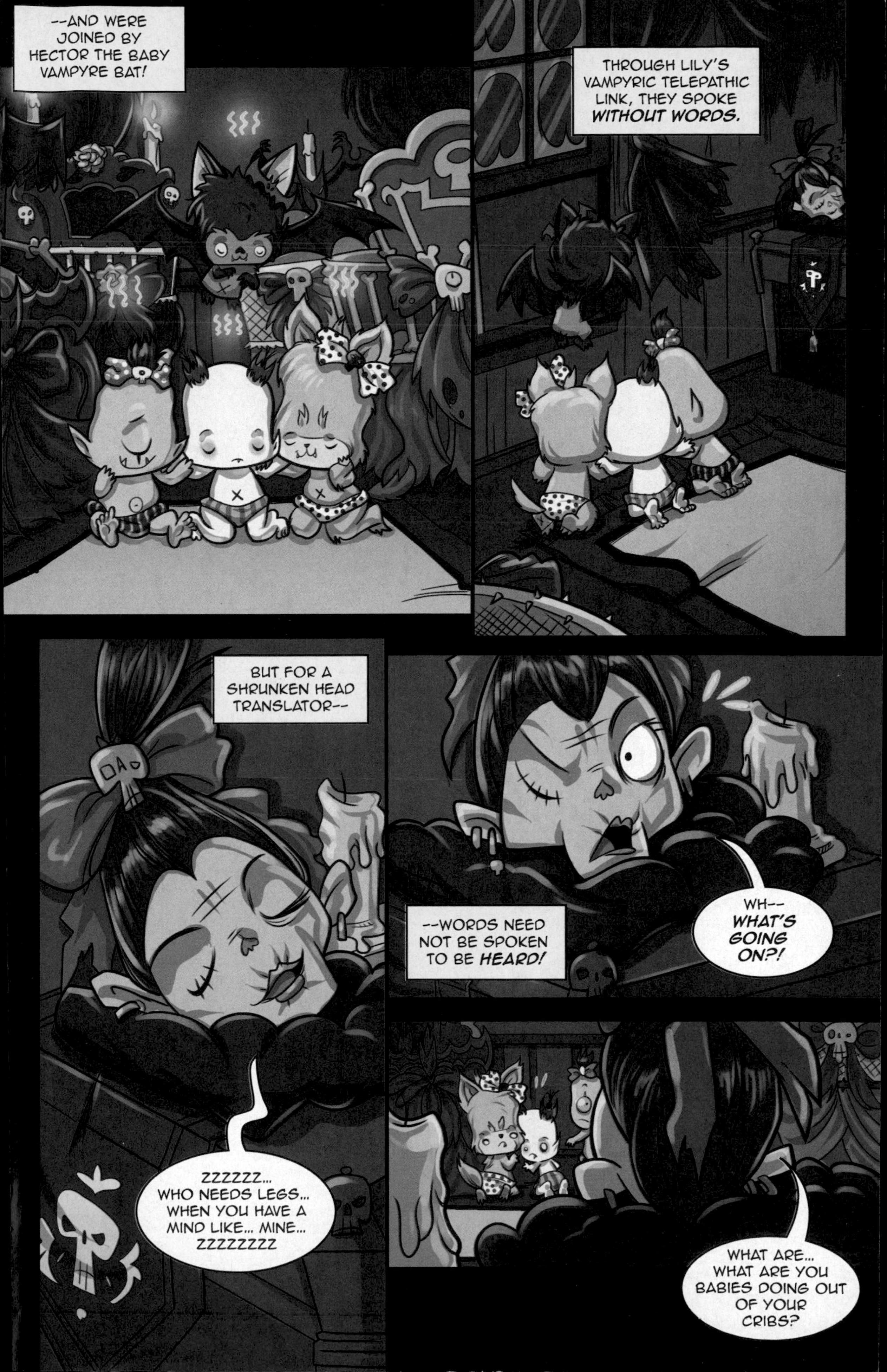
--AND WERE JOINED BY HECTOR THE BABY VAMPYRE BAT!
THROUGH LILY'S VAMPYRIC TELEPATHIC LINK, THEY SPOKE WITHOUT WORDS.
BUT FOR A SHRUNKEN HEAD TRANSLATOR--
ZZZZZZ... WHO NEEDS LEGS... WHEN YOU HAVE A MIND LIKE... MINE... ZZZZZZZZ
--WORDS NEED NOT BE SPOKEN TO BE HEARD!
WH-- WHAT'S GOING ON?!
WHAT ARE... WHAT ARE YOU BABIES DOING OUT OF YOUR CRIBS?

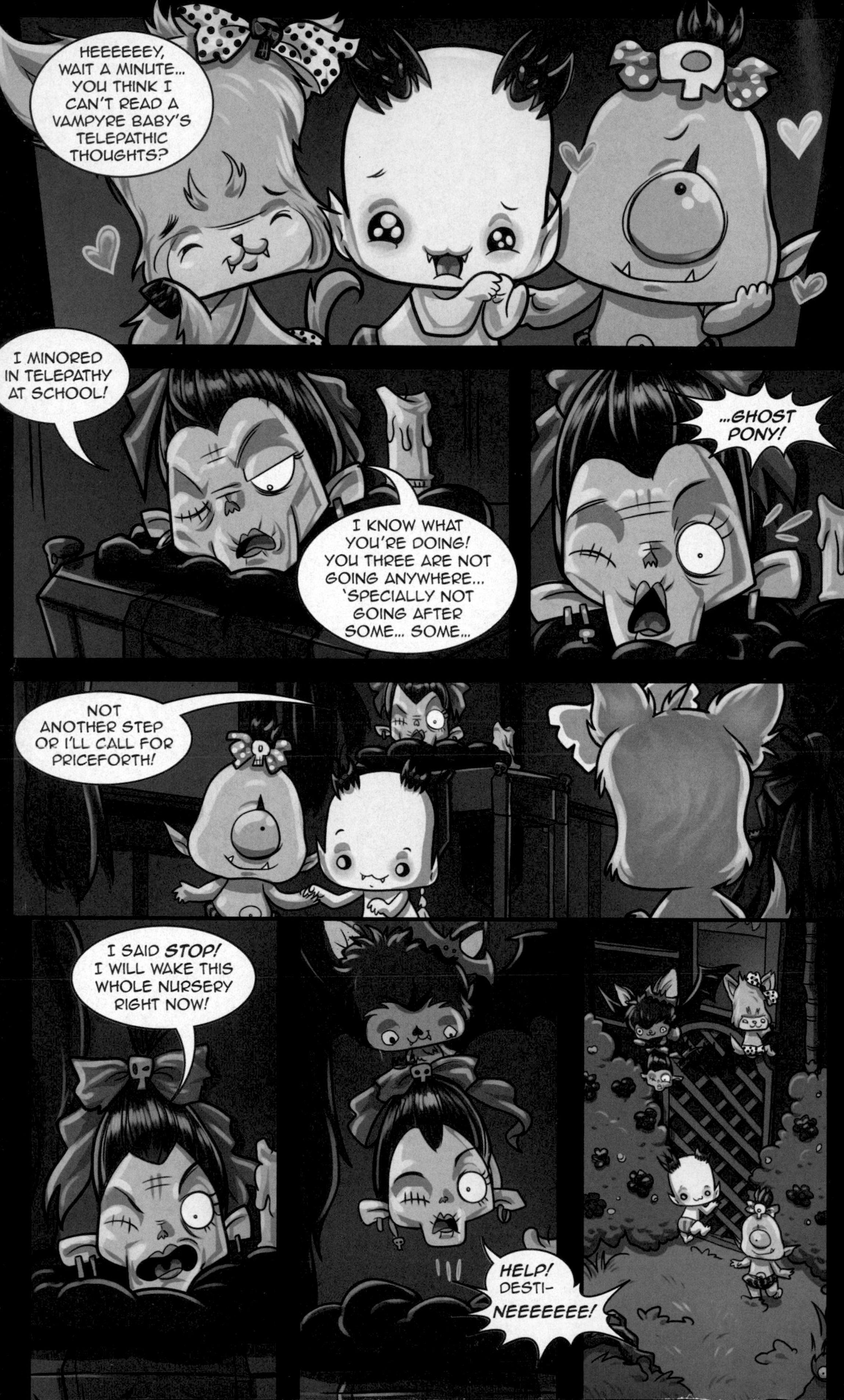
HEEEEEEY, WAIT A MINUTE... YOU THINK I CAN'T READ A VAMPYRE BABY'S TELEPATHIC THOUGHTS?
I MINORED IN TELEPATHY AT SCHOOL!
I KNOW WHAT YOU'RE DOING! YOU THREE ARE NOT GOING ANYWHERE... 'SPECIALLY NOT GOING AFTER SOME... SOME...
...GHOST PONY!
NOT ANOTHER STEP OR I'LL CALL FOR PRICEFORTH!
I SAID STOP! I WILL WAKE THIS WHOLE NURSERY RIGHT NOW!
HELP! DESTI-NEEEEEEE!

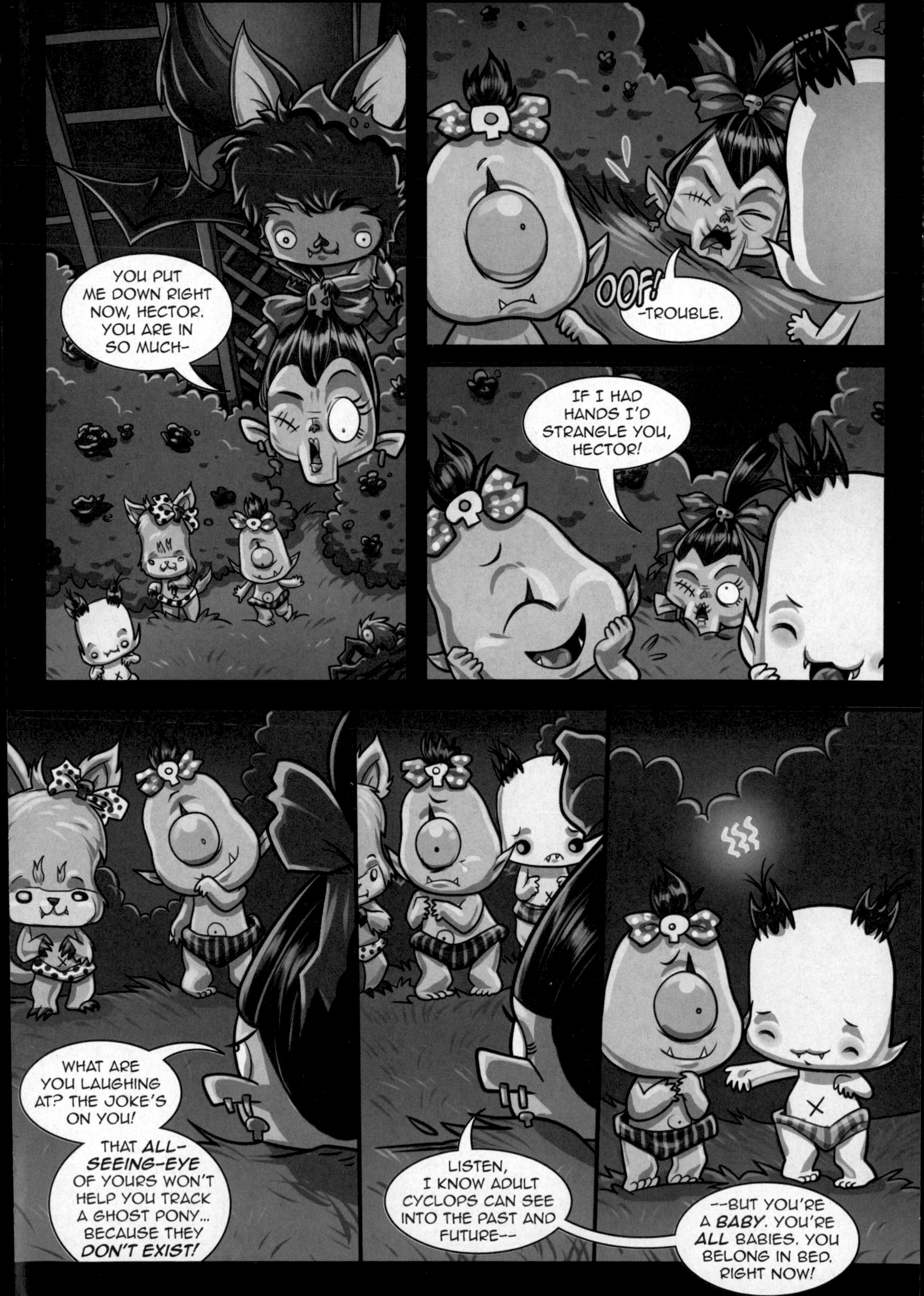
YOU PUT ME DOWN RIGHT NOW, HECTOR. YOU ARE IN SO MUCH-
OOF!
-TROUBLE.
IF I HAD HANDS I'D STRANGLE YOU, HECTOR!
WHAT ARE YOU LAUGHING AT? THE JOKE'S ON YOU!
THAT ALL-SEEING-EYE OF YOURS WON'T HELP YOU TRACK A GHOST PONY... BECAUSE THEY DON'T EXIST!
LISTEN, I KNOW ADULT CYCLOPS CAN SEE INTO THE PAST AND FUTURE--
--BUT YOU'RE A BABY. YOU'RE ALL BABIES. YOU BELONG IN BED. RIGHT NOW!

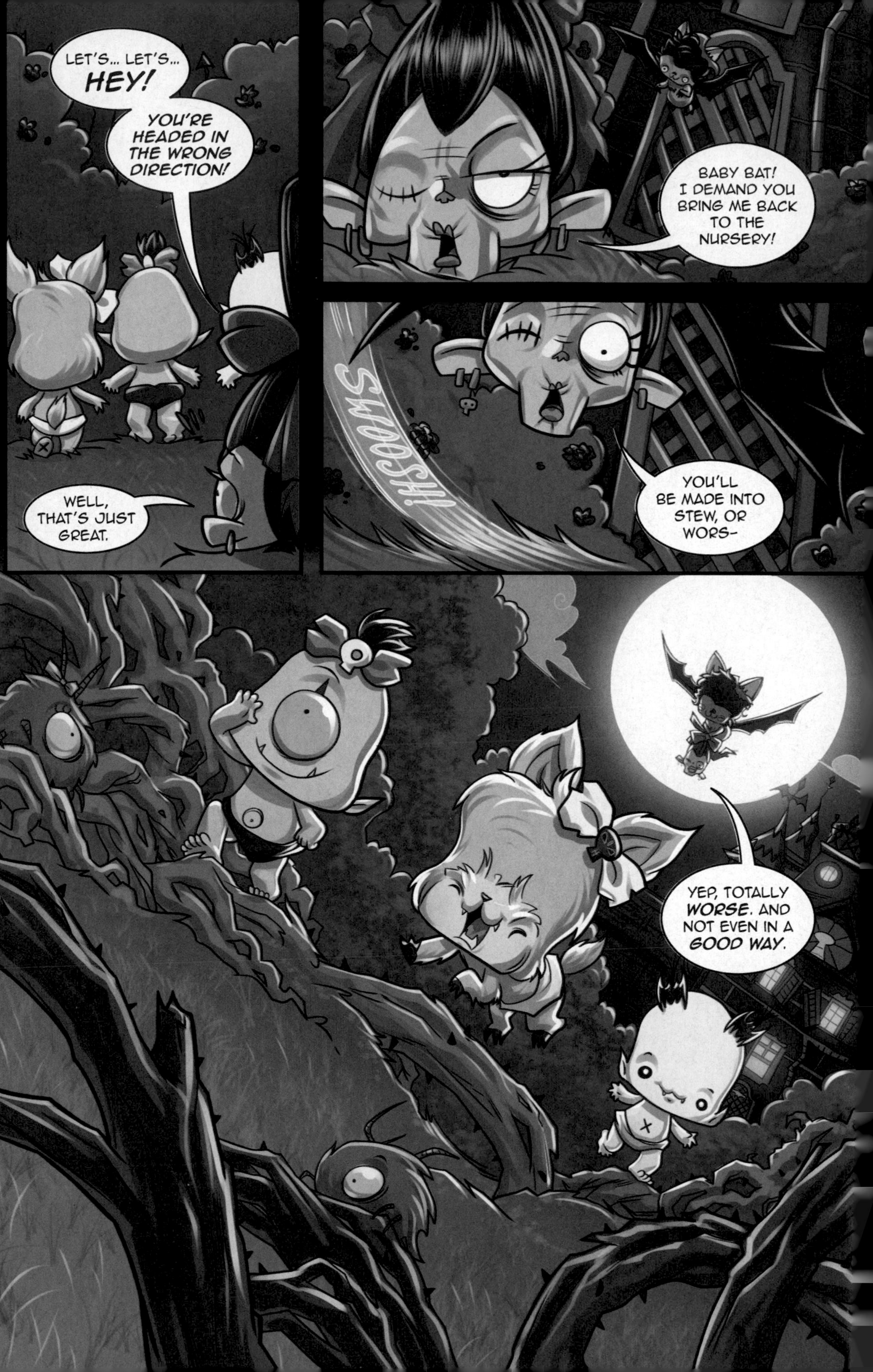
LET'S... LET'S... HEY!
YOU'RE HEADED IN THE WRONG DIRECTION!
WELL, THAT'S JUST GREAT.
BABY BAT! I DEMAND YOU BRING ME BACK TO THE NURSERY!
SWOOSH!
YOU'LL BE MADE INTO STEW, OR WORS-
YEP, TOTALLY WORSE. AND NOT EVEN IN A GOOD WAY.

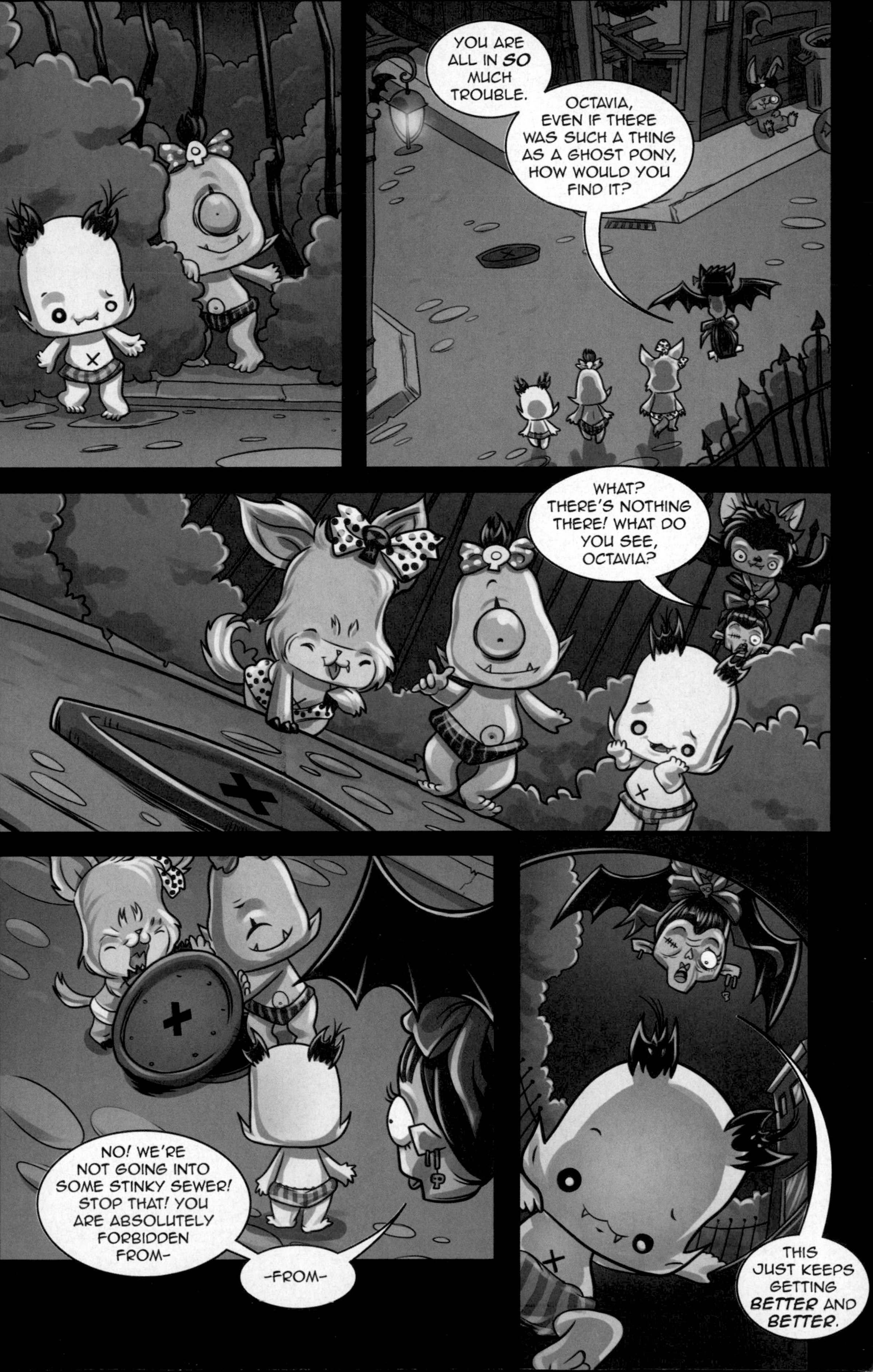
YOU ARE ALL IN SO MUCH TROUBLE.
OCTAVIA, EVEN IF THERE WAS SUCH A THING AS A GHOST PONY, HOW WOULD YOU FIND IT?
WHAT? THERE'S NOTHING THERE! WHAT DO YOU SEE, OCTAVIA?
NO! WE'RE NOT GOING INTO SOME STINKY SEWER! STOP THAT! YOU ARE ABSOLUTELY FORBIDDEN FROM-
-FROM-
THIS JUST KEEPS GETTING BETTER AND BETTER.

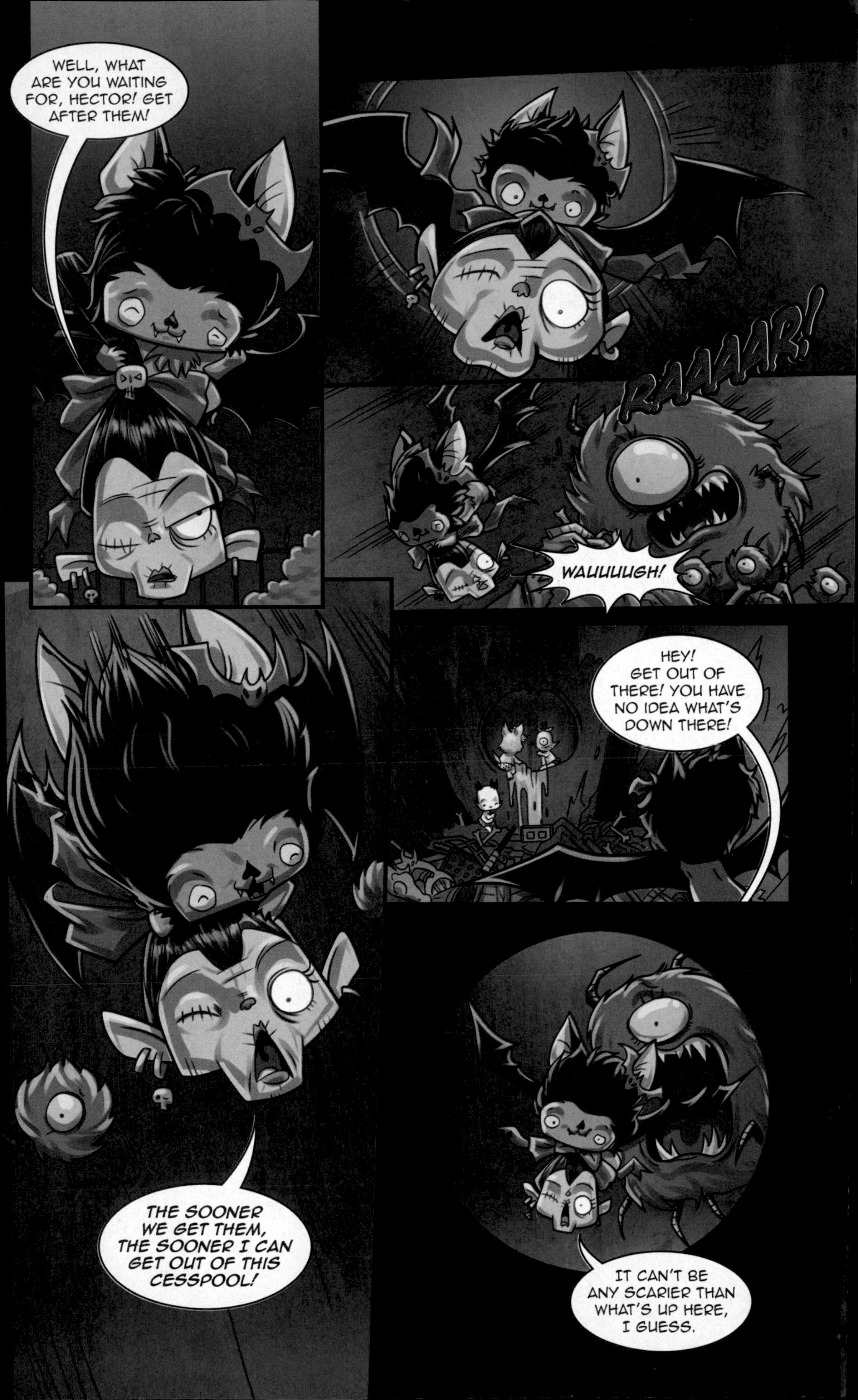

WELL, WHAT ARE YOU WAITING FOR, HECTOR! GET AFTER THEM!
RAAAAAR!
WAUUUUGH!
THE SOONER WE GET THEM, THE SOONER I CAN GET OUT OF THIS CESSPOOL!
HEY! GET OUT OF THERE! YOU HAVE NO IDEA WHAT'S DOWN THERE!
IT CAN'T BE ANY SCARIER THAN WHAT'S UP HERE, I GUESS.

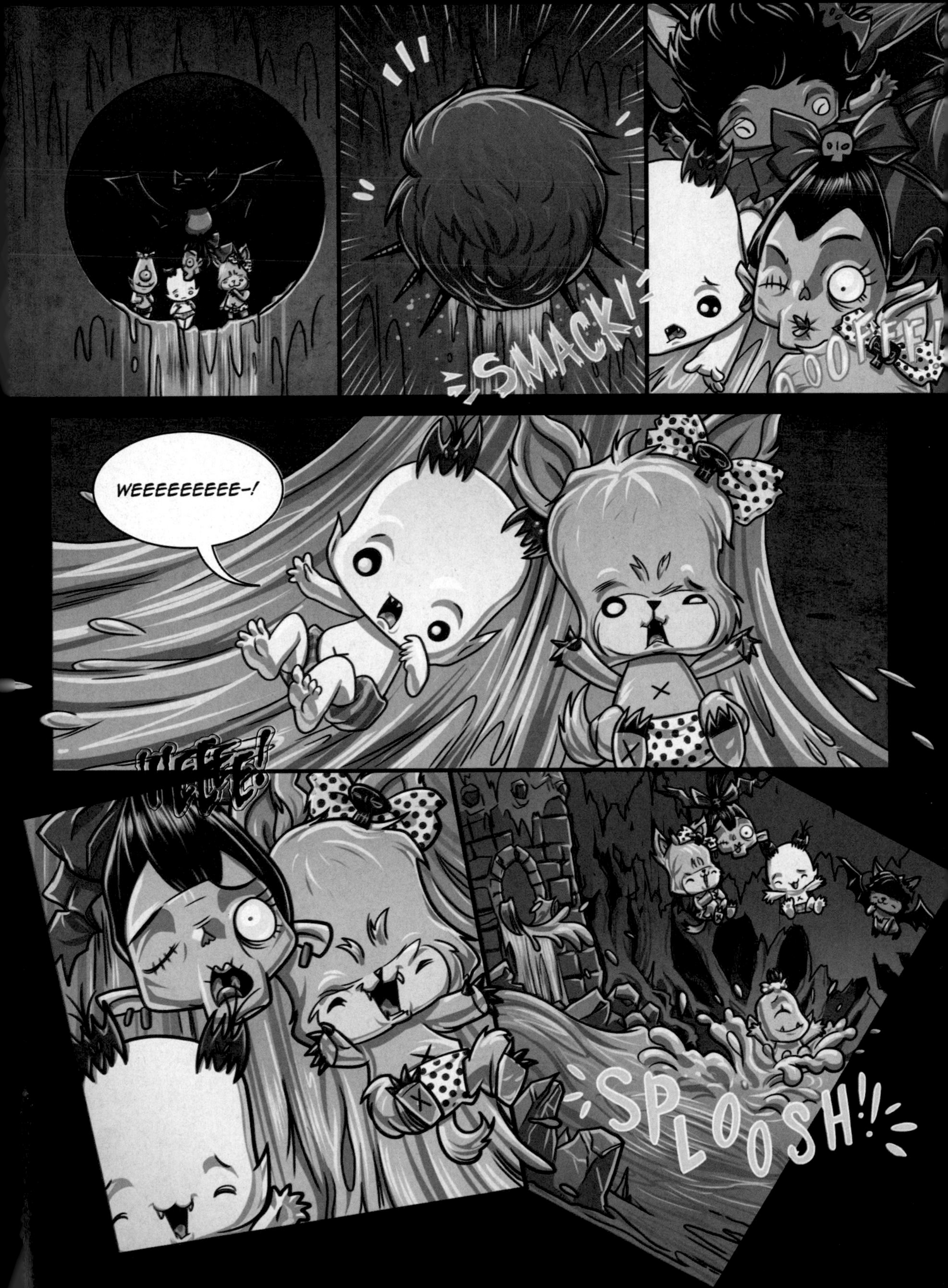
SMACK!
OOOFFF!
WEEEEEEEEE-!
SPLOOSH!!

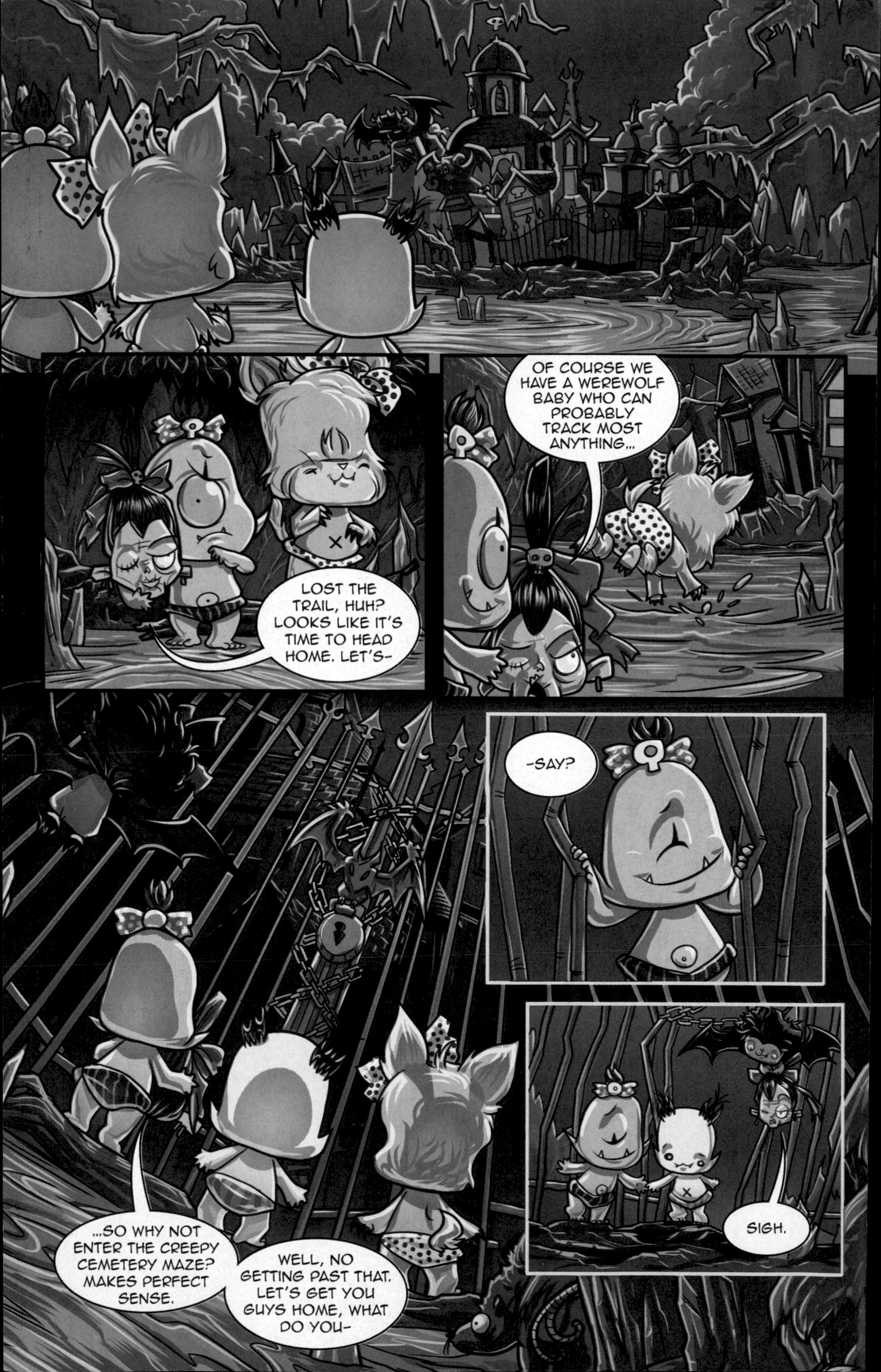
LOST THE TRAIL, HUH? LOOKS LIKE IT'S TIME TO HEAD HOME. LET'S-
OF COURSE WE HAVE A WEREWOLF BABY WHO CAN PROBABLY TRACK MOST ANYTHING...
...SO WHY NOT ENTER THE CREEPY CEMETERY MAZE? MAKES PERFECT SENSE.
WELL, NO GETTING PAST THAT. LET'S GET YOU GUYS HOME, WHAT DO YOU-
-SAY?
SIGH.

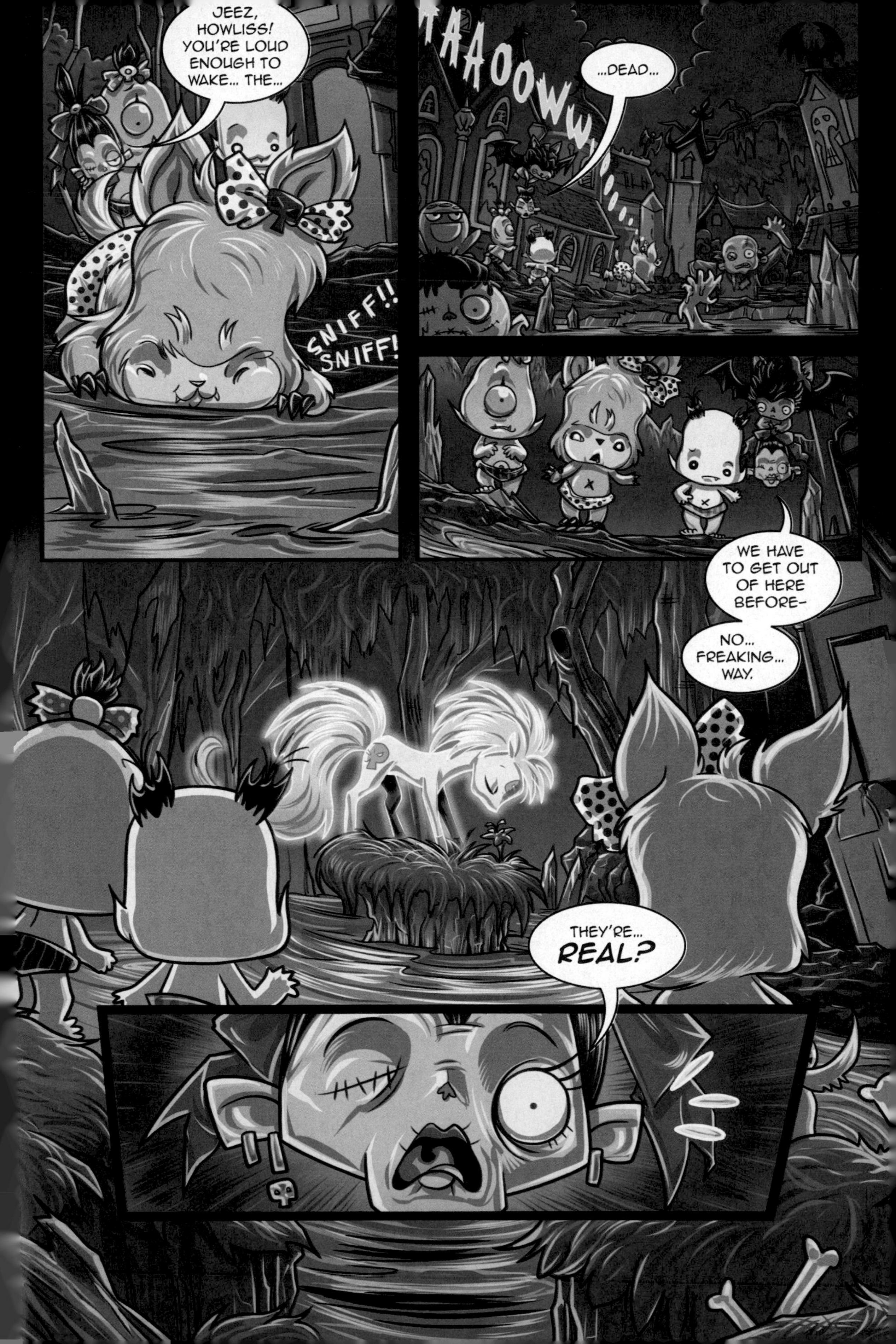
JEEZ, HOWLISS! YOU'RE LOUD ENOUGH TO WAKE... THE...
SNIFF!! SNIFF!
...DEAD...
TAAAOOWWW...
WE HAVE TO GET OUT OF HERE BEFORE-
NO... FREAKING... WAY.
THEY'RE... REAL?

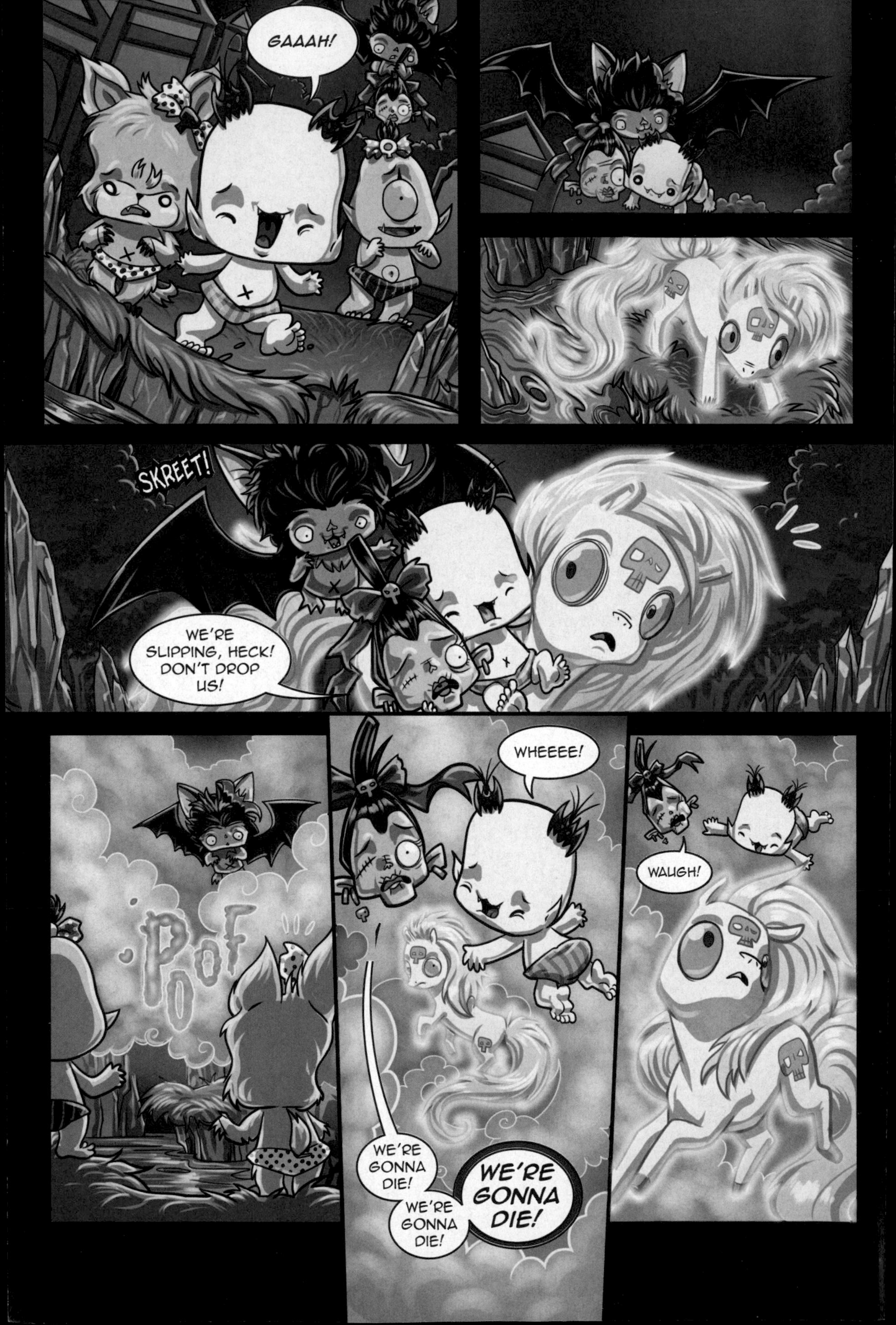
GAAAH!
SKREET!
WE'RE SLIPPING, HECK! DON'T DROP US!
POOF
WHEEEE!
WE'RE GONNA DIE!
WE'RE GONNA DIE!
WE'RE GONNA DIE!
WAUGH!

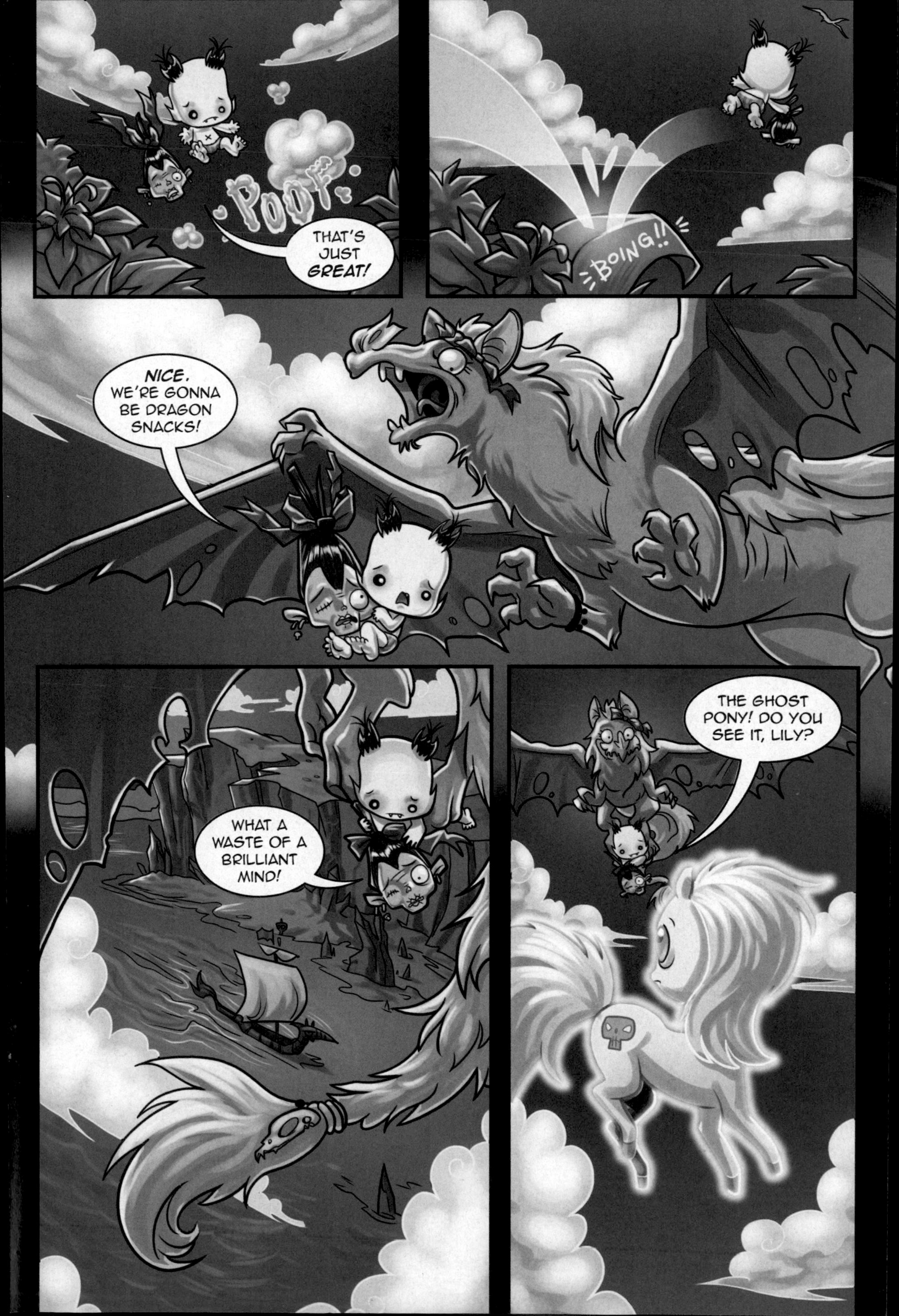
POOF
THAT'S JUST GREAT!
BOING!!
NICE. WE'RE GONNA BE DRAGON SNACKS!
WHAT A WASTE OF A BRILLIANT MIND!
THE GHOST PONY! DO YOU SEE IT, LILY?

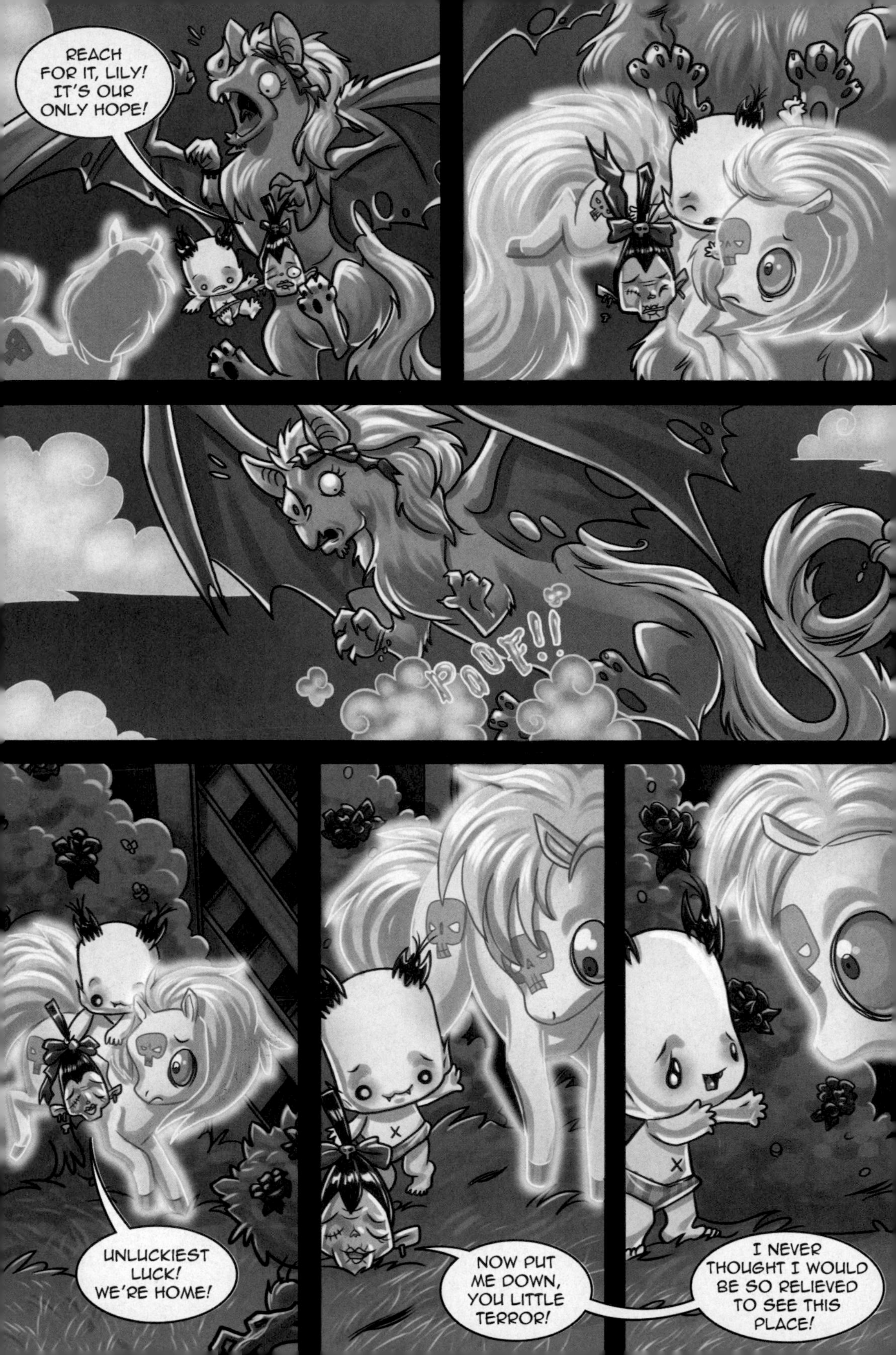
REACH FOR IT, LILY! IT'S OUR ONLY HOPE!
POOF!!
UNLUCKIEST LUCK! WE'RE HOME!
NOW PUT ME DOWN, YOU LITTLE TERROR!
I NEVER THOUGHT I WOULD BE SO RELIEVED TO SEE THIS PLACE!

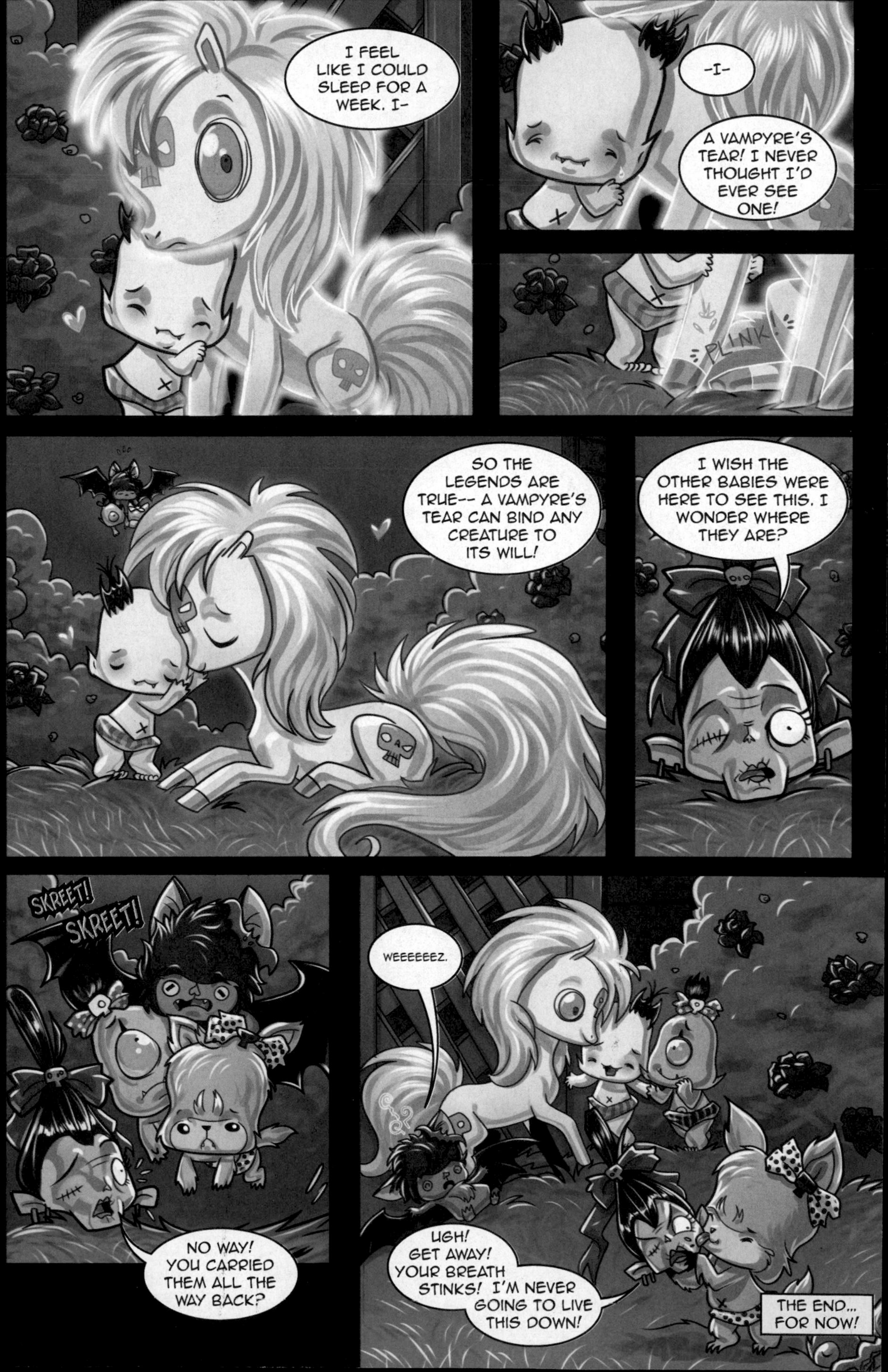

I FEEL LIKE I COULD SLEEP FOR A WEEK. I-
-I-
A VAMPYRE'S TEAR! I NEVER THOUGHT I'D EVER SEE ONE!
PLINK!
SO THE LEGENDS ARE TRUE-- A VAMPYRE'S TEAR CAN BIND ANY CREATURE TO ITS WILL!
I WISH THE OTHER BABIES WERE HERE TO SEE THIS. I WONDER WHERE THEY ARE?
SKREET! SKREET!
NO WAY! YOU CARRIED THEM ALL THE WAY BACK?
WEEEEEEZ.
UGH! GET AWAY! YOUR BREATH STINKS! I'M NEVER GOING TO LIVE THIS DOWN!
THE END... FOR NOW!

CHAPTER TWO

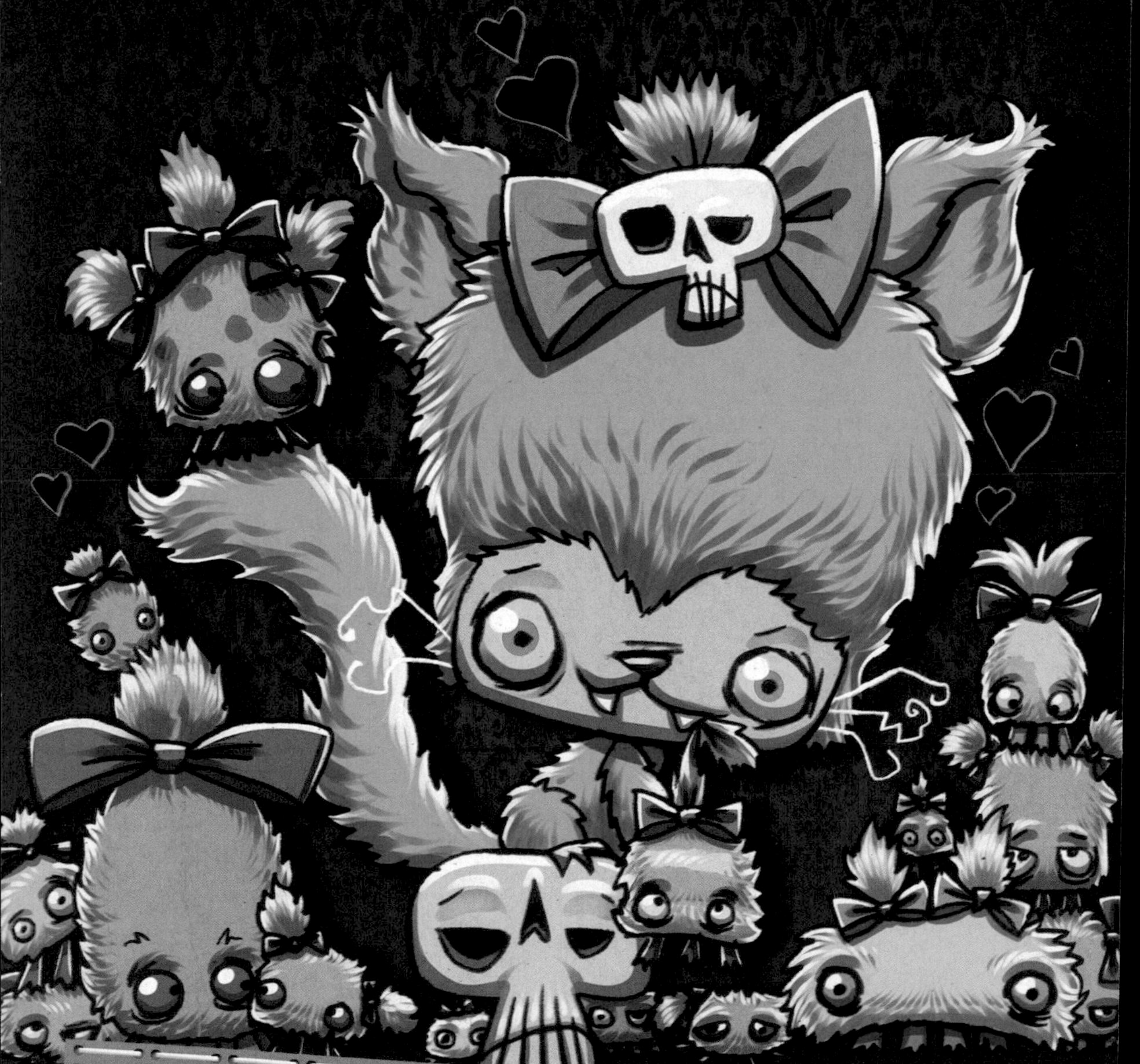

BEWARE THE BITEMARES!

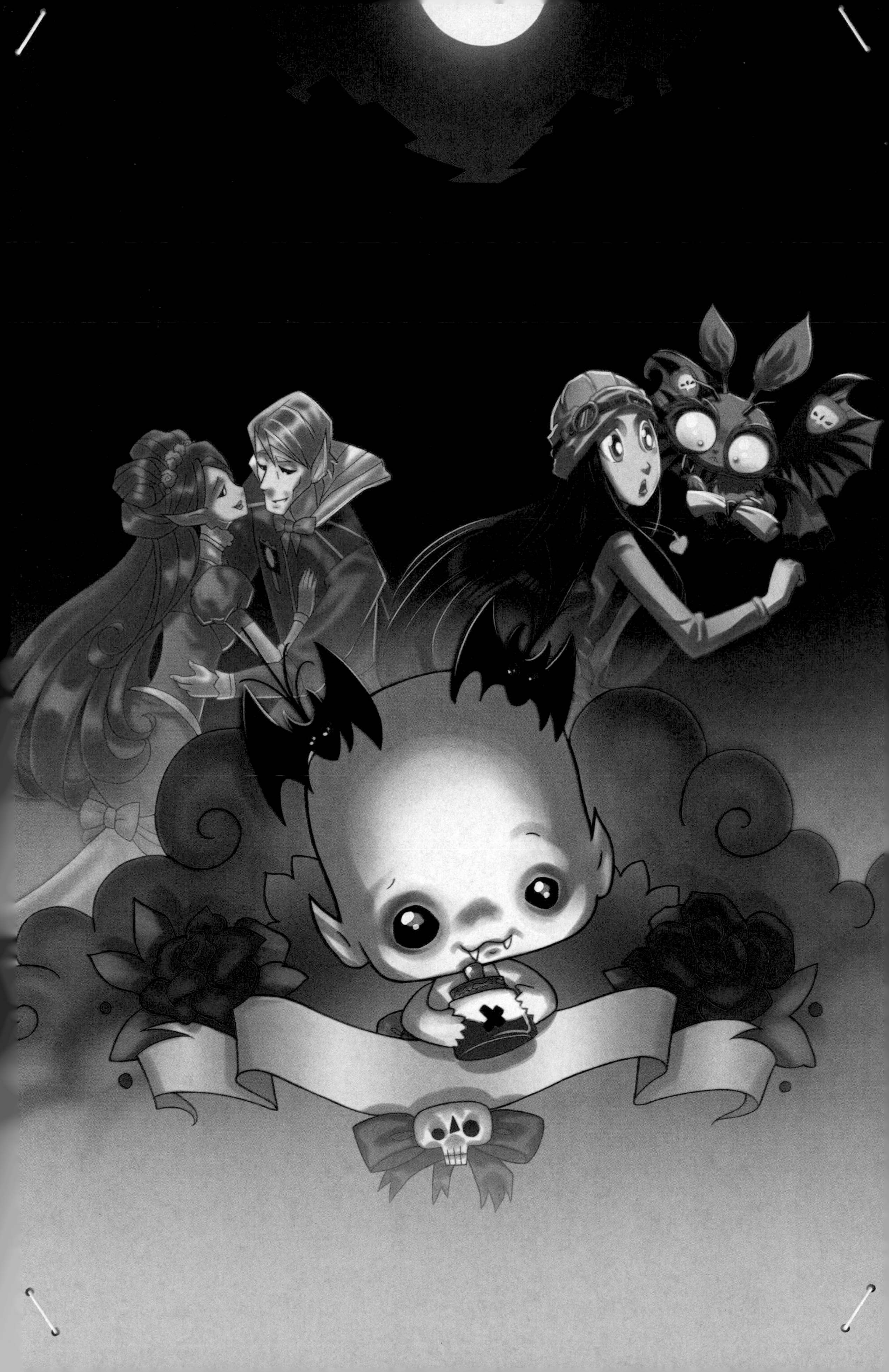

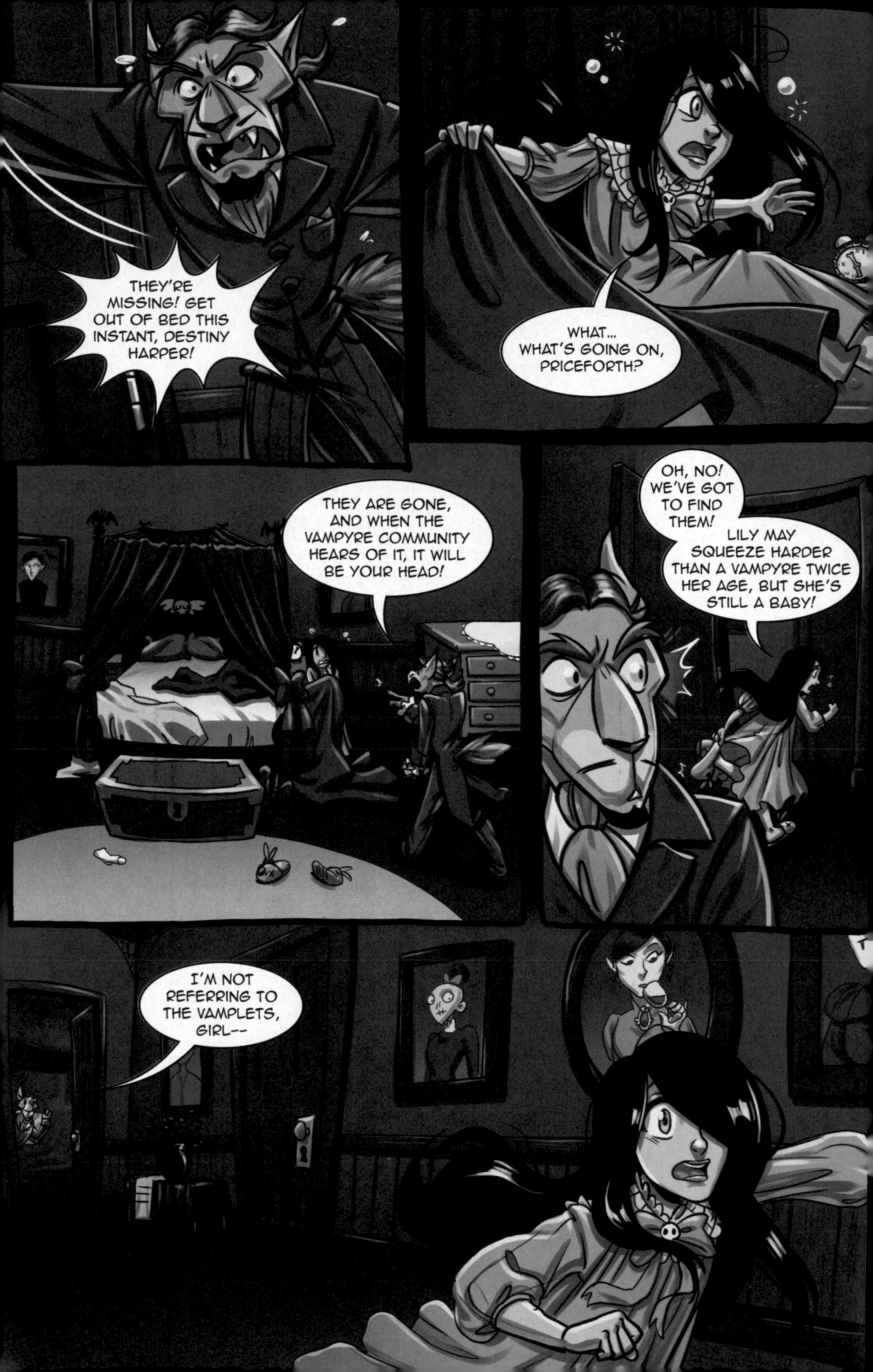
THEY'RE MISSING! GET OUT OF BED THIS INSTANT, DESTINY HARPER!
WHAT... WHAT'S GOING ON, PRICEFORTH?
THEY ARE GONE, AND WHEN THE VAMPYRE COMMUNITY HEARS OF IT, IT WILL BE YOUR HEAD!
OH, NO! WE'VE GOT TO FIND THEM!
LILY MAY SQUEEZE HARDER THAN A VAMPYRE TWICE HER AGE, BUT SHE'S STILL A BABY!
I'M NOT REFERRING TO THE VAMPLETS, GIRL--

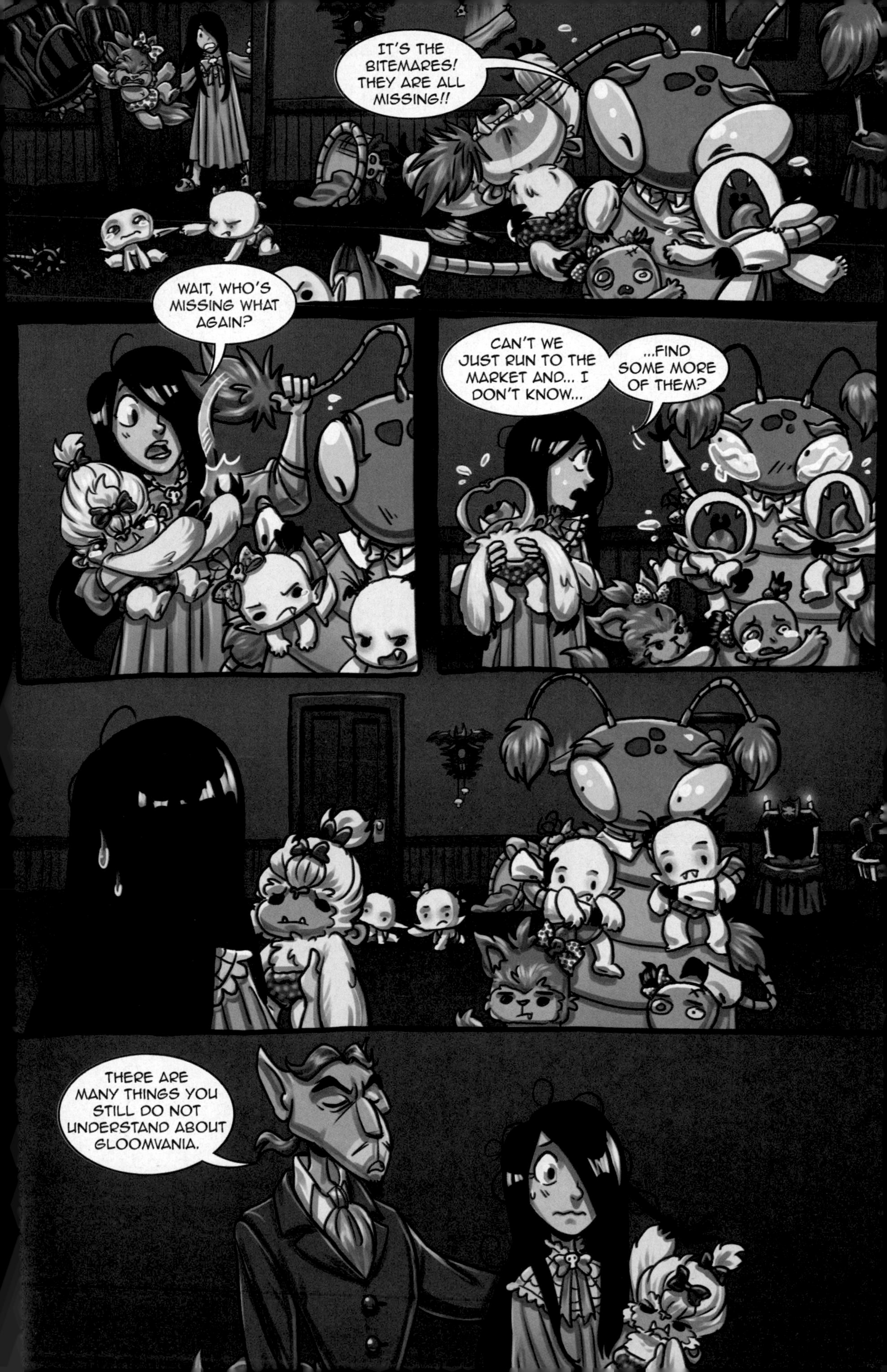

IT'S THE BITEMARES! THEY ARE ALL MISSING!!
WAIT, WHO'S MISSING WHAT AGAIN?
CAN'T WE JUST RUN TO THE MARKET AND... I DON'T KNOW...
...FIND SOME MORE OF THEM?
THERE ARE MANY THINGS YOU STILL DO NOT UNDERSTAND ABOUT GLOOMVANIA.

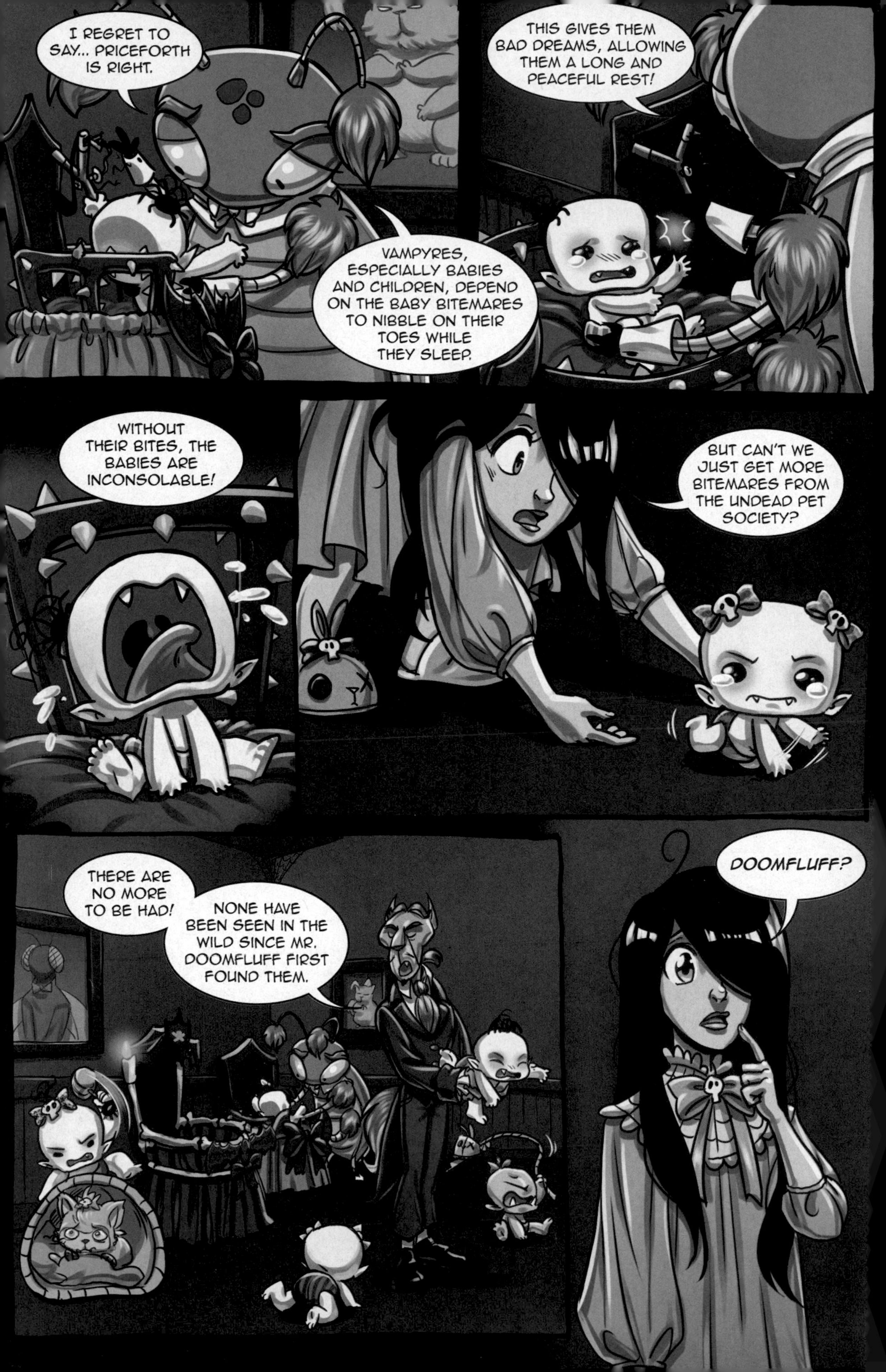
I REGRET TO SAY... PRICEFORTH IS RIGHT.
VAMPYRES, ESPECIALLY BABIES AND CHILDREN, DEPEND ON THE BABY BITEMARES TO NIBBLE ON THEIR TOES WHILE THEY SLEEP.
THIS GIVES THEM BAD DREAMS, ALLOWING THEM A LONG AND PEACEFUL REST!
WITHOUT THEIR BITES, THE BABIES ARE INCONSOLABLE!
BUT CAN'T WE JUST GET MORE BITEMARES FROM THE UNDEAD PET SOCIETY?
THERE ARE NO MORE TO BE HAD!
NONE HAVE BEEN SEEN IN THE WILD SINCE MR. DOOMFLUFF FIRST FOUND THEM.
DOOMFLUFF?

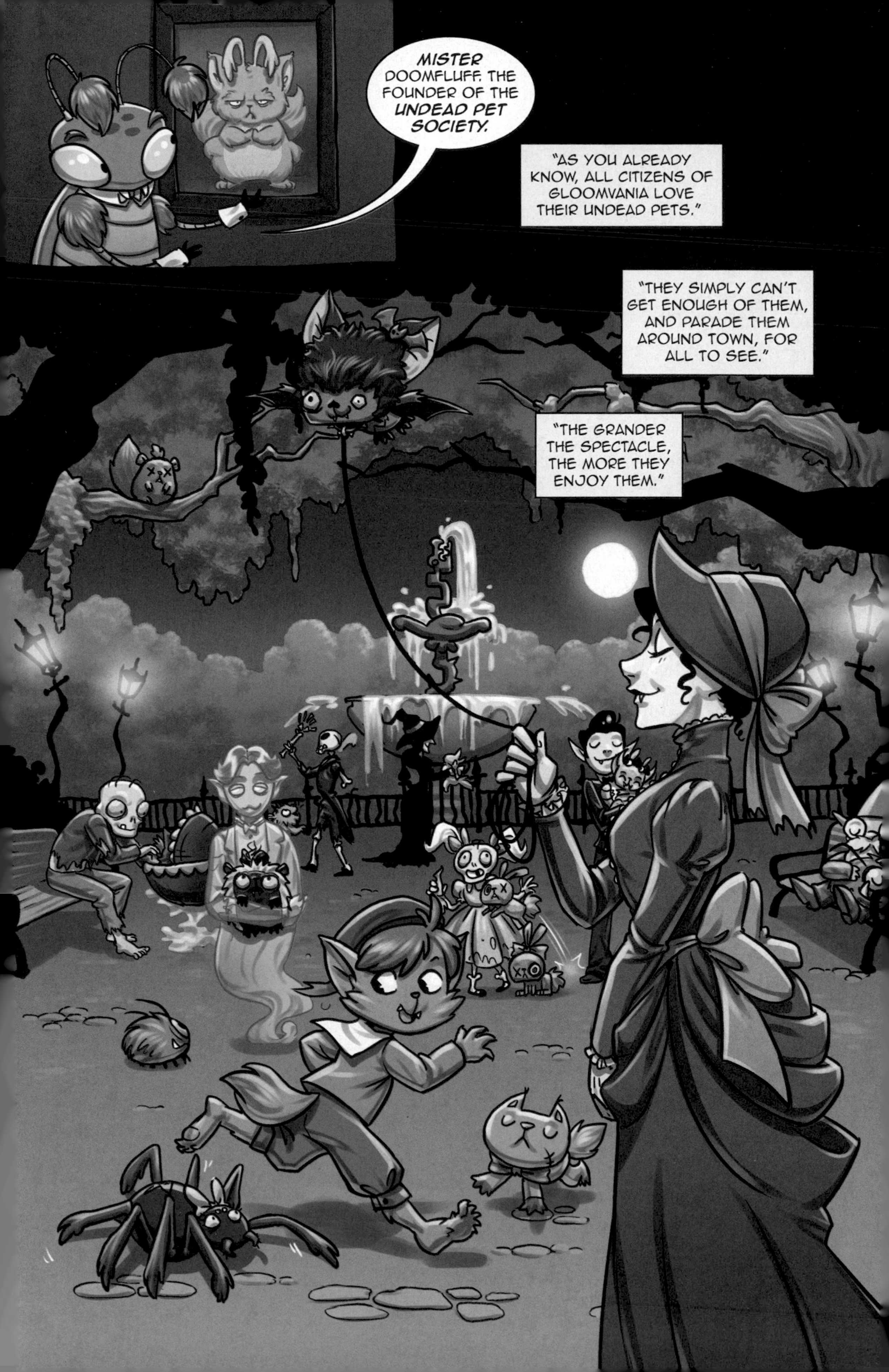
MISTER DOOMFLUFF. THE FOUNDER OF THE UNDEAD PET SOCIETY.
"AS YOU ALREADY KNOW, ALL CITIZENS OF GLOOMVANIA LOVE THEIR UNDEAD PETS."
"THEY SIMPLY CAN'T GET ENOUGH OF THEM, AND PARADE THEM AROUND TOWN, FOR ALL TO SEE."
"THE GRANDER THE SPECTACLE, THE MORE THEY ENJOY THEM."

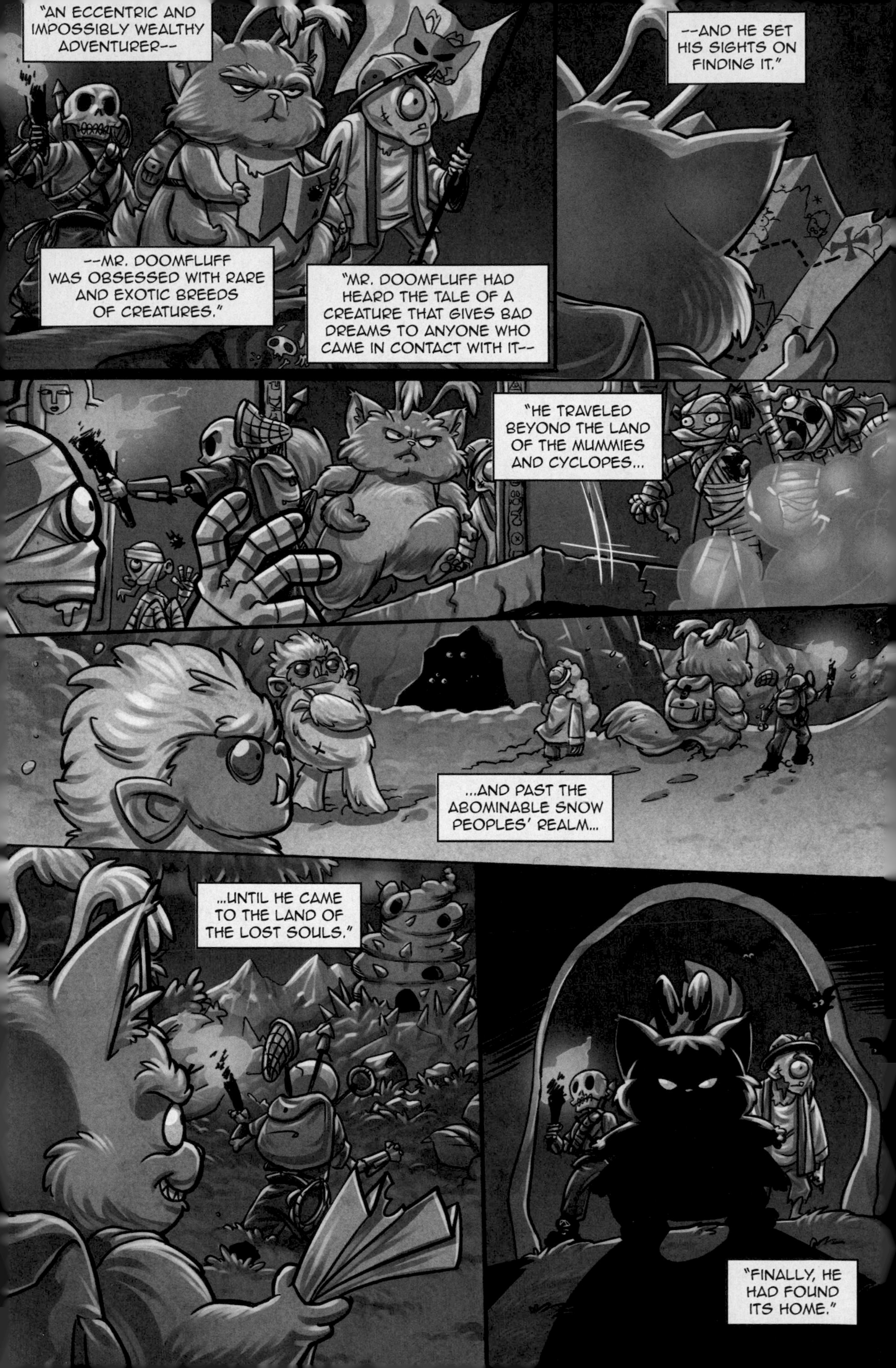
"AN ECCENTRIC AND IMPOSSIBLY WEALTHY ADVENTURER--
--MR. DOOMFLUFF WAS OBSESSED WITH RARE AND EXOTIC BREEDS OF CREATURES."
"MR. DOOMFLUFF HAD HEARD THE TALE OF A CREATURE THAT GIVES BAD DREAMS TO ANYONE WHO CAME IN CONTACT WITH IT--
--AND HE SET HIS SIGHTS ON FINDING IT."
"HE TRAVELED BEYOND THE LAND OF THE MUMMIES AND CYCLOPES...
...AND PAST THE ABOMINABLE SNOW PEOPLES' REALM...
...UNTIL HE CAME TO THE LAND OF THE LOST SOULS."
"FINALLY, HE HAD FOUND ITS HOME."

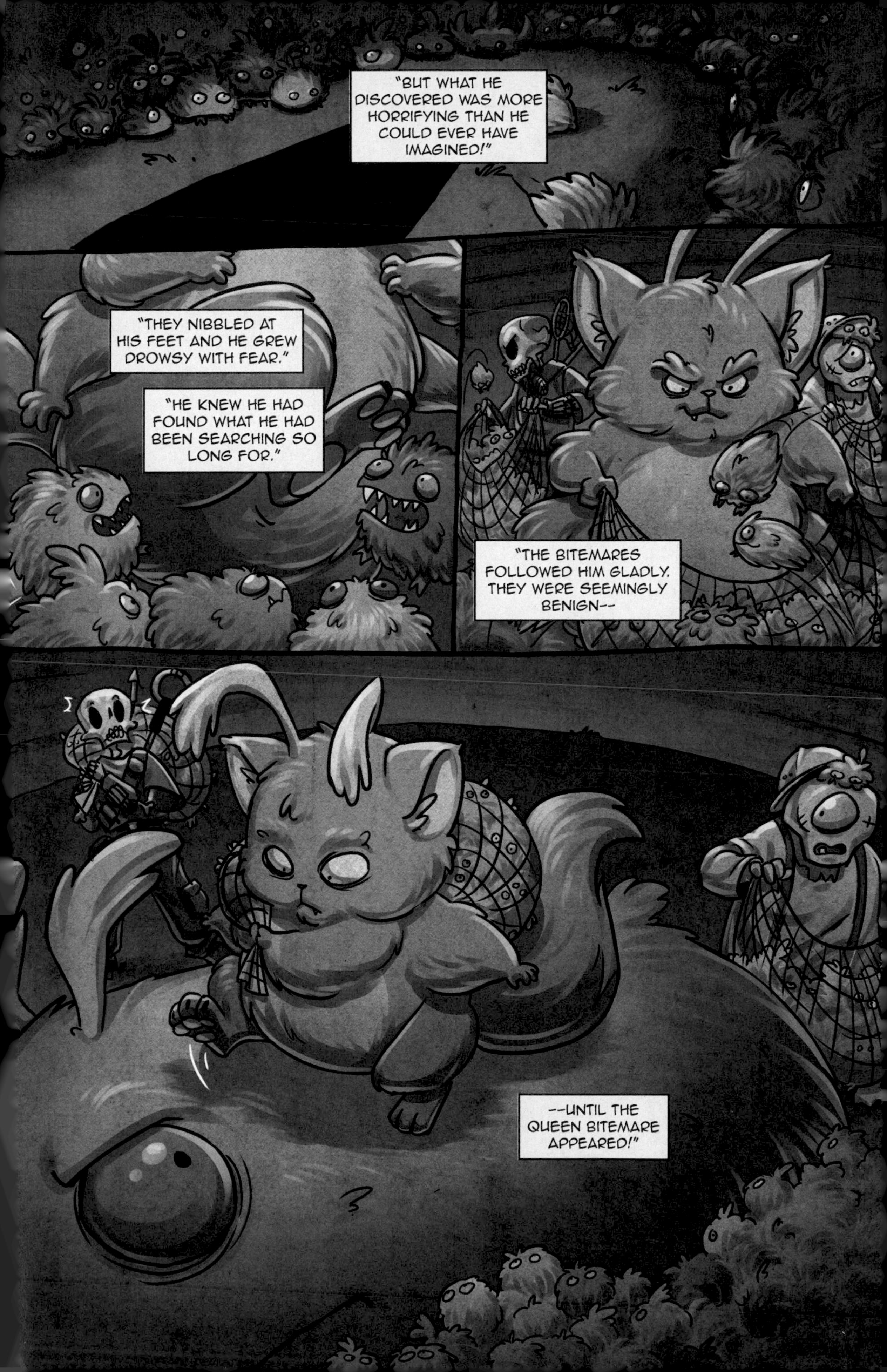
"BUT WHAT HE DISCOVERED WAS MORE HORRIFYING THAN HE COULD EVER HAVE IMAGINED!"
"THEY NIBBLED AT HIS FEET AND HE GREW DROWSY WITH FEAR."
"HE KNEW HE HAD FOUND WHAT HE HAD BEEN SEARCHING SO LONG FOR."
"THE BITEMARES FOLLOWED HIM GLADLY. THEY WERE SEEMINGLY BENIGN--
--UNTIL THE QUEEN BITEMARE APPEARED!"

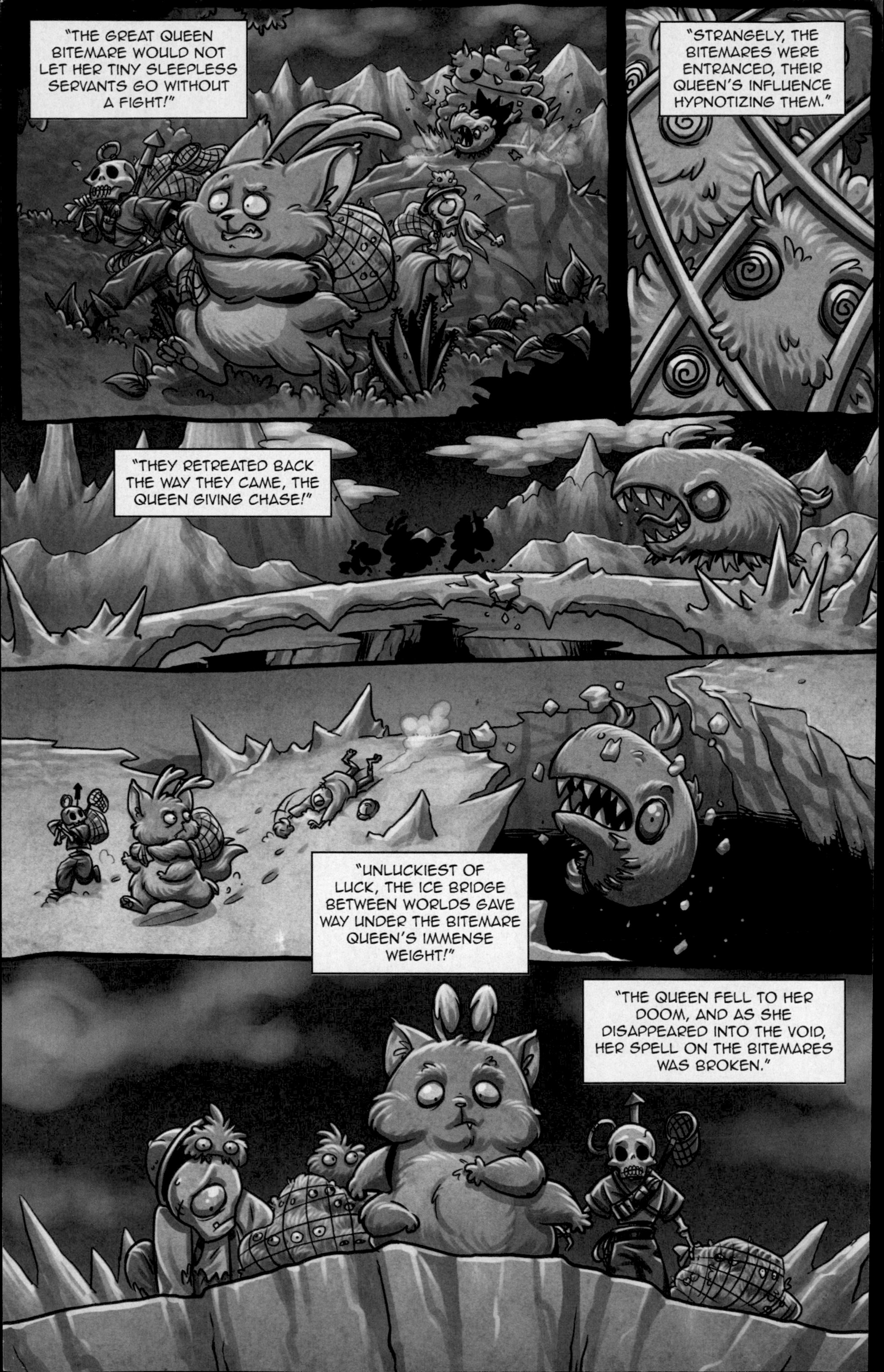
"THE GREAT QUEEN BITEMARE WOULD NOT LET HER TINY SLEEPLESS SERVANTS GO WITHOUT A FIGHT!"
"STRANGELY, THE BITEMARES WERE ENTRANCED, THEIR QUEEN'S INFLUENCE HYPNOTIZING THEM."
"THEY RETREATED BACK THE WAY THEY CAME, THE QUEEN GIVING CHASE!"
"UNLUCKIEST OF LUCK, THE ICE BRIDGE BETWEEN WORLDS GAVE WAY UNDER THE BITEMARE QUEEN'S IMMENSE WEIGHT!"
"THE QUEEN FELL TO HER DOOM, AND AS SHE DISAPPEARED INTO THE VOID, HER SPELL ON THE BITEMARES WAS BROKEN."

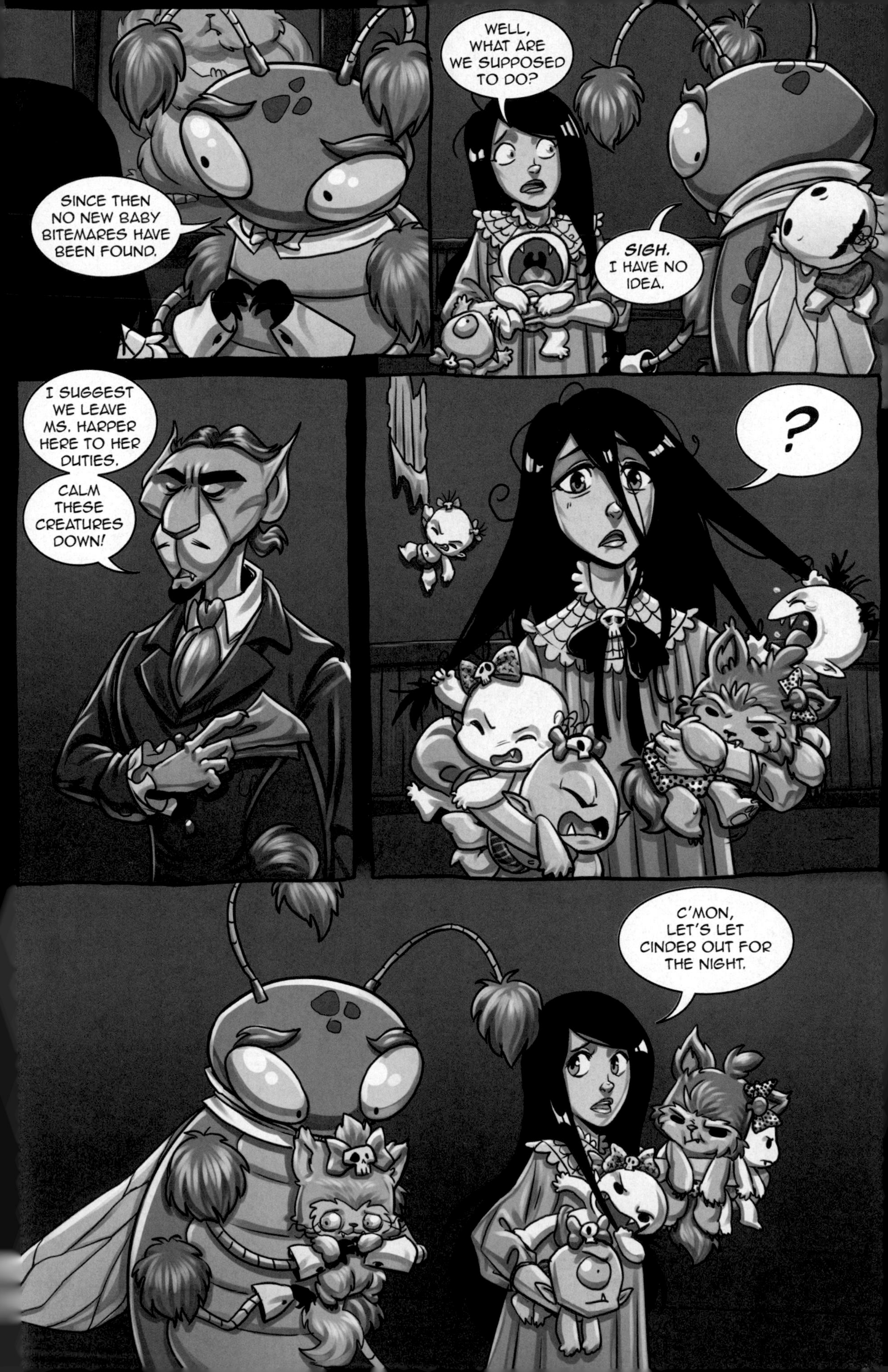
SINCE THEN NO NEW BABY BITEMARES HAVE BEEN FOUND.
WELL, WHAT ARE WE SUPPOSED TO DO?
SIGH. I HAVE NO IDEA.
I SUGGEST WE LEAVE MS. HARPER HERE TO HER DUTIES.
CALM THESE CREATURES DOWN!
?
C'MON, LET'S LET CINDER OUT FOR THE NIGHT.

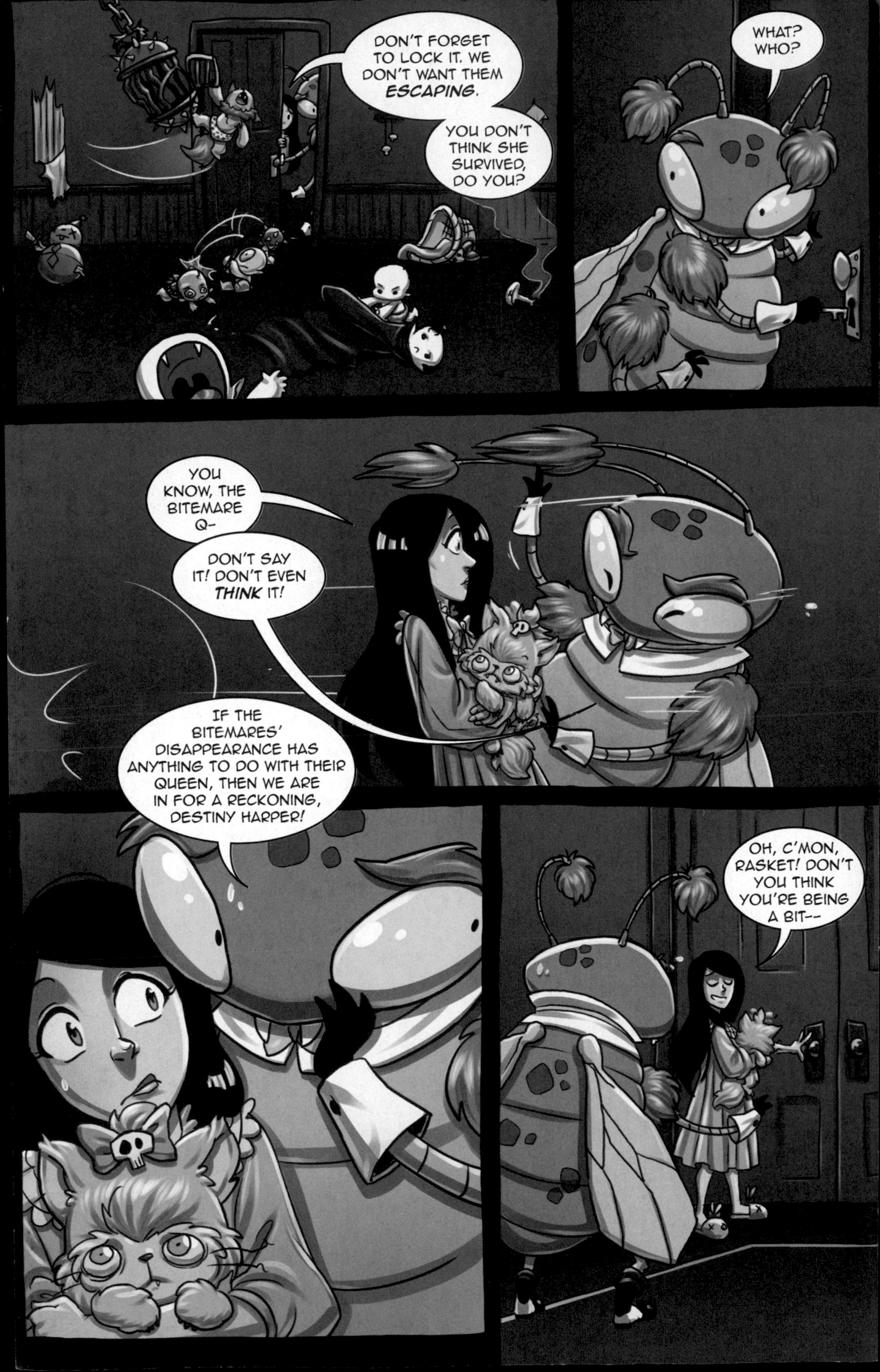
DON'T FORGET TO LOCK IT. WE DON'T WANT THEM ESCAPING.
YOU DON'T THINK SHE SURVIVED, DO YOU?
WHAT? WHO?
YOU KNOW, THE BITEMARE Q-
DON'T SAY IT! DON'T EVEN THINK IT!
IF THE BITEMARES' DISAPPEARANCE HAS ANYTHING TO DO WITH THEIR QUEEN, THEN WE ARE IN FOR A RECKONING, DESTINY HARPER!
OH, C'MON, RASKET! DON'T YOU THINK YOU'RE BEING A BIT--

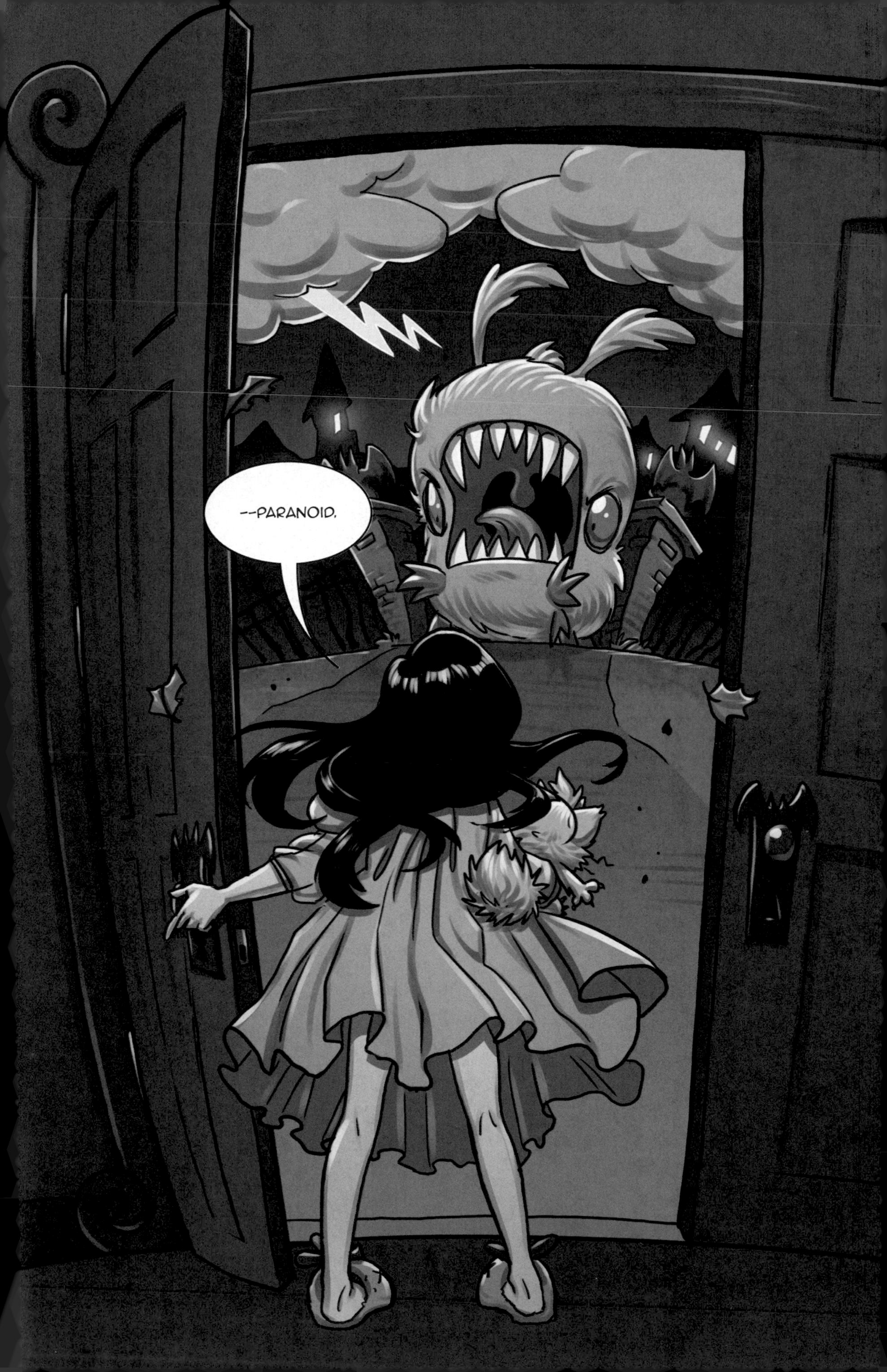
--PARANOID.

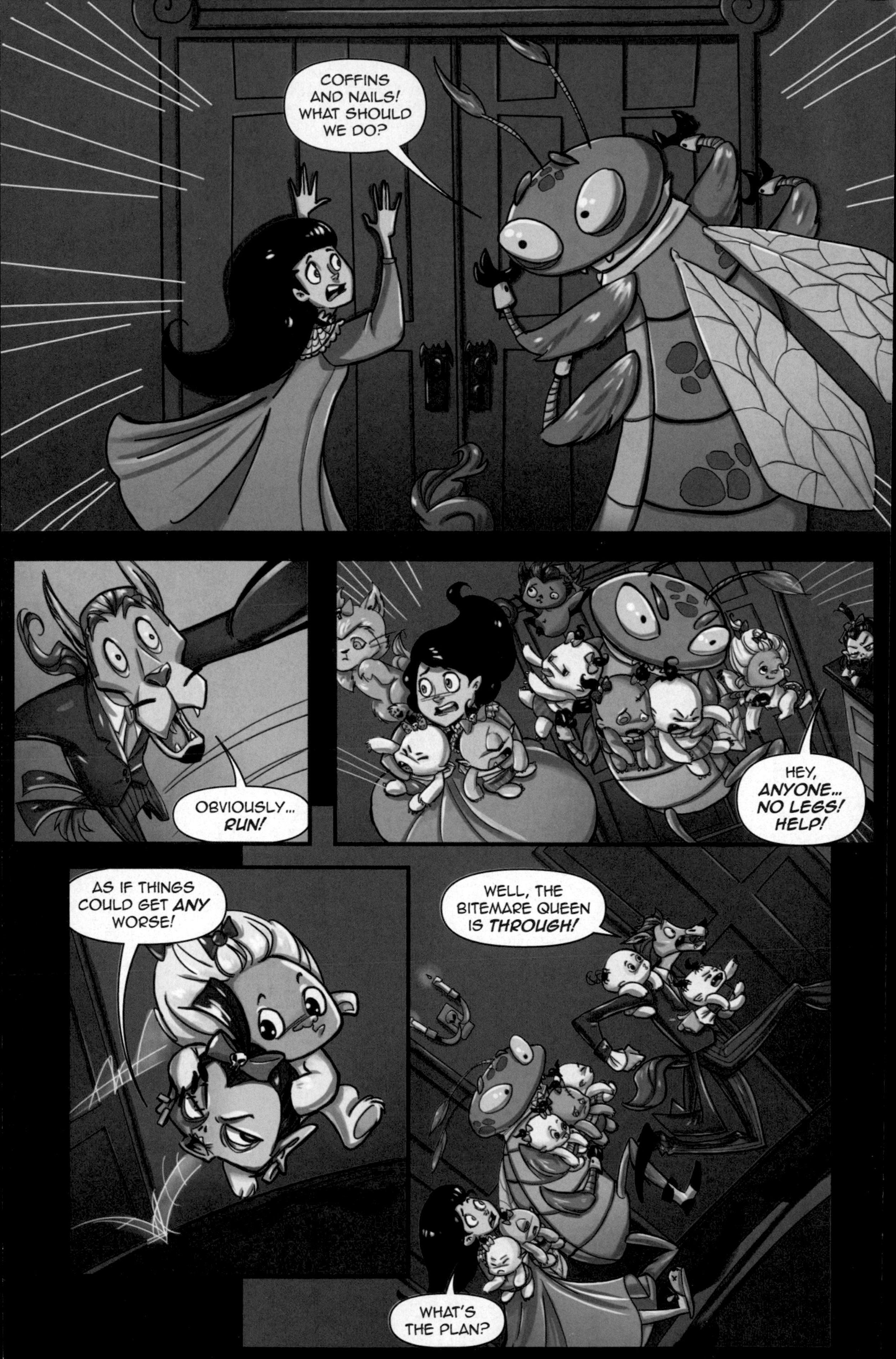
COFFINS AND NAILS! WHAT SHOULD WE DO?
OBVIOUSLY... RUN!
HEY, ANYONE... NO LEGS! HELP!
AS IF THINGS COULD GET ANY WORSE!
WELL, THE BITEMARE QUEEN IS THROUGH!
WHAT'S THE PLAN?

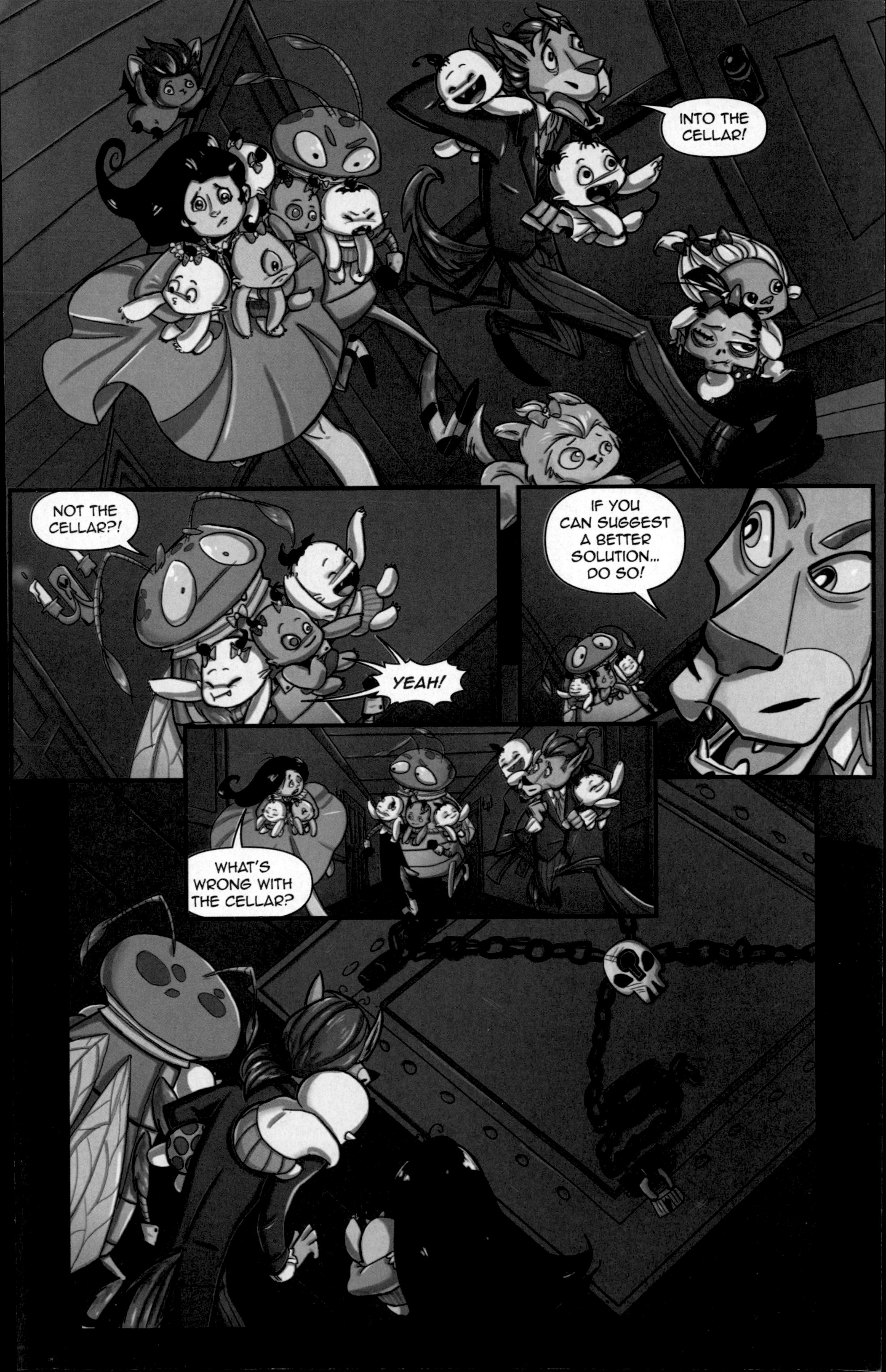
INTO THE CELLAR!
NOT THE CELLAR?!
YEAH!
IF YOU CAN SUGGEST A BETTER SOLUTION... DO SO!
WHAT'S WRONG WITH THE CELLAR?

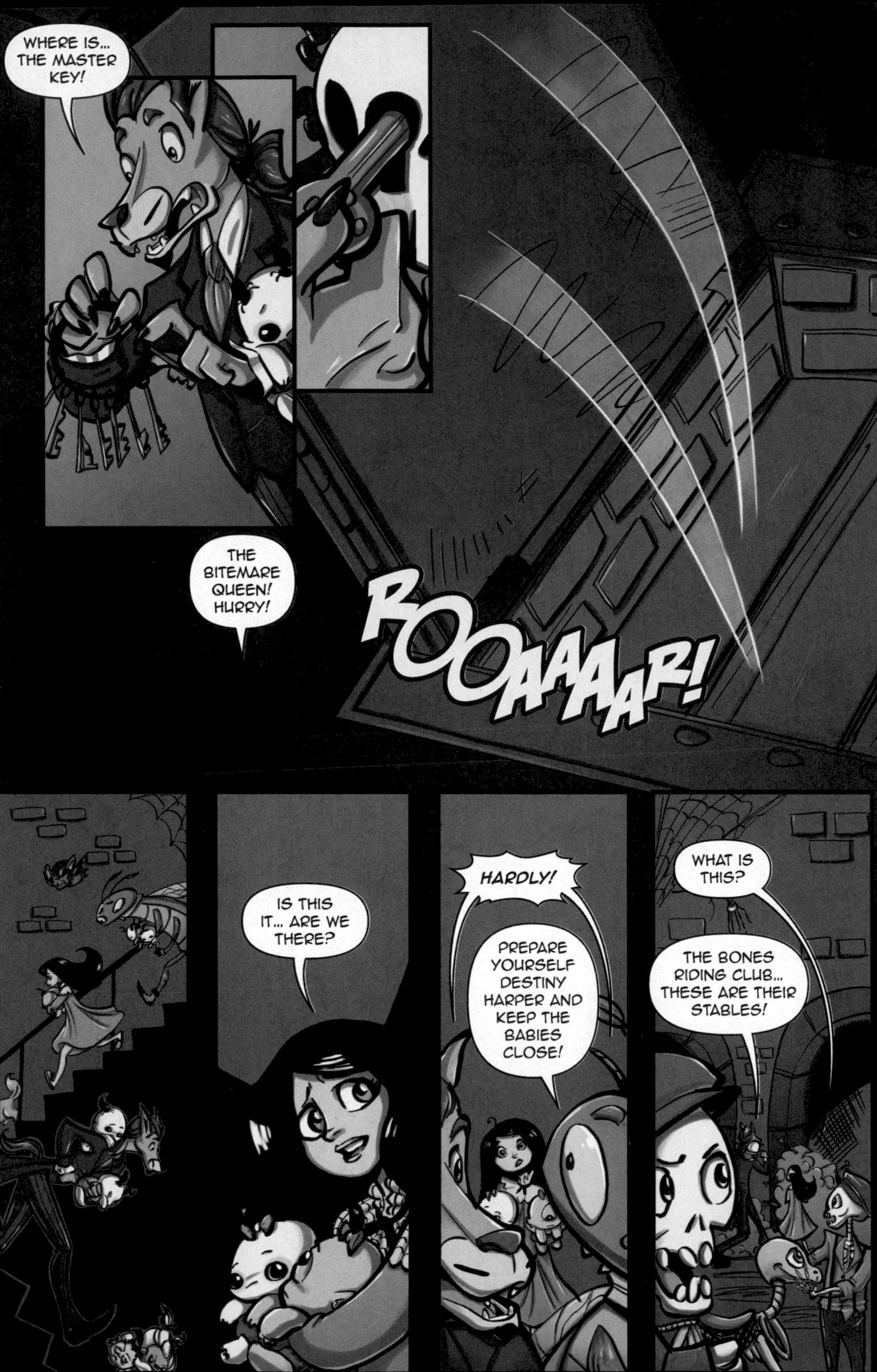
WHERE IS... THE MASTER KEY!
THE BITEMARE QUEEN! HURRY!
ROOAAAAAR!
IS THIS IT... ARE WE THERE?
HARDLY!
PREPARE YOURSELF DESTINY HARPER AND KEEP THE BABIES CLOSE!
WHAT IS THIS?
THE BONES RIDING CLUB... THESE ARE THEIR STABLES!

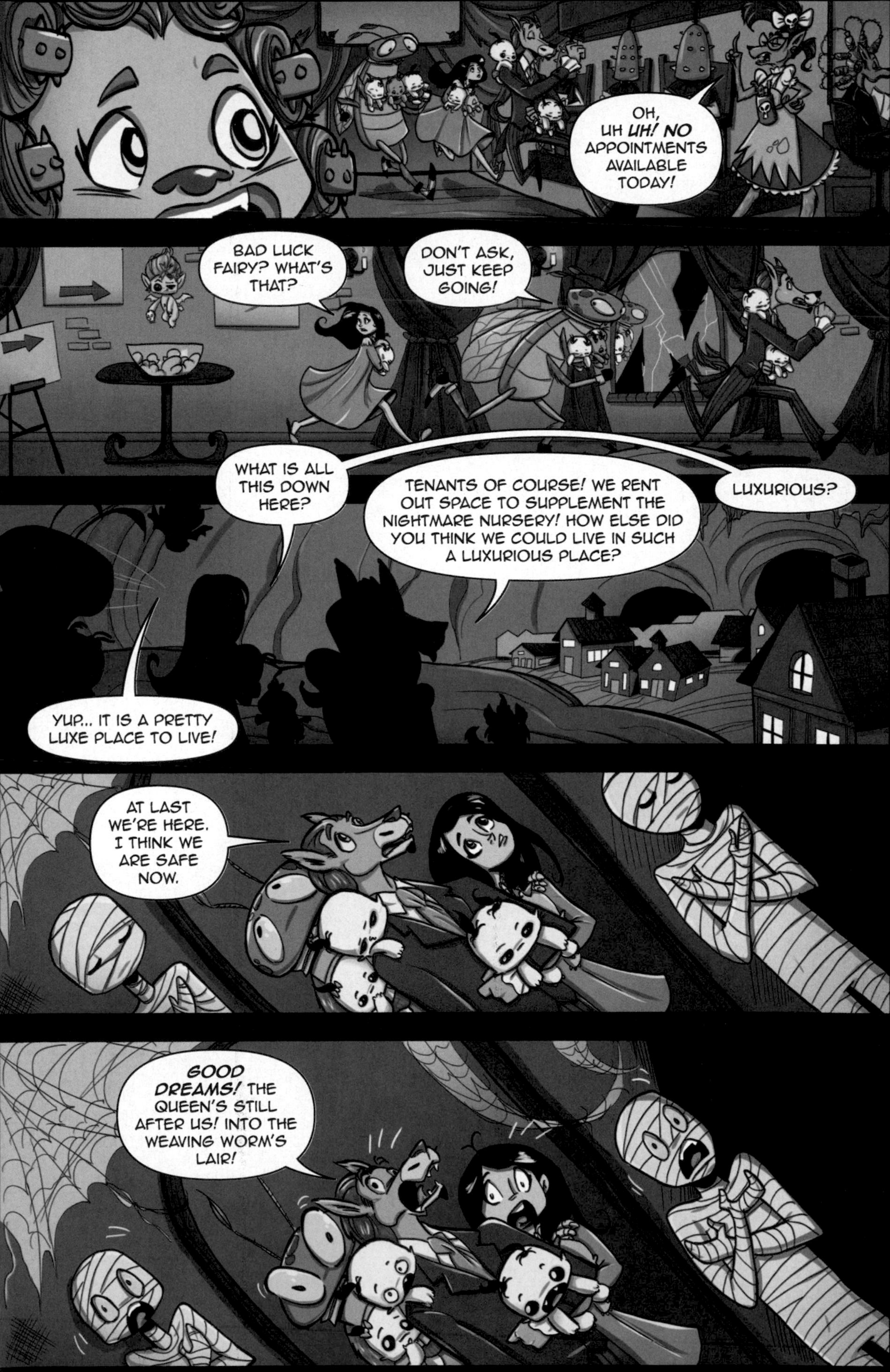
OH, UH UH! NO APPOINTMENTS AVAILABLE TODAY!
BAD LUCK FAIRY? WHAT'S THAT?
DON'T ASK, JUST KEEP GOING!
WHAT IS ALL THIS DOWN HERE?
TENANTS OF COURSE! WE RENT OUT SPACE TO SUPPLEMENT THE NIGHTMARE NURSERY! HOW ELSE DID YOU THINK WE COULD LIVE IN SUCH A LUXURIOUS PLACE?
LUXURIOUS?
YUP... IT IS A PRETTY LUXE PLACE TO LIVE!
AT LAST WE'RE HERE. I THINK WE ARE SAFE NOW.
GOOD DREAMS! THE QUEEN'S STILL AFTER US! INTO THE WEAVING WORM'S LAIR!

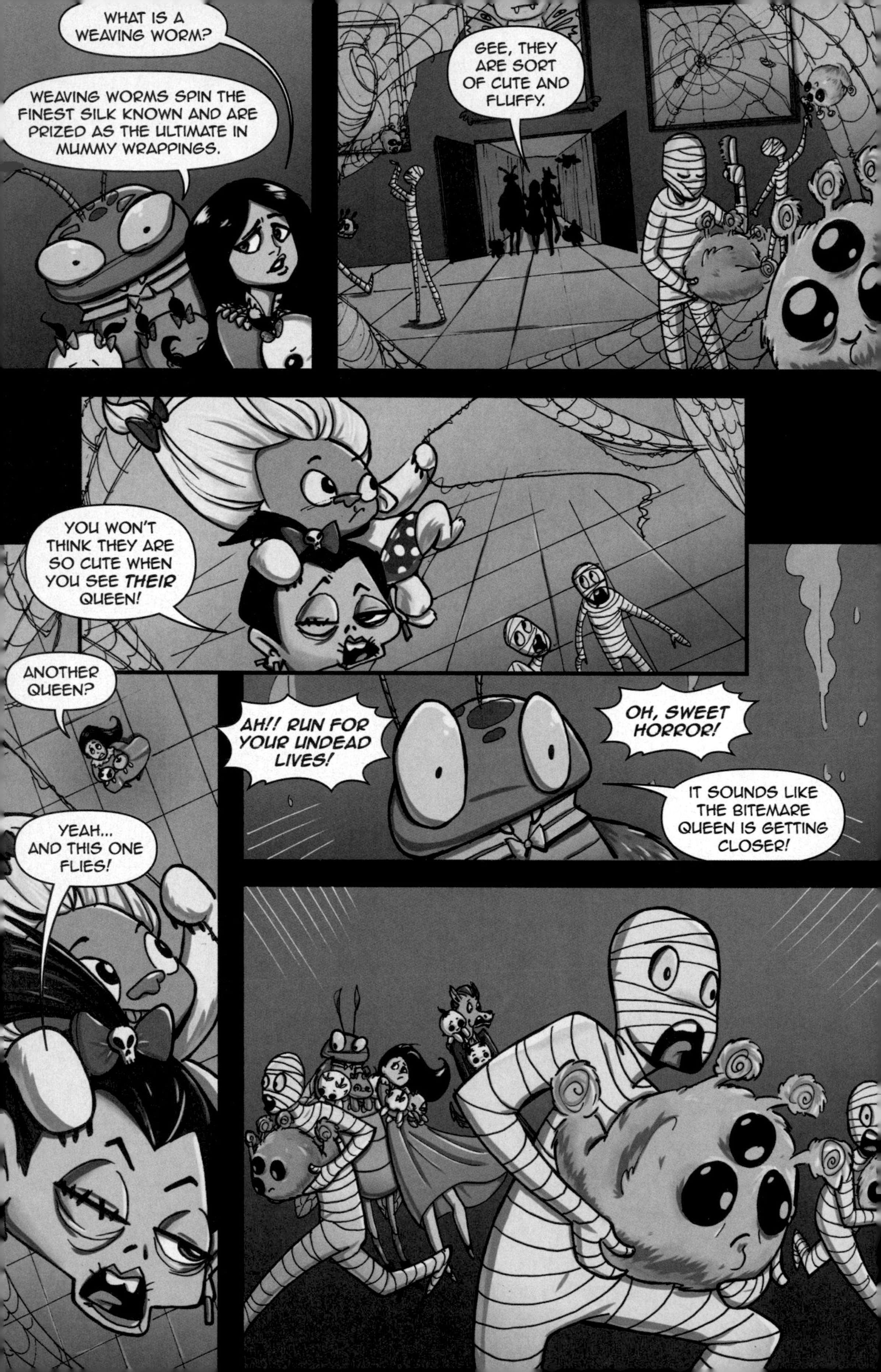
WHAT IS A WEAVING WORM?
WEAVING WORMS SPIN THE FINEST SILK KNOWN AND ARE PRIZED AS THE ULTIMATE IN MUMMY WRAPPINGS.
GEE, THEY ARE SORT OF CUTE AND FLUFFY.
YOU WON'T THINK THEY ARE SO CUTE WHEN YOU SEE THEIR QUEEN!
ANOTHER QUEEN?
YEAH... AND THIS ONE FLIES!
AH!! RUN FOR YOUR UNDEAD LIVES!
OH, SWEET HORROR!
IT SOUNDS LIKE THE BITEMARE QUEEN IS GETTING CLOSER!

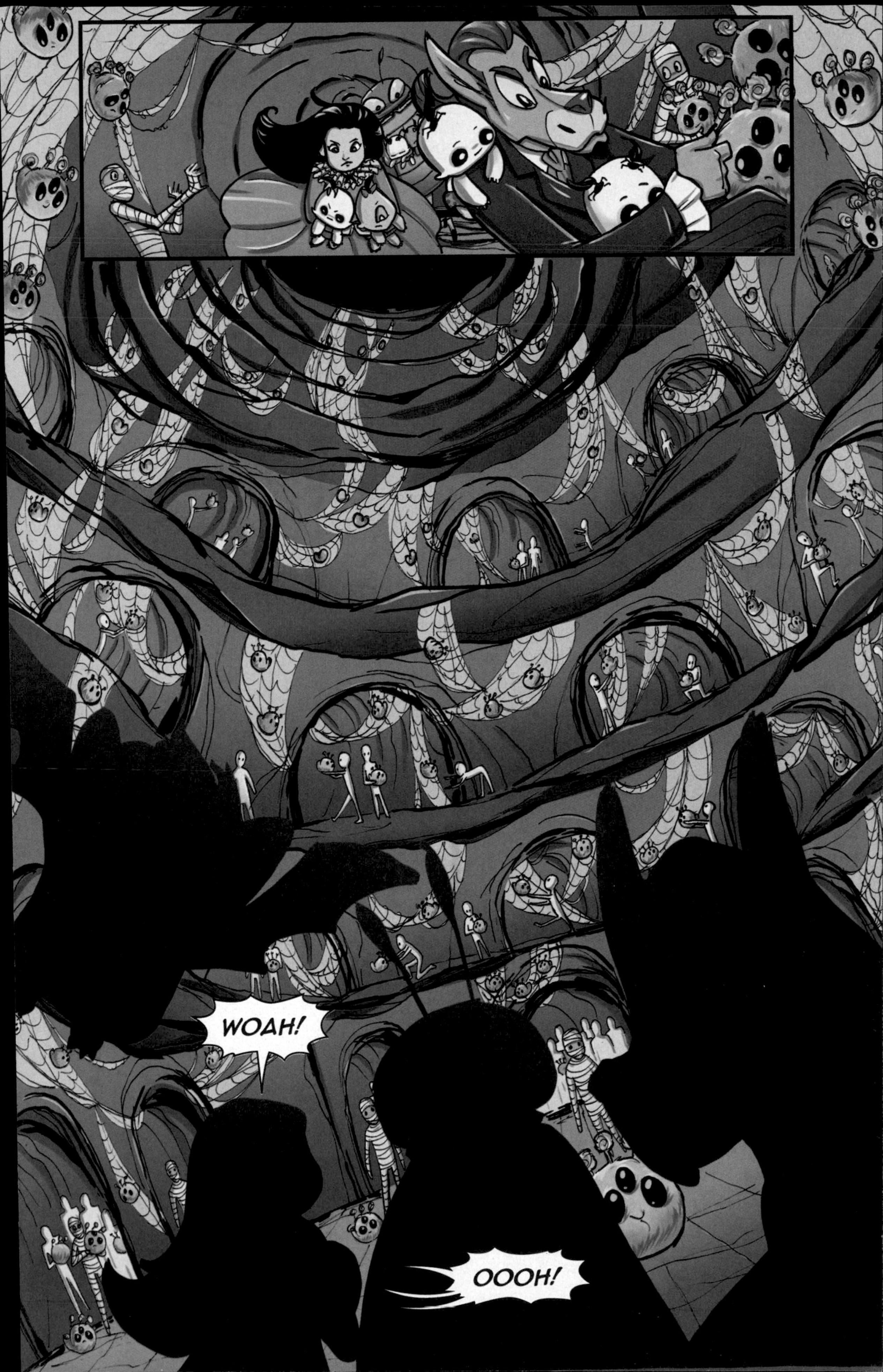
WOAH!
OOOH!

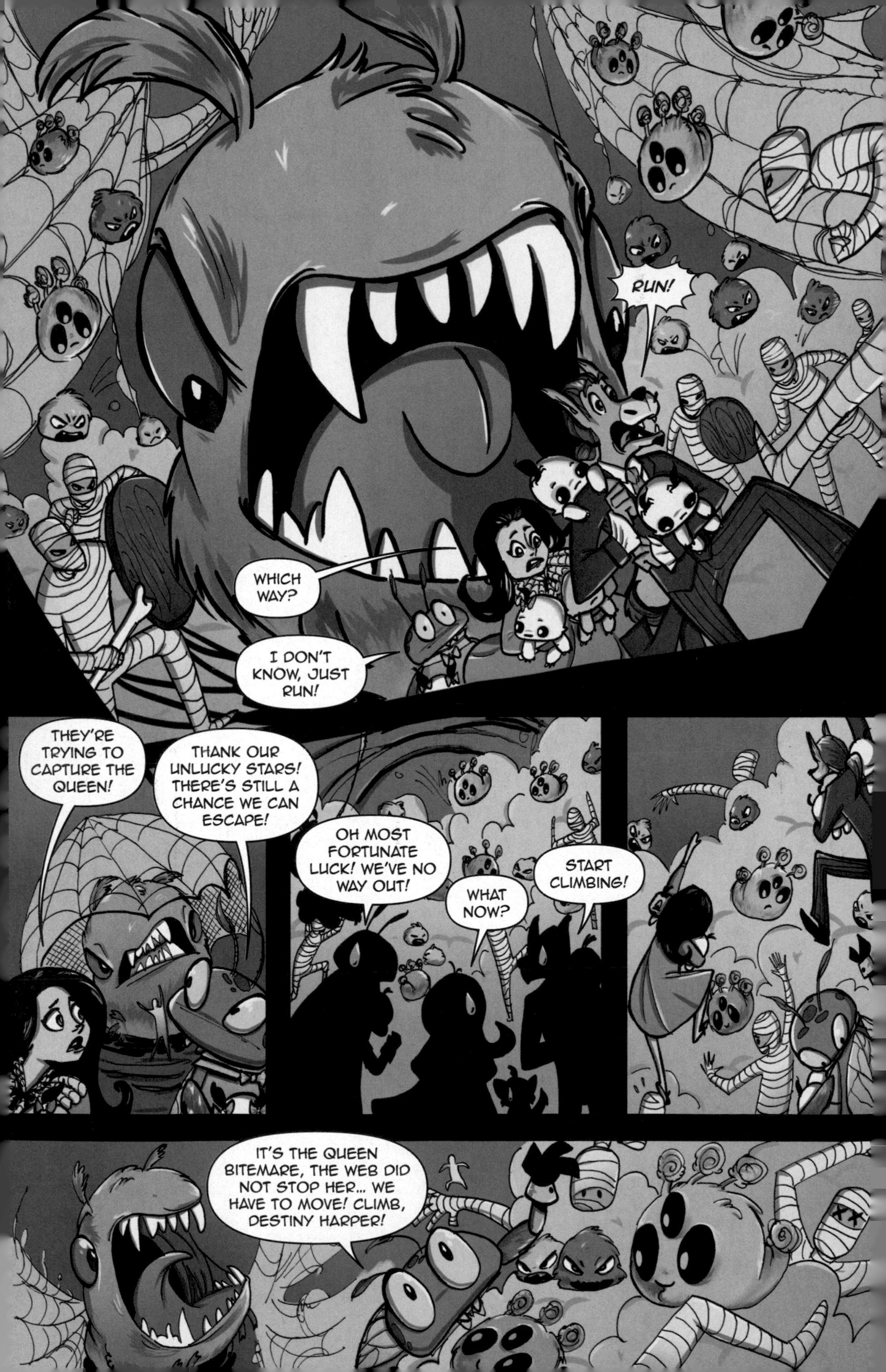
RUN!
WHICH WAY?
I DON'T KNOW, JUST RUN!
THEY'RE TRYING TO CAPTURE THE QUEEN!
THANK OUR UNLUCKY STARS! THERE'S STILL A CHANCE WE CAN ESCAPE!
OH MOST FORTUNATE LUCK! WE'VE NO WAY OUT!
WHAT NOW?
START CLIMBING!
IT'S THE QUEEN BITEMARE, THE WEB DID NOT STOP HER... WE HAVE TO MOVE! CLIMB, DESTINY HARPER!

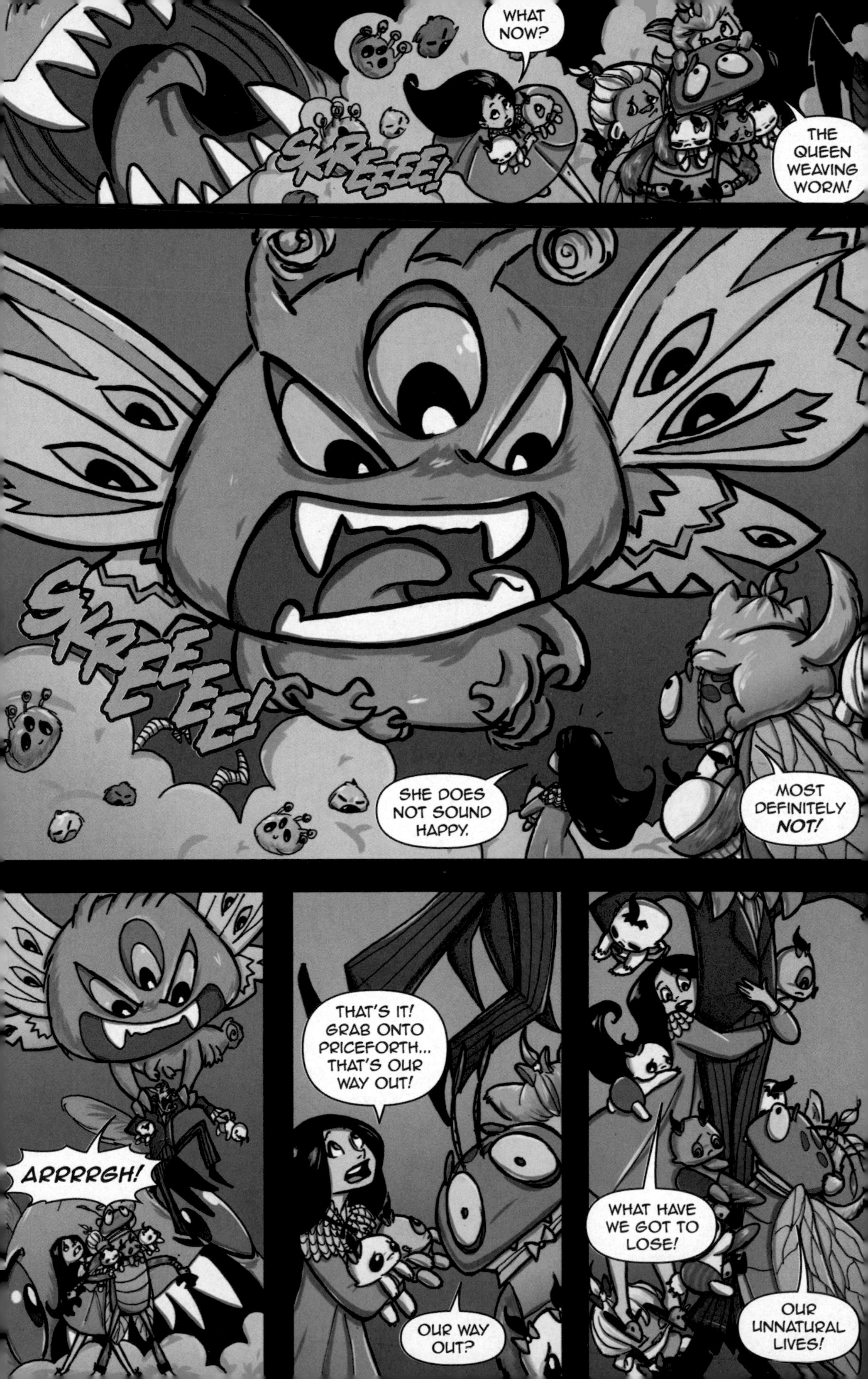
WHAT NOW?
SKREEEEE!
THE QUEEN WEAVING WORM!
SKREEEEE!
SHE DOES NOT SOUND HAPPY.
MOST DEFINITELY NOT!
ARRRRGH!
THAT'S IT! GRAB ONTO PRICEFORTH... THAT'S OUR WAY OUT!
OUR WAY OUT?
WHAT HAVE WE GOT TO LOSE!
OUR UNNATURAL LIVES!

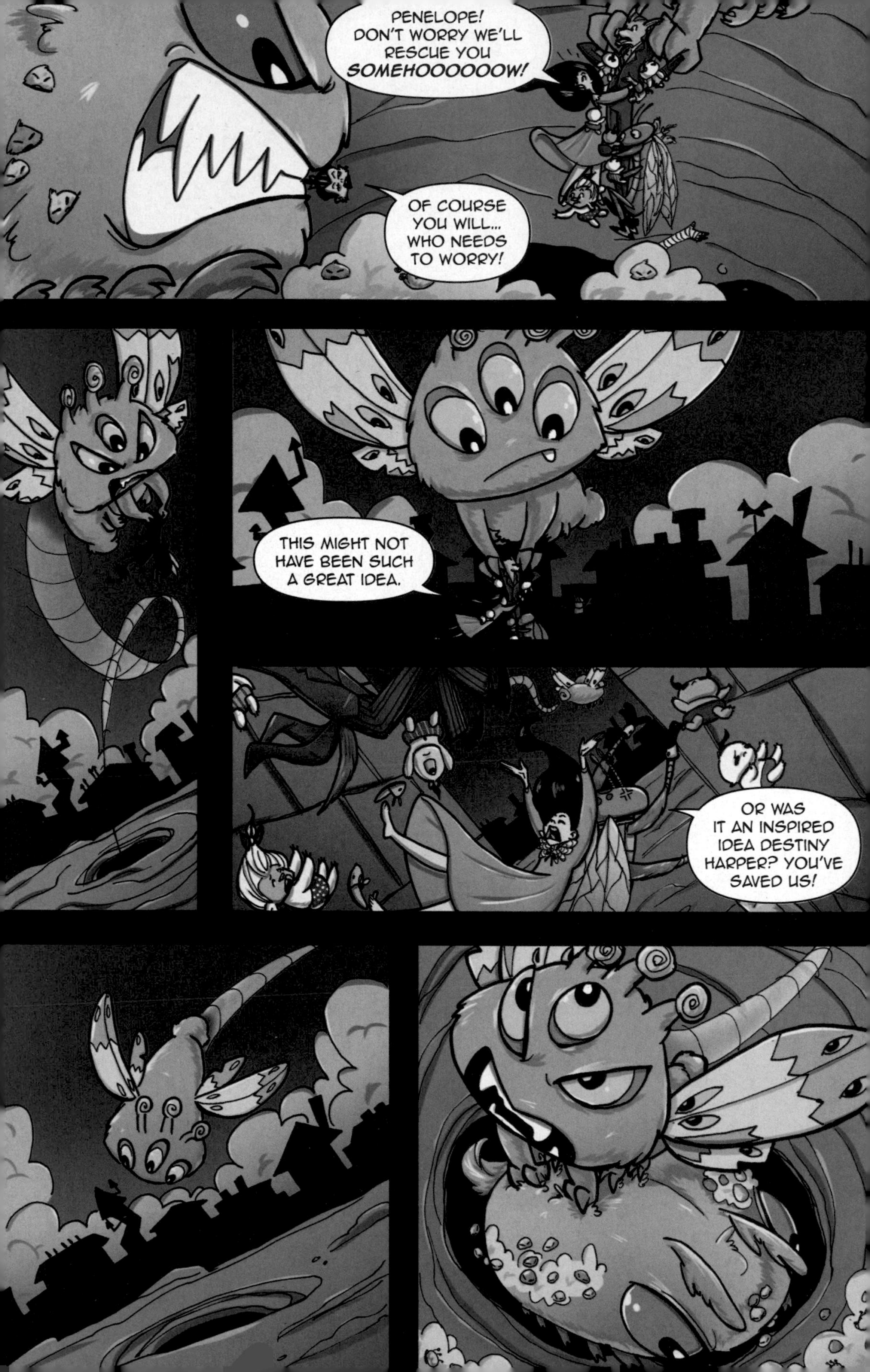
PENELOPE! DON'T WORRY WE'LL RESCUE YOU *SOMEHOOOOOOW!*
OF COURSE YOU WILL... WHO NEEDS TO WORRY!
THIS MIGHT NOT HAVE BEEN SUCH A GREAT IDEA.
OR WAS IT AN INSPIRED IDEA DESTINY HARPER? YOU'VE SAVED US!

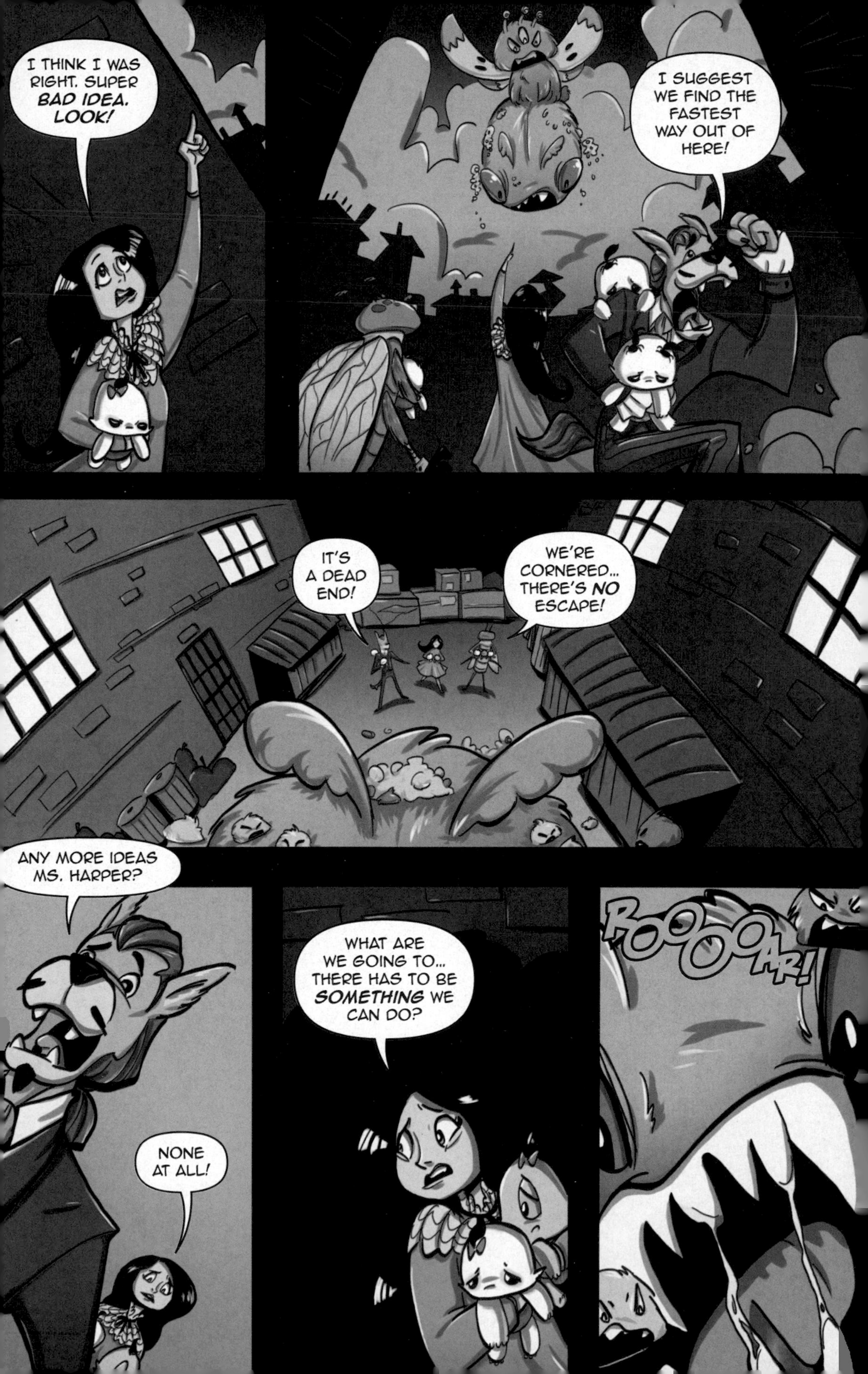
I THINK I WAS RIGHT. SUPER BAD IDEA. LOOK!
I SUGGEST WE FIND THE FASTEST WAY OUT OF HERE!
IT'S A DEAD END!
WE'RE CORNERED... THERE'S NO ESCAPE!
ANY MORE IDEAS MS. HARPER?
NONE AT ALL!
WHAT ARE WE GOING TO... THERE HAS TO BE SOMETHING WE CAN DO?
ROOOOOAR!

LOOK IT'S CINDER!

STUPID CREATURE THINKS SHE CAN CHALLENGE THE QUEEN BITEMARE!

OH, NO... SHE'LL BE KILLED!

GRRRRRR!

HEEEEELP!

÷GASP!÷

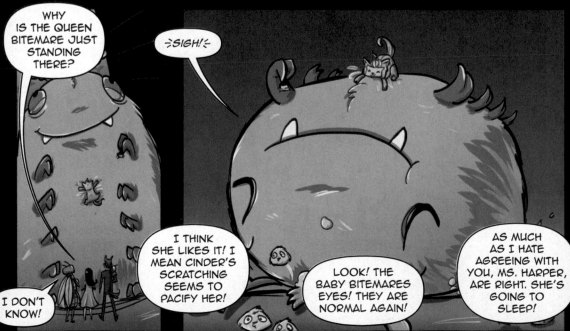

WHY IS THE QUEEN BITEMARE JUST STANDING THERE?

÷SIGH!÷

I DON'T KNOW!

I THINK SHE LIKES IT! I MEAN CINDER'S SCRATCHING SEEMS TO PACIFY HER!

LOOK! THE BABY BITEMARES EYES! THEY ARE NORMAL AGAIN!

AS MUCH AS I HATE AGREEING WITH YOU, MS. HARPER, ARE RIGHT. SHE'S GOING TO SLEEP!

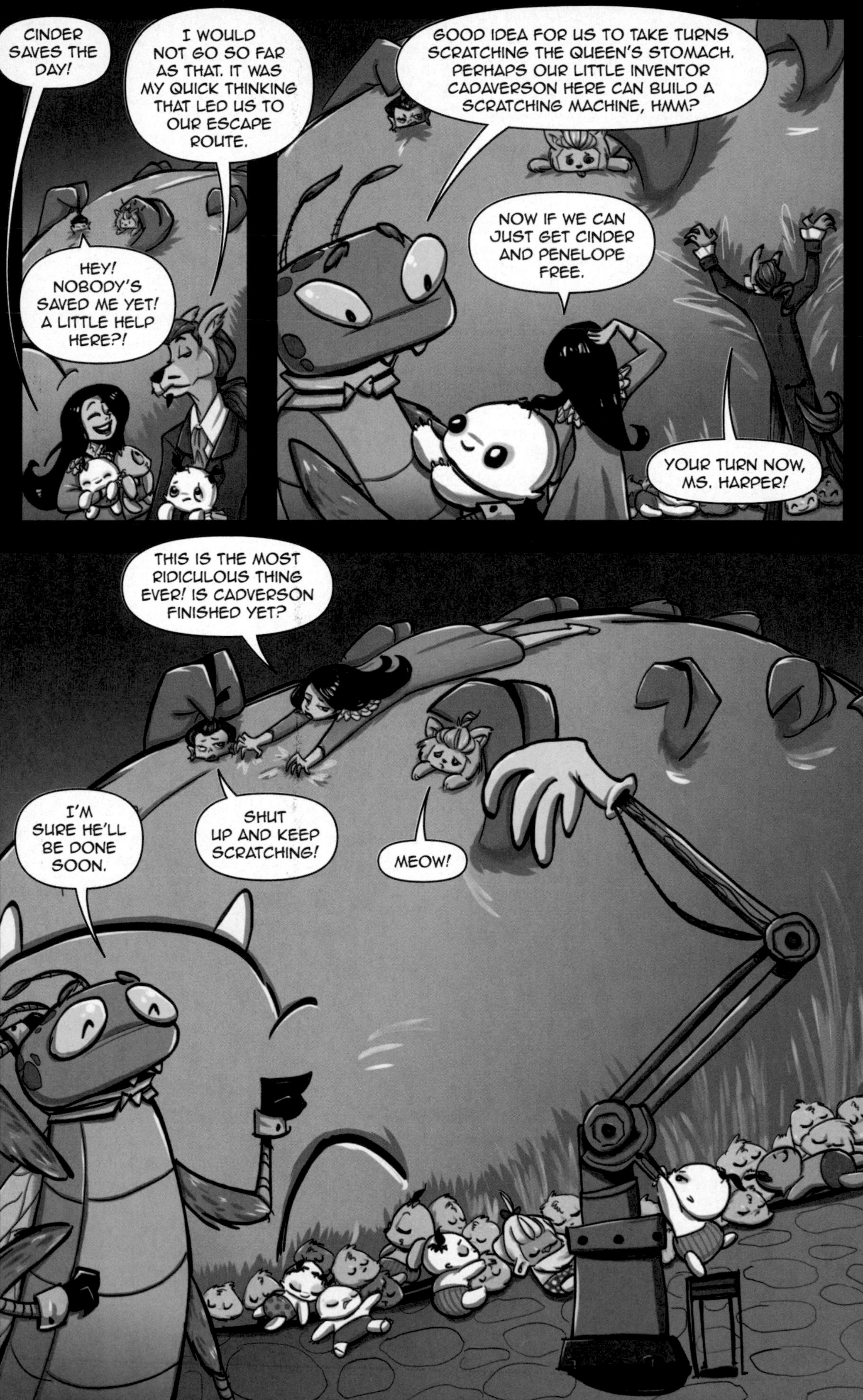
CINDER SAVES THE DAY!
I WOULD NOT GO SO FAR AS THAT. IT WAS MY QUICK THINKING THAT LED US TO OUR ESCAPE ROUTE.
HEY! NOBODY'S SAVED ME YET! A LITTLE HELP HERE?!
GOOD IDEA FOR US TO TAKE TURNS SCRATCHING THE QUEEN'S STOMACH. PERHAPS OUR LITTLE INVENTOR CADAVERSON HERE CAN BUILD A SCRATCHING MACHINE, HMM?
NOW IF WE CAN JUST GET CINDER AND PENELOPE FREE.
YOUR TURN NOW, MS. HARPER!
THIS IS THE MOST RIDICULOUS THING EVER! IS CADVERSON FINISHED YET?
I'M SURE HE'LL BE DONE SOON.
SHUT UP AND KEEP SCRATCHING!
MEOW!

CHAPTER THREE

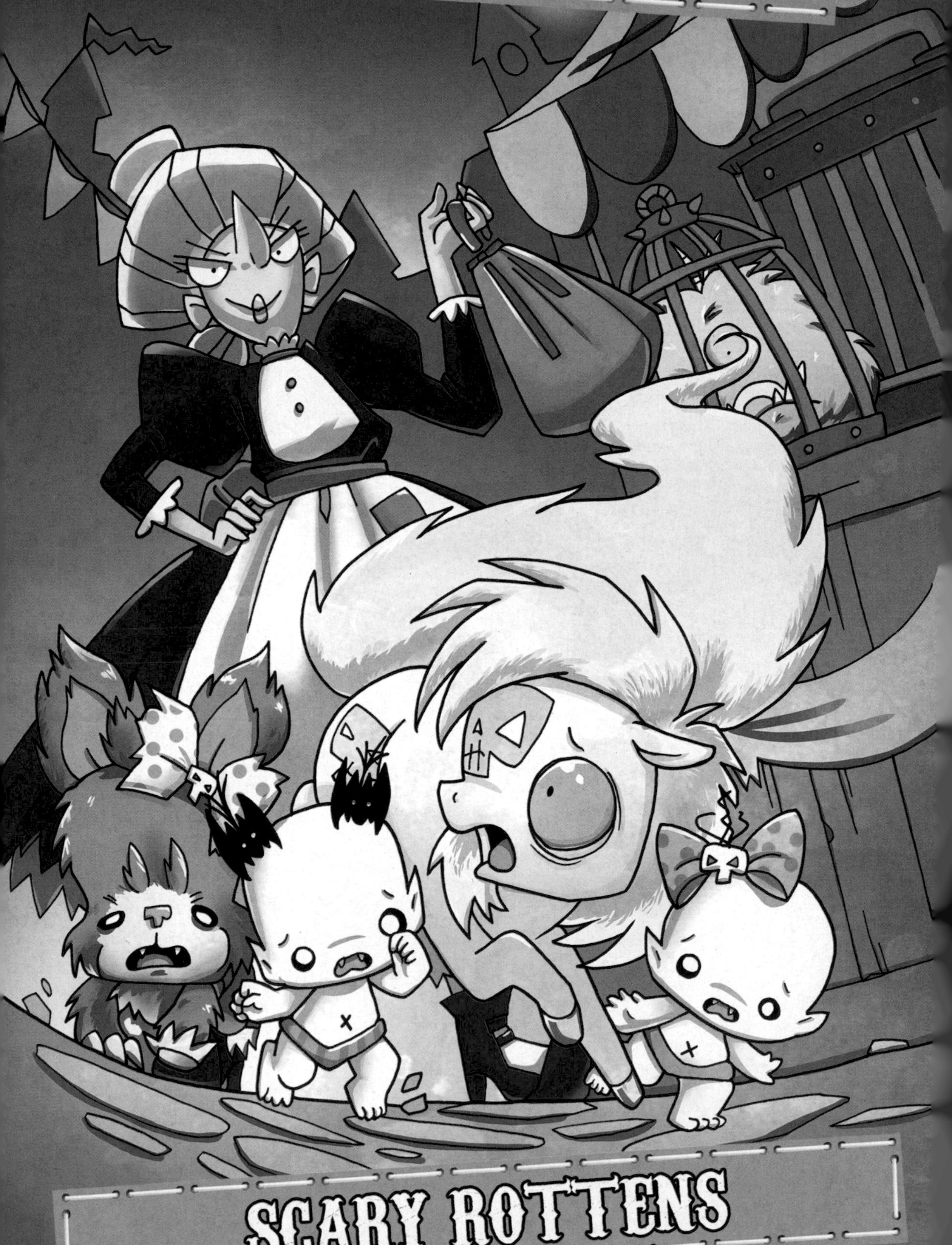

SCARY ROTTENS

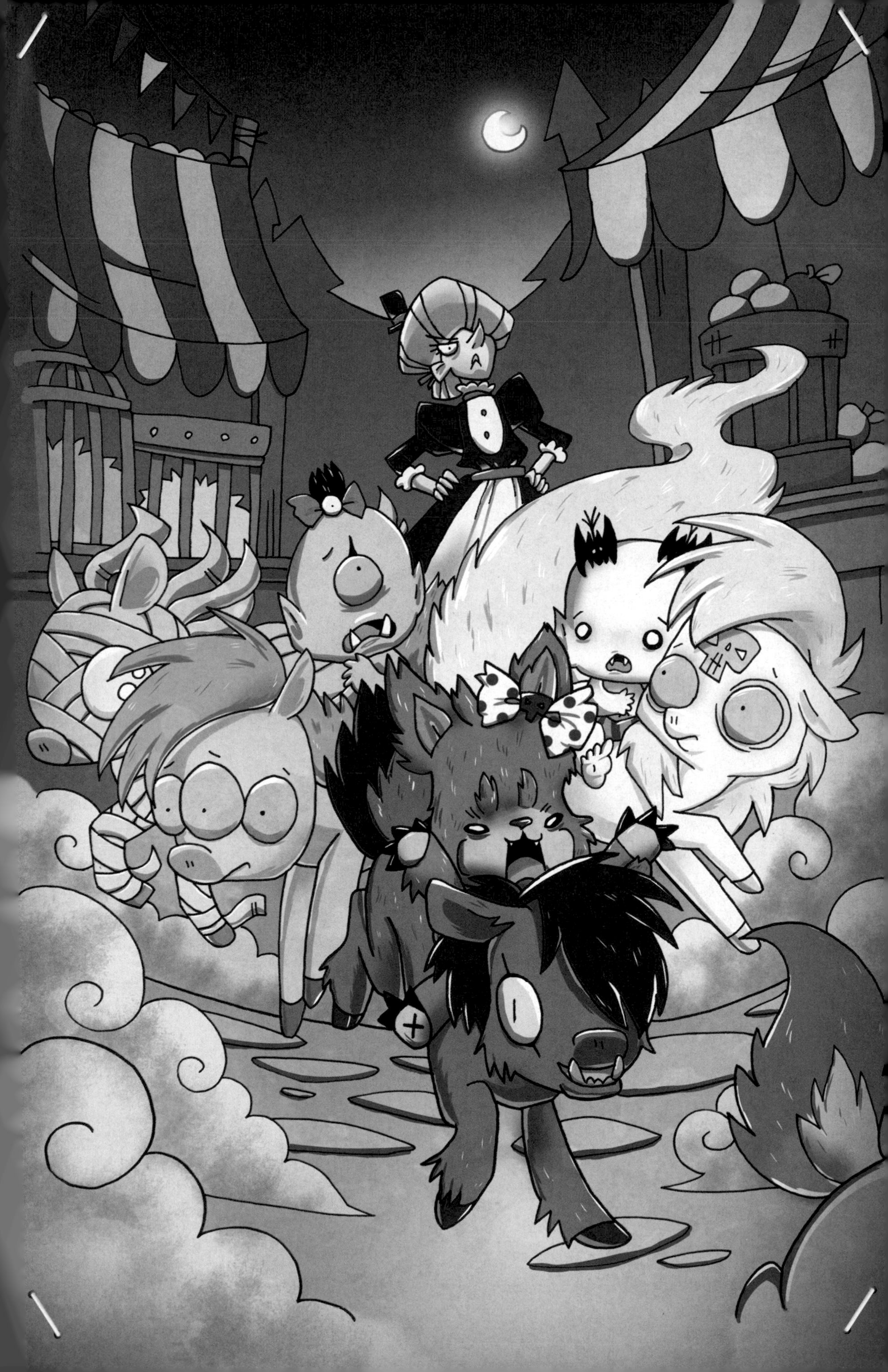

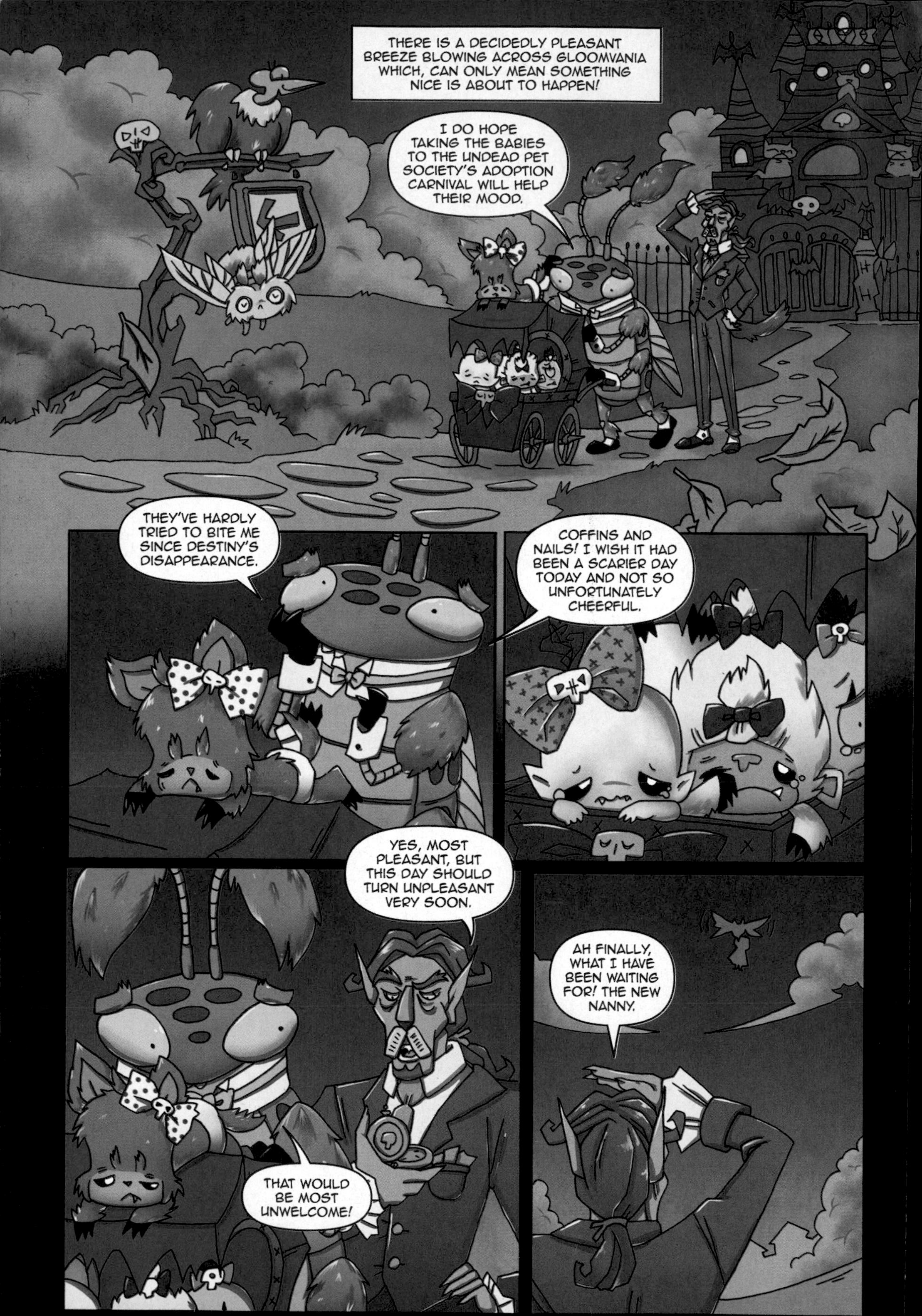
THERE IS A DECIDEDLY PLEASANT BREEZE BLOWING ACROSS GLOOMVANIA WHICH, CAN ONLY MEAN SOMETHING NICE IS ABOUT TO HAPPEN!
I DO HOPE TAKING THE BABIES TO THE UNDEAD PET SOCIETY'S ADOPTION CARNIVAL WILL HELP THEIR MOOD.
THEY'VE HARDLY TRIED TO BITE ME SINCE DESTINY'S DISAPPEARANCE.
COFFINS AND NAILS! I WISH IT HAD BEEN A SCARIER DAY TODAY AND NOT SO UNFORTUNATELY CHEERFUL.
YES, MOST PLEASANT, BUT THIS DAY SHOULD TURN UNPLEASANT VERY SOON.
THAT WOULD BE MOST UNWELCOME!
AH FINALLY, WHAT I HAVE BEEN WAITING FOR! THE NEW NANNY.

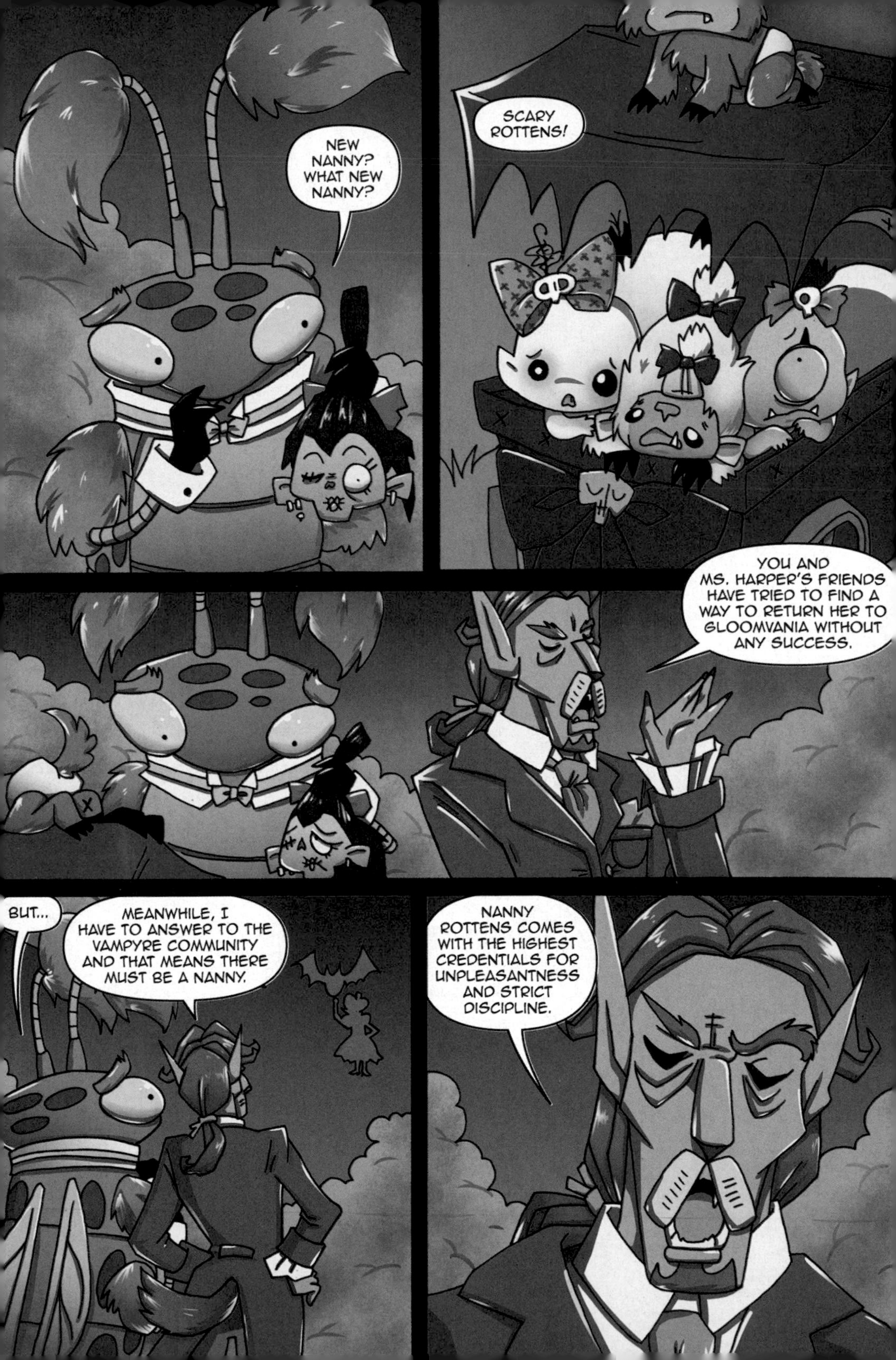
NEW NANNY? WHAT NEW NANNY?
SCARY ROTTENS!
YOU AND MS. HARPER'S FRIENDS HAVE TRIED TO FIND A WAY TO RETURN HER TO GLOOMVANIA WITHOUT ANY SUCCESS.
BUT...
MEANWHILE, I HAVE TO ANSWER TO THE VAMPYRE COMMUNITY AND THAT MEANS THERE MUST BE A NANNY.
NANNY ROTTENS COMES WITH THE HIGHEST CREDENTIALS FOR UNPLEASANTNESS AND STRICT DISCIPLINE.

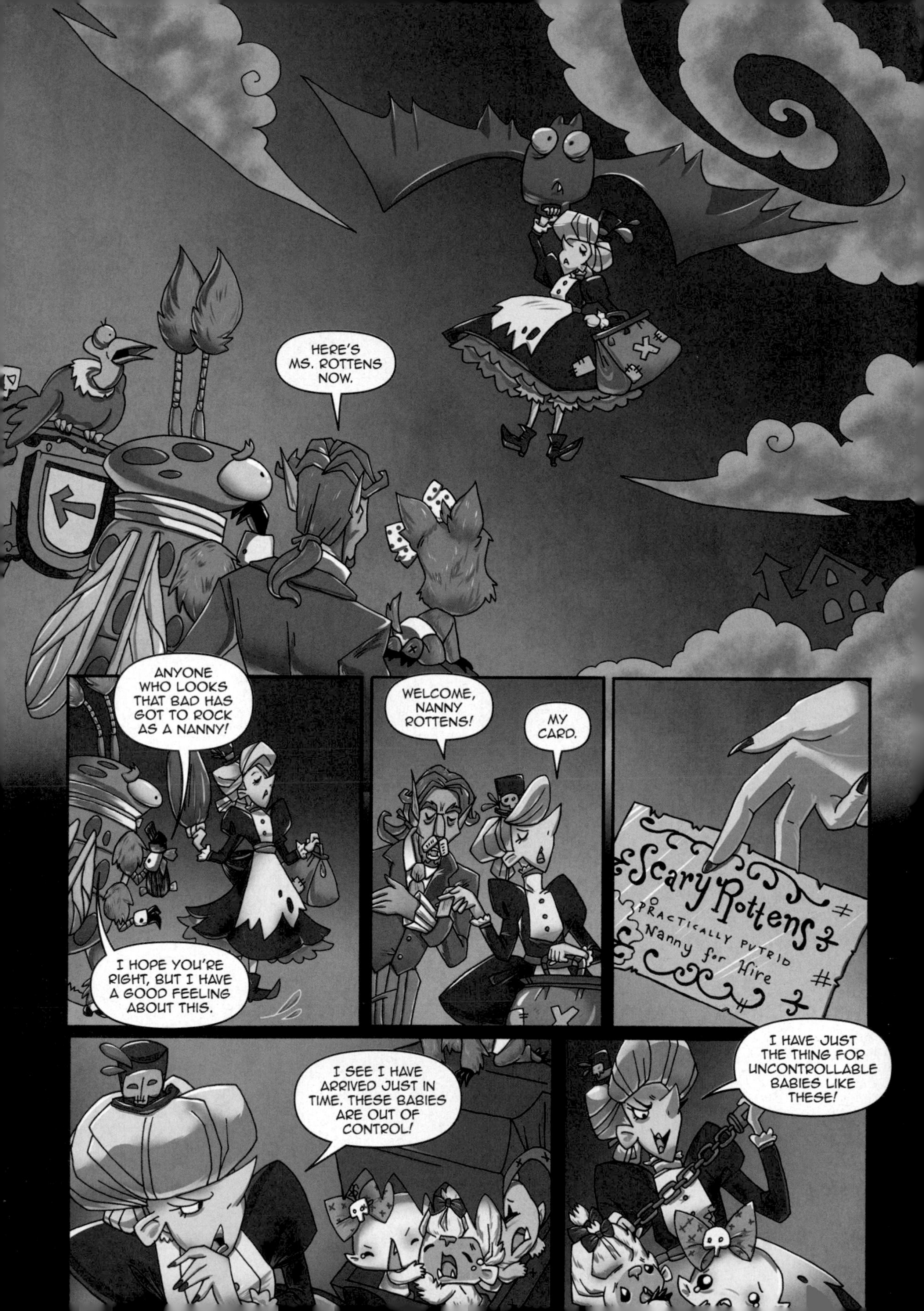
HERE'S MS. ROTTENS NOW.
ANYONE WHO LOOKS THAT BAD HAS GOT TO ROCK AS A NANNY!
I HOPE YOU'RE RIGHT, BUT I HAVE A GOOD FEELING ABOUT THIS.
WELCOME, NANNY ROTTENS!
MY CARD.
Scary Rottens
PRACTICALLY PUTRID
Nanny for Hire
I SEE I HAVE ARRIVED JUST IN TIME. THESE BABIES ARE OUT OF CONTROL!
I HAVE JUST THE THING FOR UNCONTROLLABLE BABIES LIKE THESE!

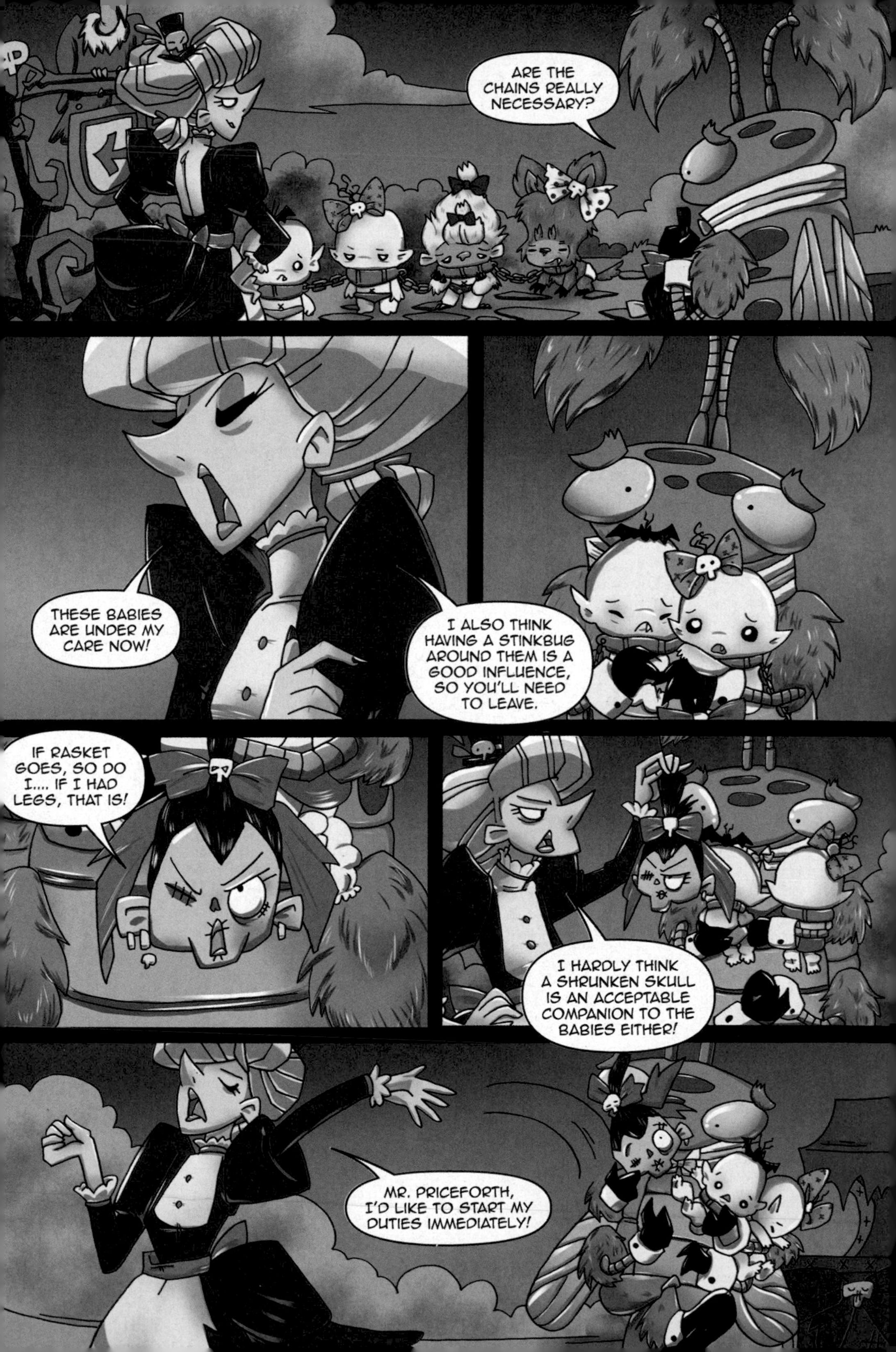
ARE THE CHAINS REALLY NECESSARY?
THESE BABIES ARE UNDER MY CARE NOW!
I ALSO THINK HAVING A STINKBUG AROUND THEM IS A GOOD INFLUENCE, SO YOU'LL NEED TO LEAVE.
IF RASKET GOES, SO DO I.... IF I HAD LEGS, THAT IS!
I HARDLY THINK A SHRUNKEN SKULL IS AN ACCEPTABLE COMPANION TO THE BABIES EITHER!
MR. PRICEFORTH, I'D LIKE TO START MY DUTIES IMMEDIATELY!

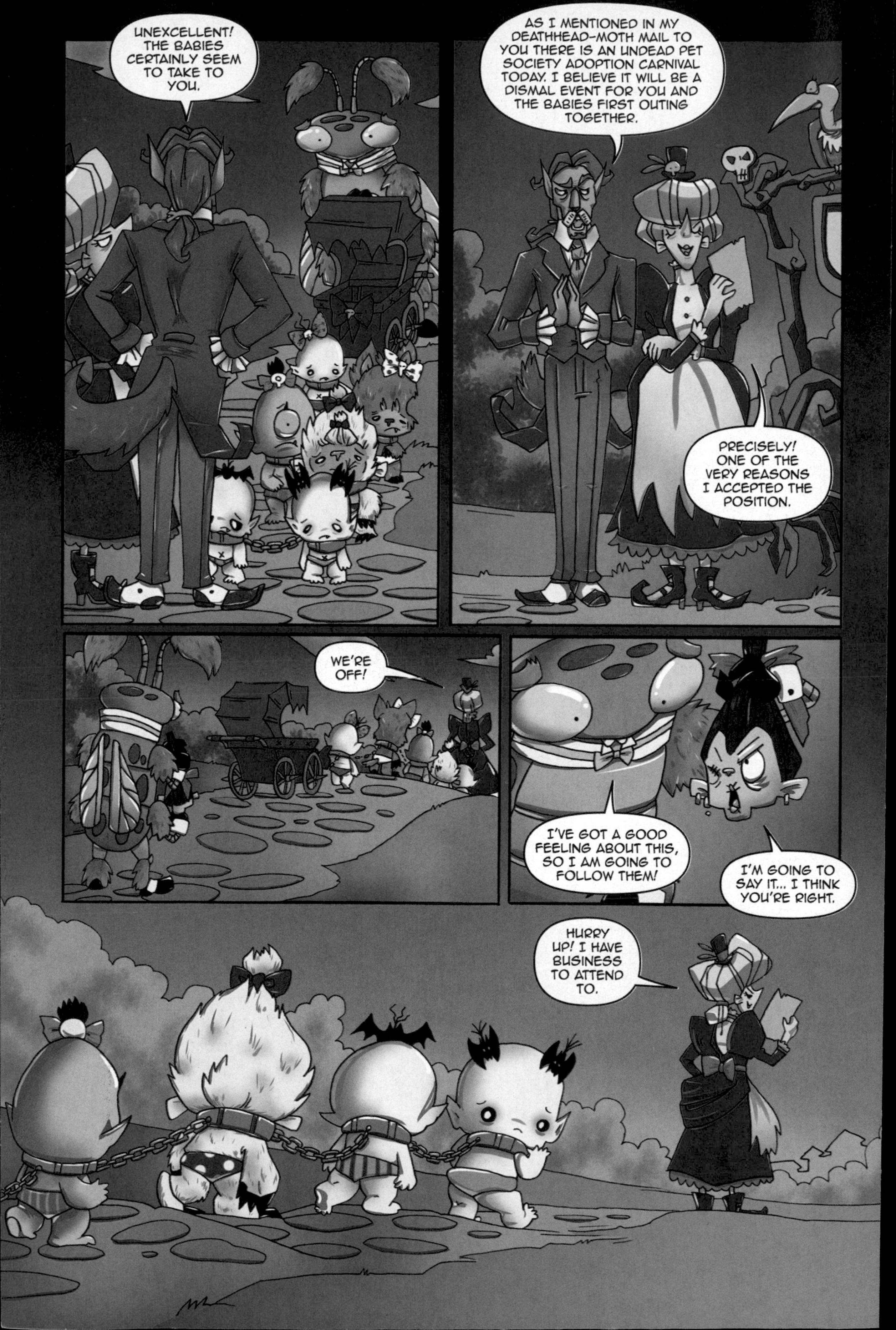
UNEXCELLENT! THE BABIES CERTAINLY SEEM TO TAKE TO YOU.
AS I MENTIONED IN MY DEATHHEAD-MOTH MAIL TO YOU THERE IS AN UNDEAD PET SOCIETY ADOPTION CARNIVAL TODAY. I BELIEVE IT WILL BE A DISMAL EVENT FOR YOU AND THE BABIES FIRST OUTING TOGETHER.
PRECISELY! ONE OF THE VERY REASONS I ACCEPTED THE POSITION.
WE'RE OFF!
I'VE GOT A GOOD FEELING ABOUT THIS, SO I AM GOING TO FOLLOW THEM!
I'M GOING TO SAY IT... I THINK YOU'RE RIGHT.
HURRY UP! I HAVE BUSINESS TO ATTEND TO.

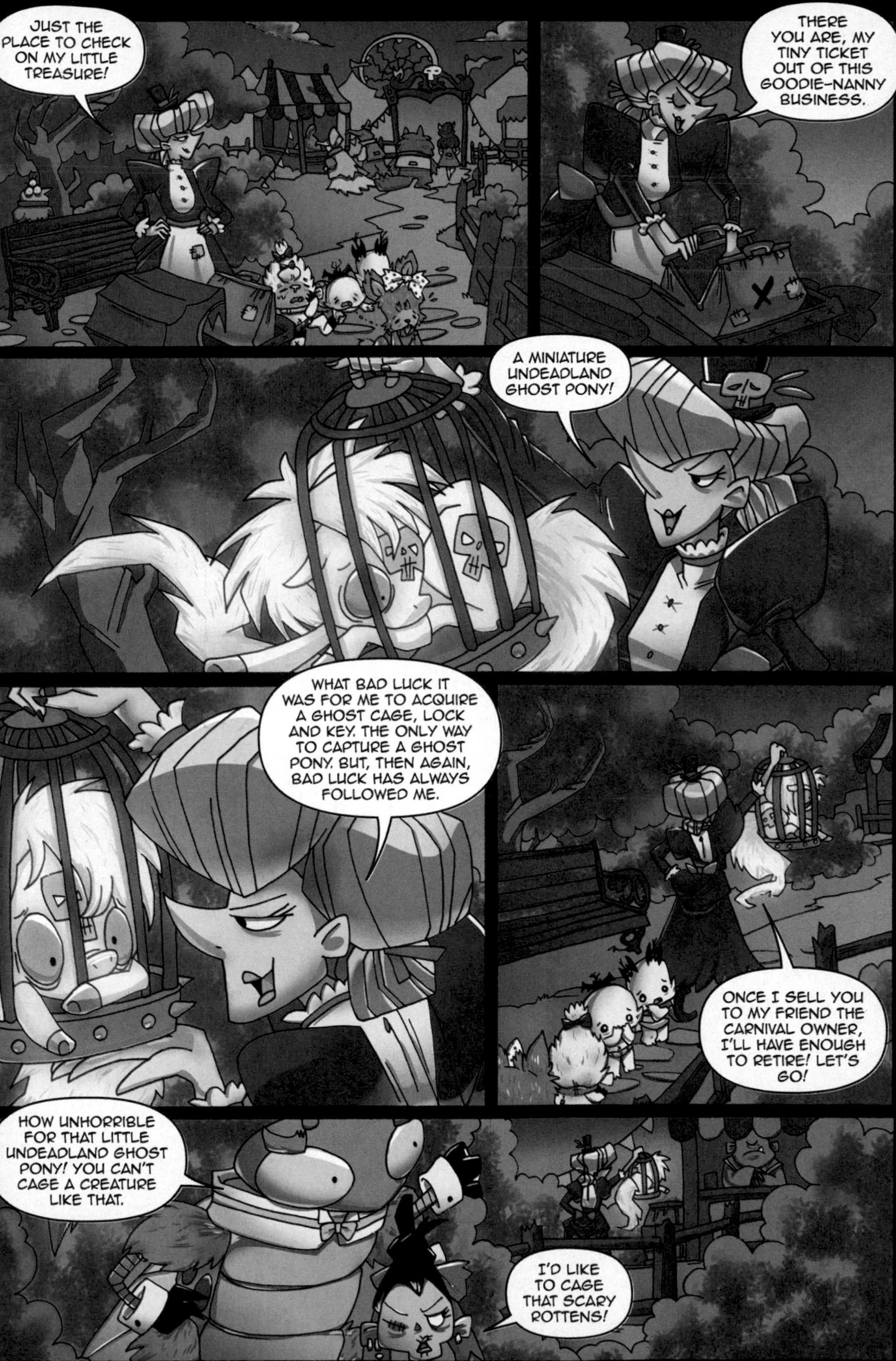
JUST THE PLACE TO CHECK ON MY LITTLE TREASURE!
THERE YOU ARE, MY TINY TICKET OUT OF THIS GOODIE-NANNY BUSINESS.
A MINIATURE UNDEADLAND GHOST PONY!
WHAT BAD LUCK IT WAS FOR ME TO ACQUIRE A GHOST CAGE, LOCK AND KEY. THE ONLY WAY TO CAPTURE A GHOST PONY. BUT, THEN AGAIN, BAD LUCK HAS ALWAYS FOLLOWED ME.
ONCE I SELL YOU TO MY FRIEND THE CARNIVAL OWNER, I'LL HAVE ENOUGH TO RETIRE! LET'S GO!
HOW UNHORRIBLE FOR THAT LITTLE UNDEADLAND GHOST PONY! YOU CAN'T CAGE A CREATURE LIKE THAT.
I'D LIKE TO CAGE THAT SCARY ROTTENS!

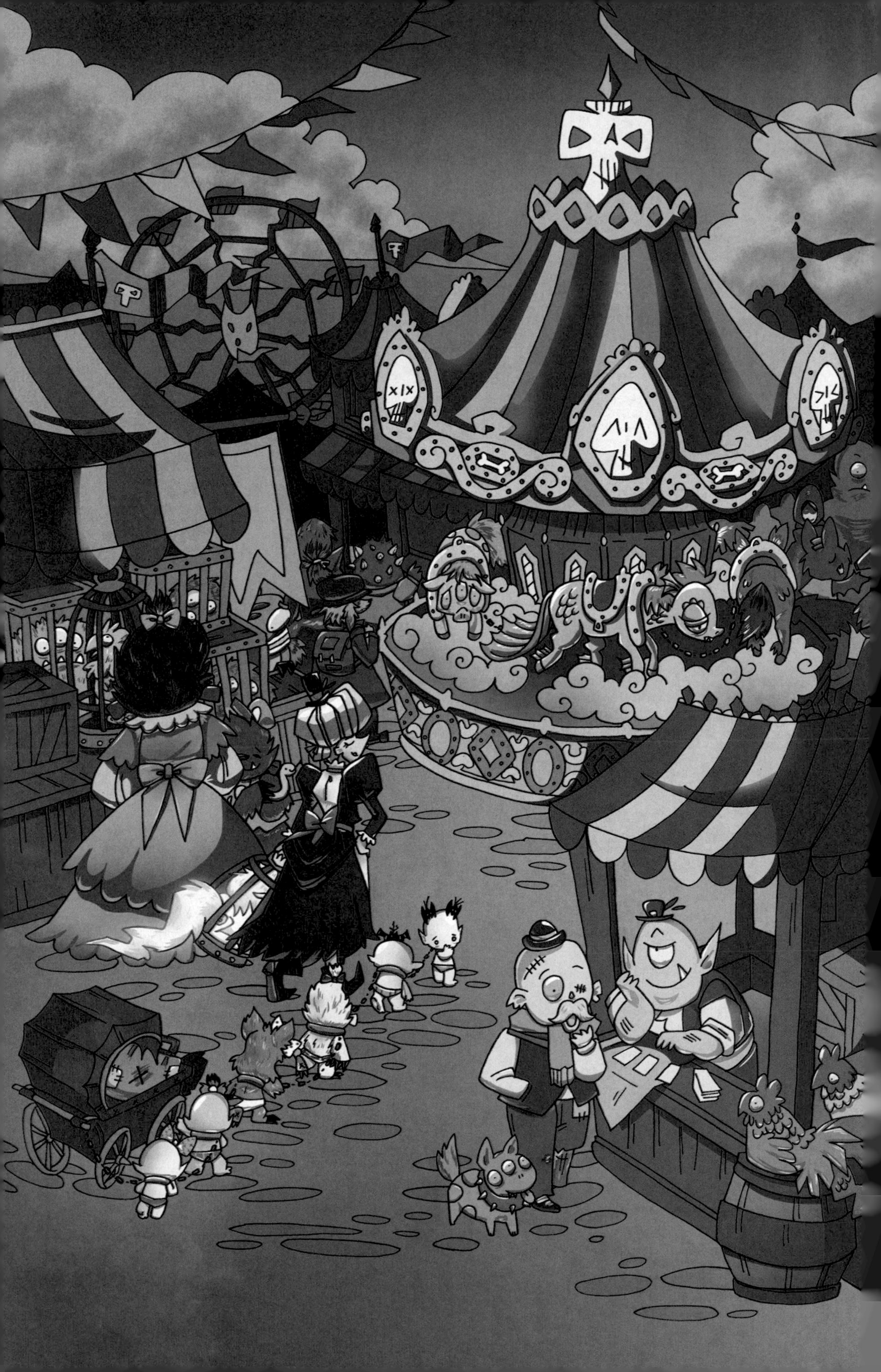

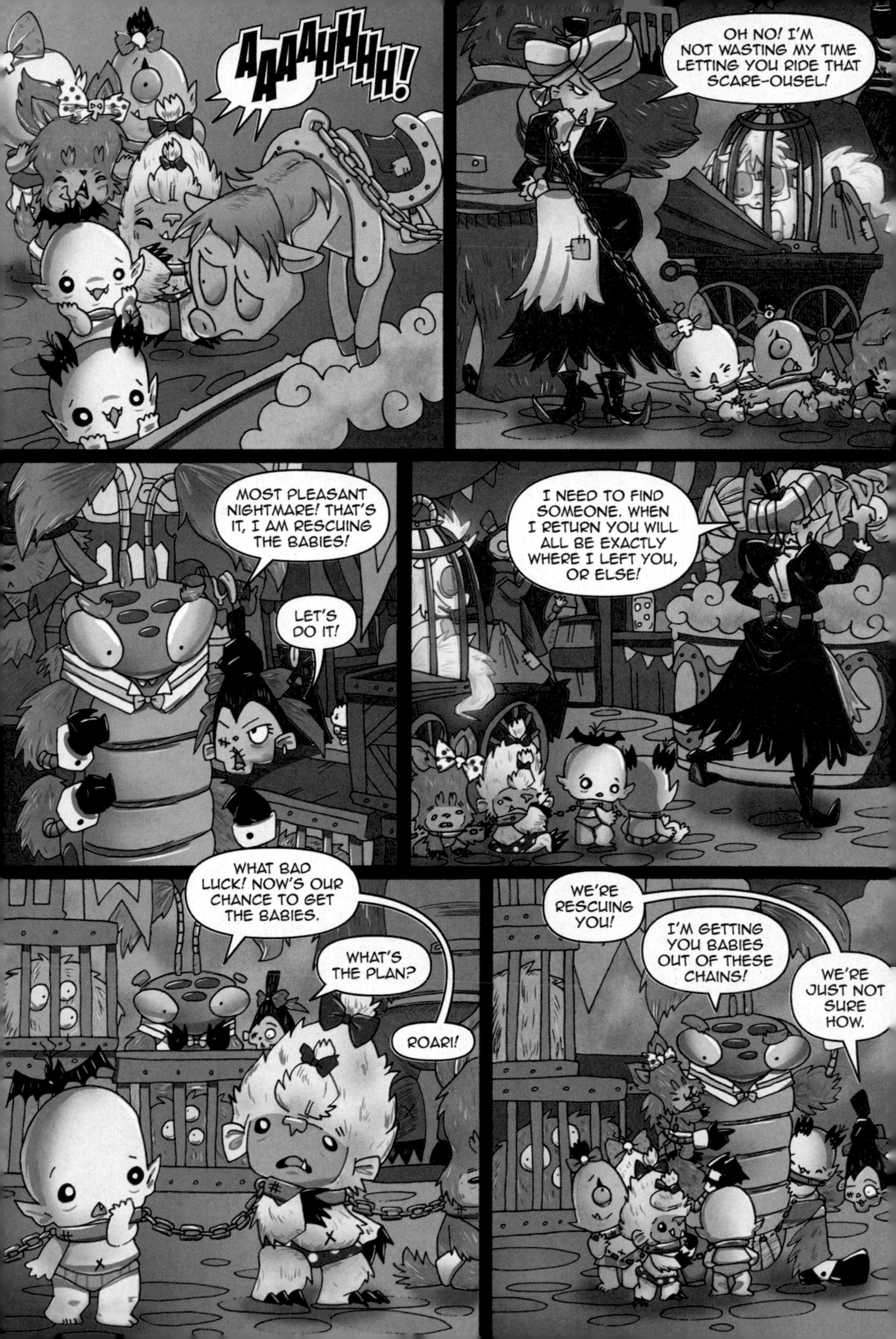
AAAAHHHH!
OH NO! I'M NOT WASTING MY TIME LETTING YOU RIDE THAT SCARE-OUSEL!
MOST PLEASANT NIGHTMARE! THAT'S IT, I AM RESCUING THE BABIES!
LET'S DO IT!
I NEED TO FIND SOMEONE. WHEN I RETURN YOU WILL ALL BE EXACTLY WHERE I LEFT YOU, OR ELSE!
WHAT BAD LUCK! NOW'S OUR CHANCE TO GET THE BABIES.
WHAT'S THE PLAN?
ROAR!
WE'RE RESCUING YOU!
I'M GETTING YOU BABIES OUT OF THESE CHAINS!
WE'RE JUST NOT SURE HOW.

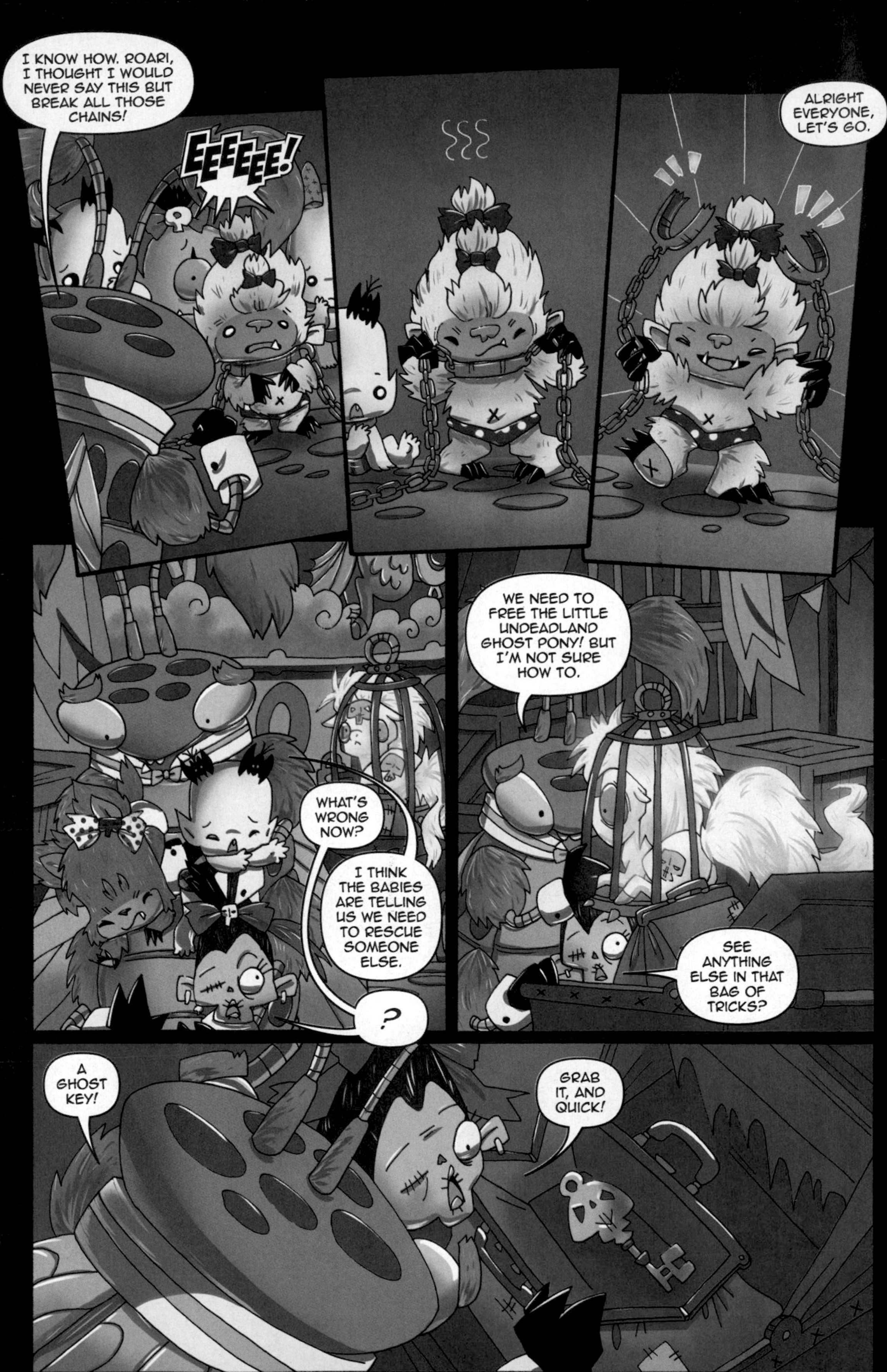
I KNOW HOW. ROARI, I THOUGHT I WOULD NEVER SAY THIS BUT BREAK ALL THOSE CHAINS!
EEEEEE!
ALRIGHT EVERYONE, LET'S GO.
WHAT'S WRONG NOW?
I THINK THE BABIES ARE TELLING US WE NEED TO RESCUE SOMEONE ELSE.
?
WE NEED TO FREE THE LITTLE UNDEADLAND GHOST PONY! BUT I'M NOT SURE HOW TO.
SEE ANYTHING ELSE IN THAT BAG OF TRICKS?
A GHOST KEY!
GRAB IT, AND QUICK!

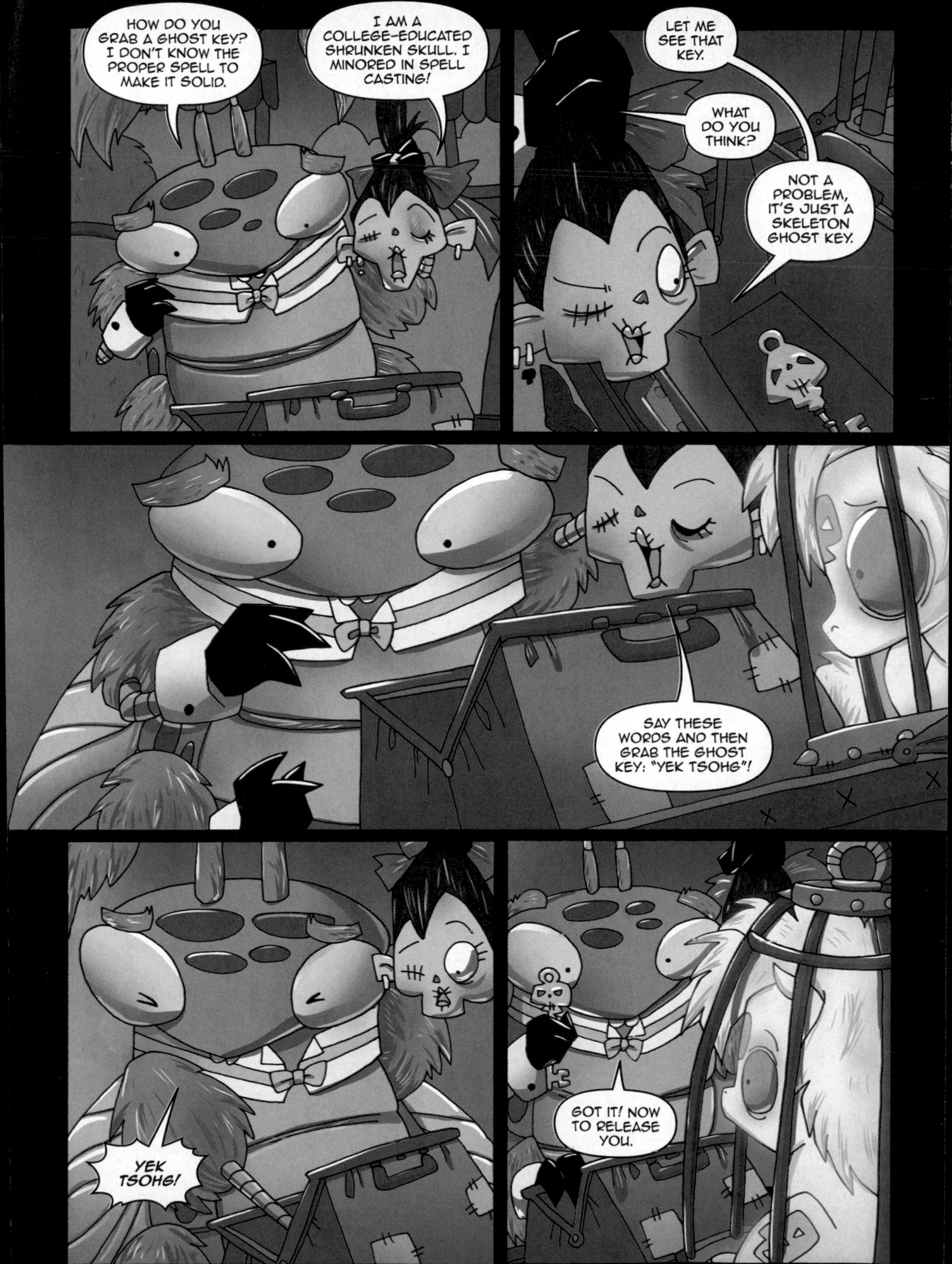
HOW DO YOU GRAB A GHOST KEY? I DON'T KNOW THE PROPER SPELL TO MAKE IT SOLID.
I AM A COLLEGE-EDUCATED SHRUNKEN SKULL. I MINORED IN SPELL CASTING!
LET ME SEE THAT KEY.
WHAT DO YOU THINK?
NOT A PROBLEM, IT'S JUST A SKELETON GHOST KEY.
SAY THESE WORDS AND THEN GRAB THE GHOST KEY: "YEK TSOHG"!
YEK TSOHG!
GOT IT! NOW TO RELEASE YOU.

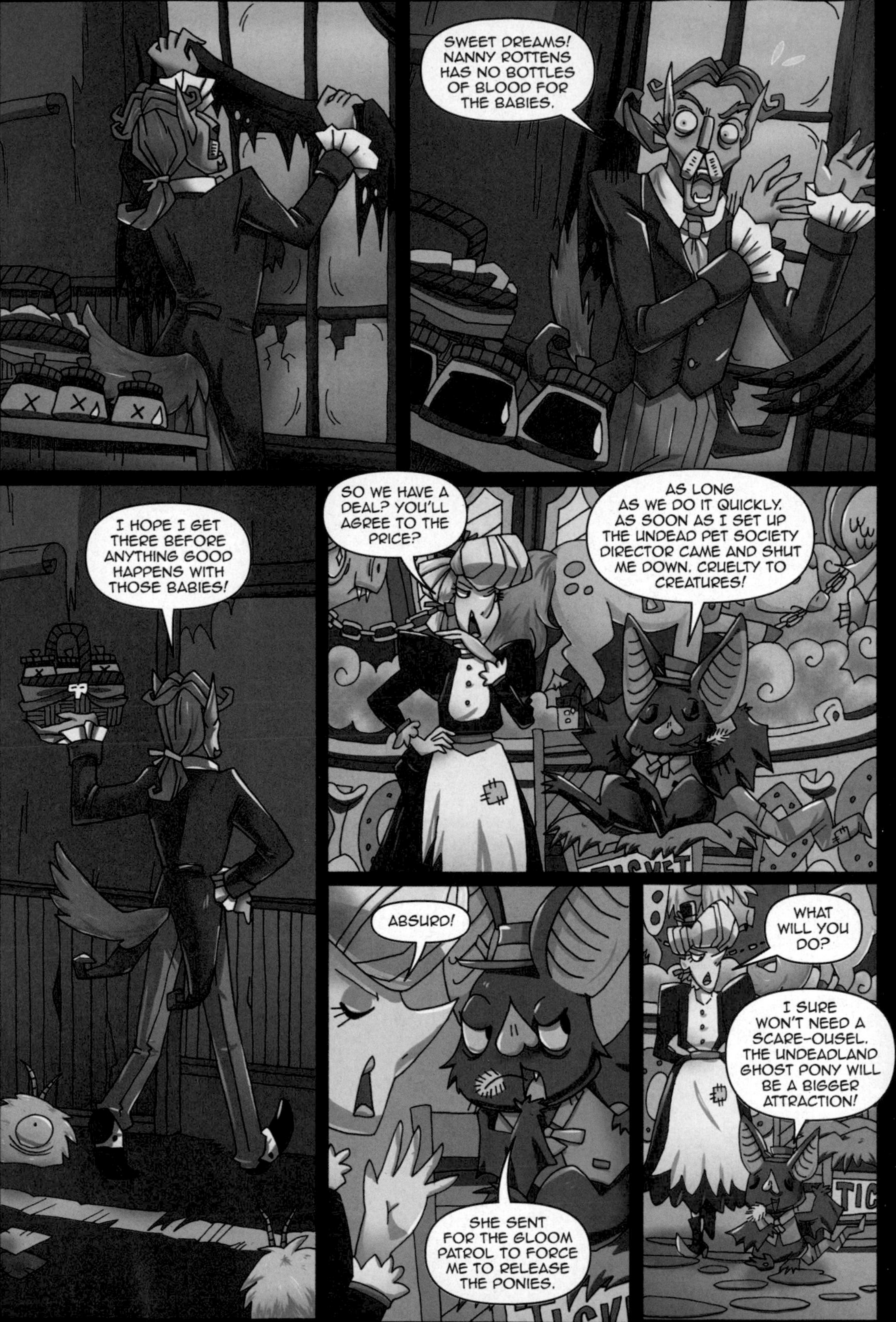
SWEET DREAMS! NANNY ROTTENS HAS NO BOTTLES OF BLOOD FOR THE BABIES.
I HOPE I GET THERE BEFORE ANYTHING GOOD HAPPENS WITH THOSE BABIES!
SO WE HAVE A DEAL? YOU'LL AGREE TO THE PRICE?
AS LONG AS WE DO IT QUICKLY. AS SOON AS I SET UP THE UNDEAD PET SOCIETY DIRECTOR CAME AND SHUT ME DOWN. CRUELTY TO CREATURES!
ABSURD!
SHE SENT FOR THE GLOOM PATROL TO FORCE ME TO RELEASE THE PONIES.
WHAT WILL YOU DO?
I SURE WON'T NEED A SCARE-OUSEL. THE UNDEADLAND GHOST PONY WILL BE A BIGGER ATTRACTION!

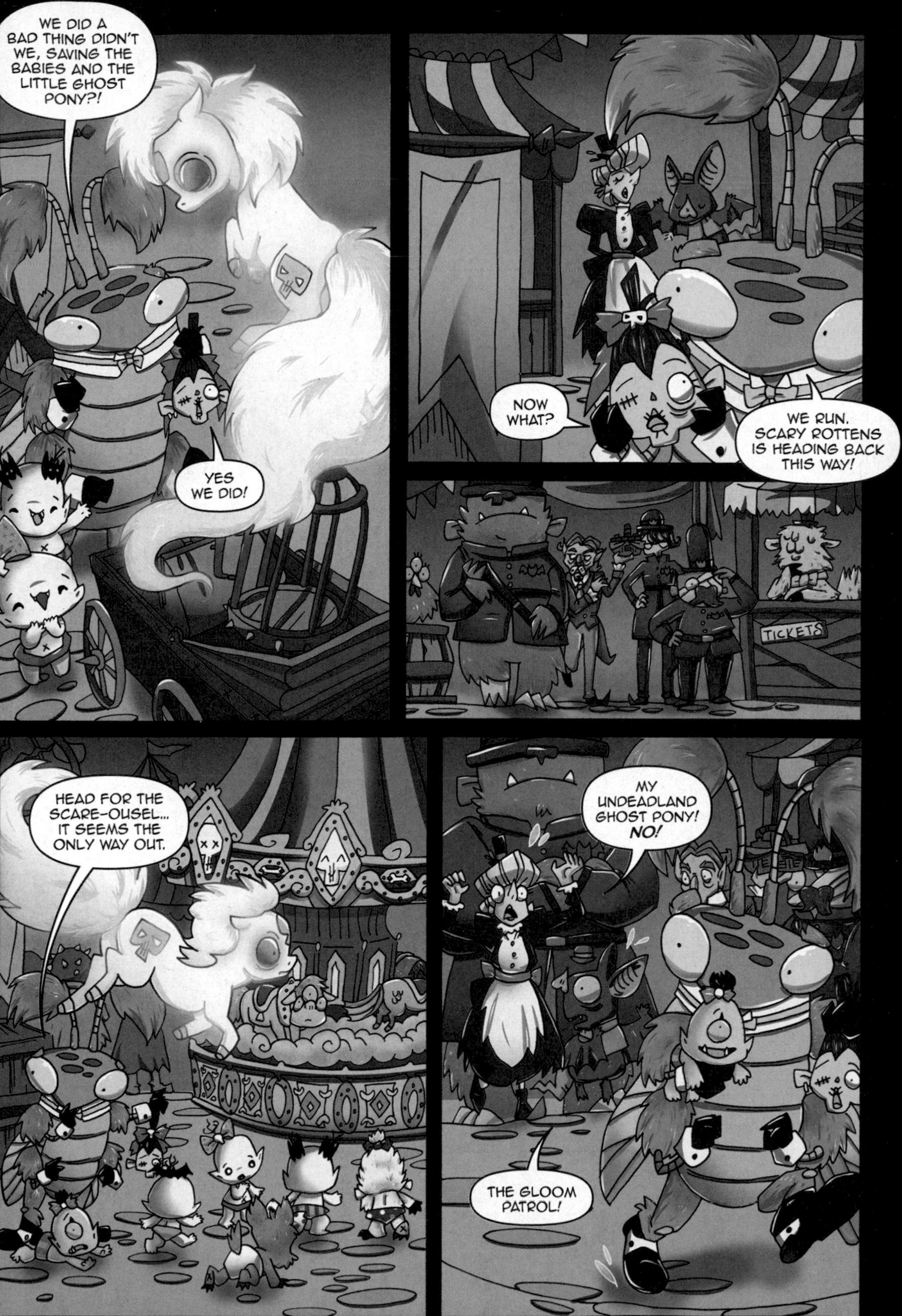
WE DID A BAD THING DIDN'T WE, SAVING THE BABIES AND THE LITTLE GHOST PONY?!
YES WE DID!
NOW WHAT?
WE RUN. SCARY ROTTENS IS HEADING BACK THIS WAY!
TICKETS
HEAD FOR THE SCARE-OUSEL... IT SEEMS THE ONLY WAY OUT.
MY UNDEADLAND GHOST PONY! **NO!**
THE GLOOM PATROL!

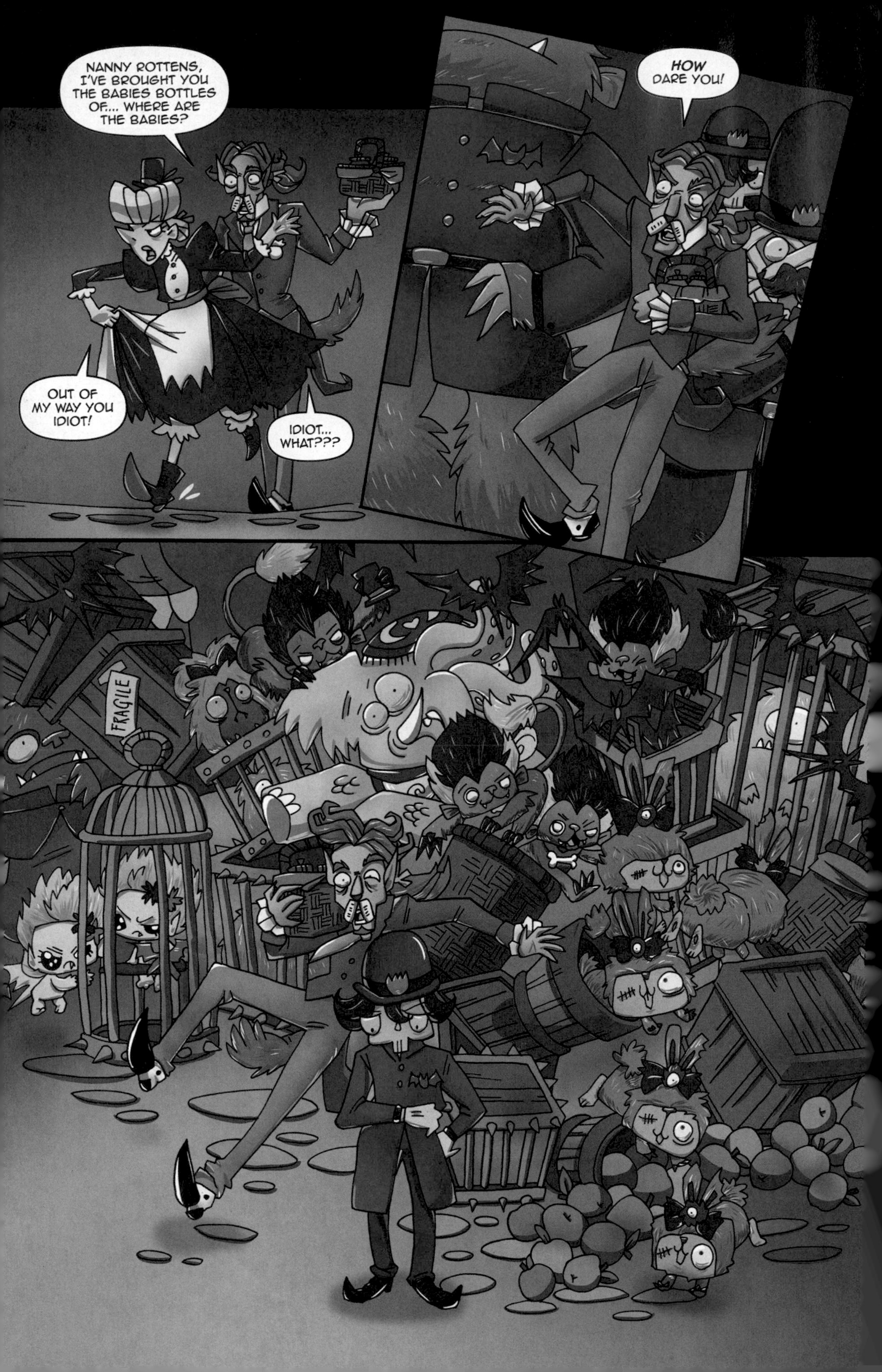

NANNY ROTTENS, I'VE BROUGHT YOU THE BABIES BOTTLES OF... WHERE ARE THE BABIES?
OUT OF MY WAY YOU IDIOT!
IDIOT... WHAT???
HOW DARE YOU!
FRAGILE

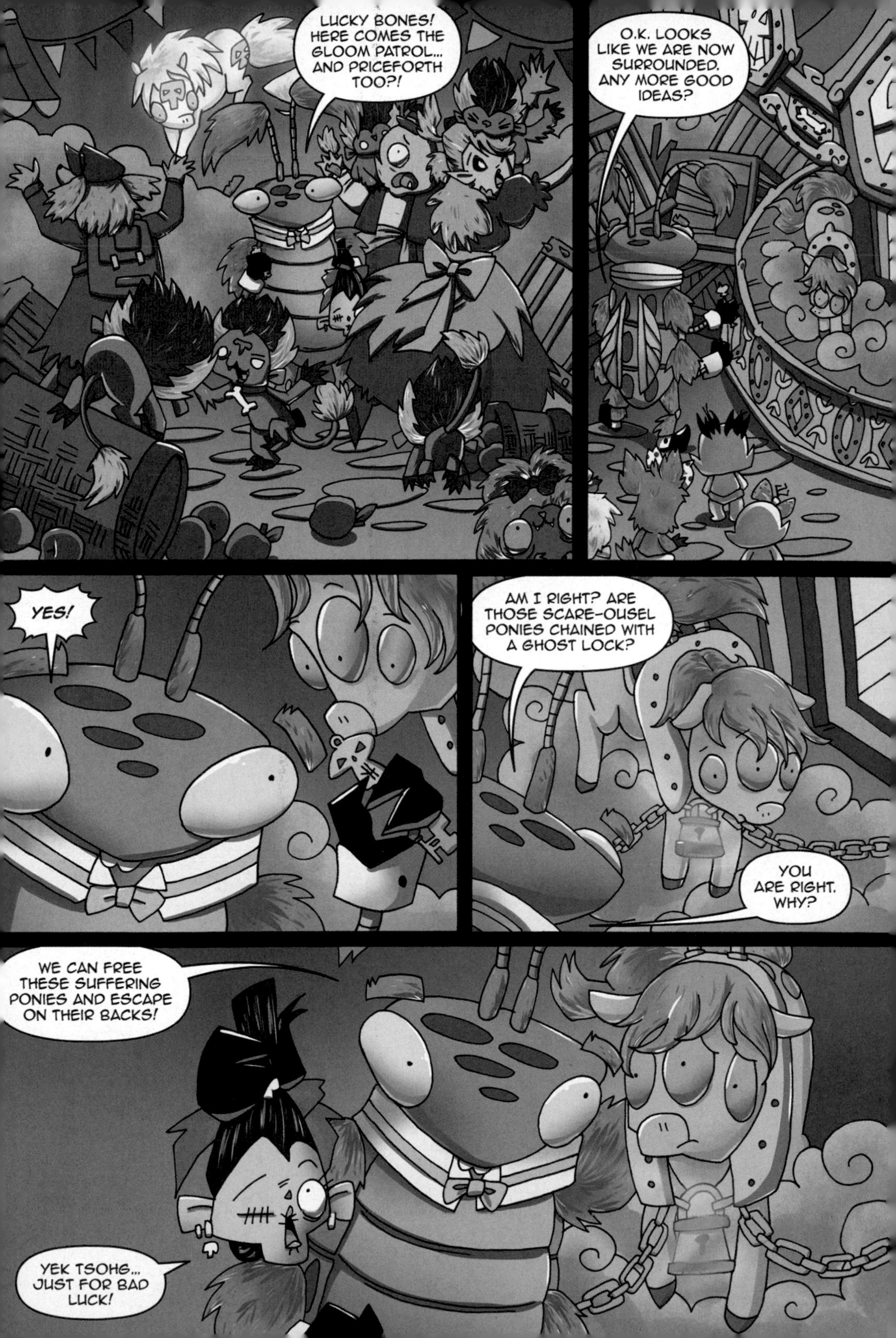
LUCKY BONES! HERE COMES THE GLOOM PATROL... AND PRICEFORTH TOO?!
O.K. LOOKS LIKE WE ARE NOW SURROUNDED. ANY MORE GOOD IDEAS?
YES!
AM I RIGHT? ARE THOSE SCARE-OUSEL PONIES CHAINED WITH A GHOST LOCK?
YOU ARE RIGHT. WHY?
WE CAN FREE THESE SUFFERING PONIES AND ESCAPE ON THEIR BACKS!
YEK TSOHG... JUST FOR BAD LUCK!

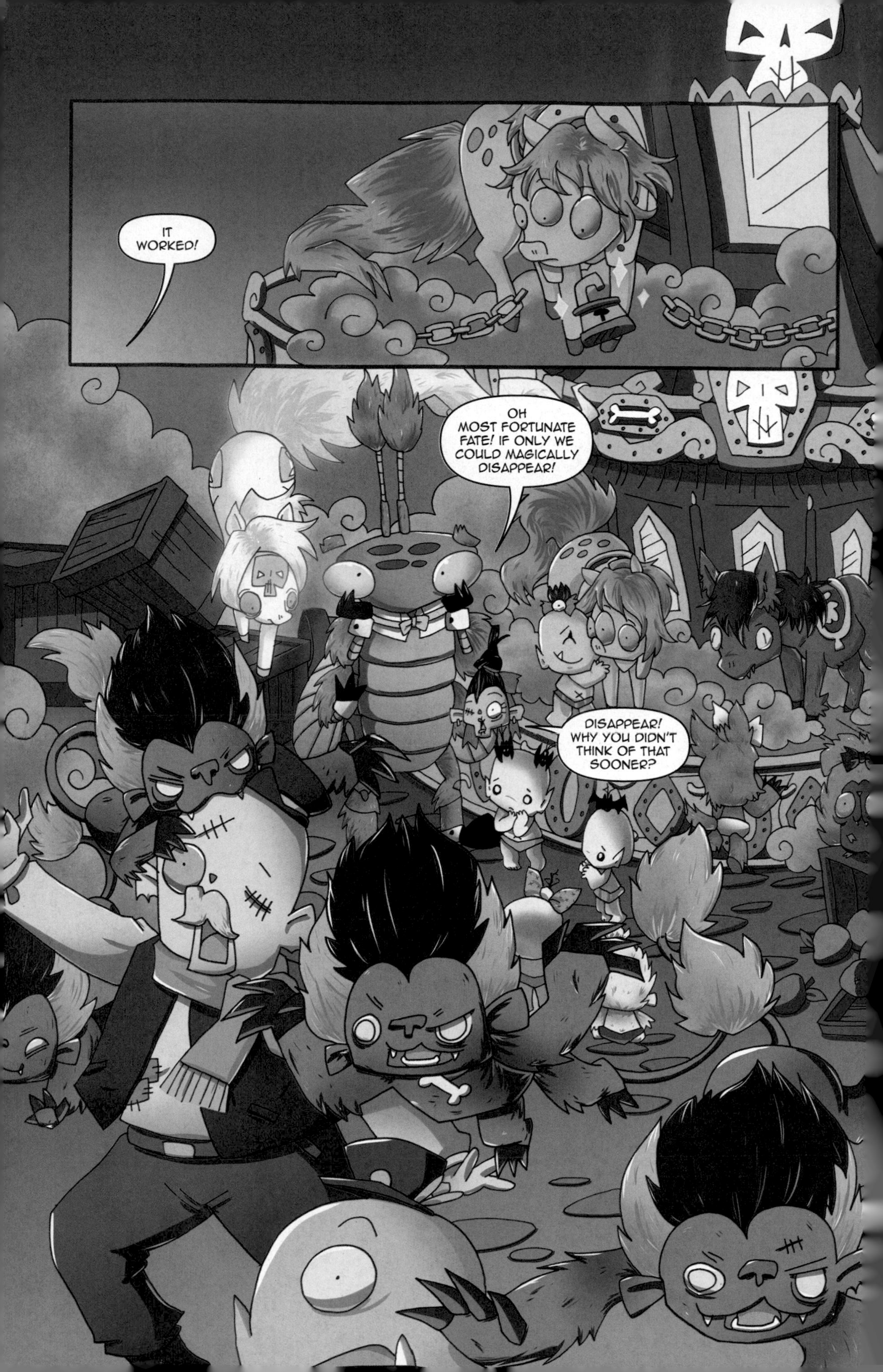
IT WORKED!
OH MOST FORTUNATE FATE! IF ONLY WE COULD MAGICALLY DISAPPEAR!
DISAPPEAR! WHY YOU DIDN'T THINK OF THAT SOONER?

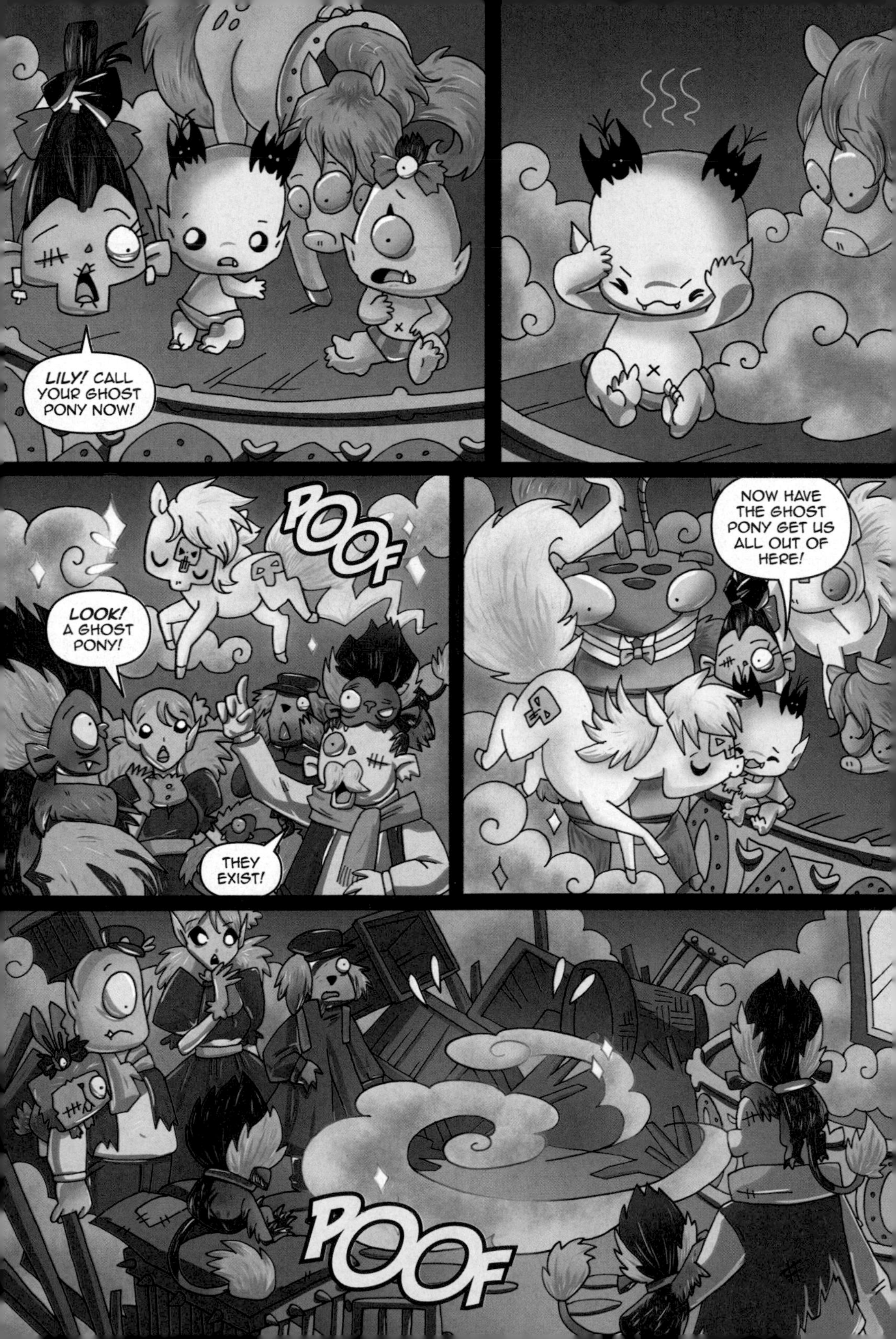
LILY! CALL YOUR GHOST PONY NOW!
POOF
LOOK! A GHOST PONY!
THEY EXIST!
NOW HAVE THE GHOST PONY GET US ALL OUT OF HERE!
POOF

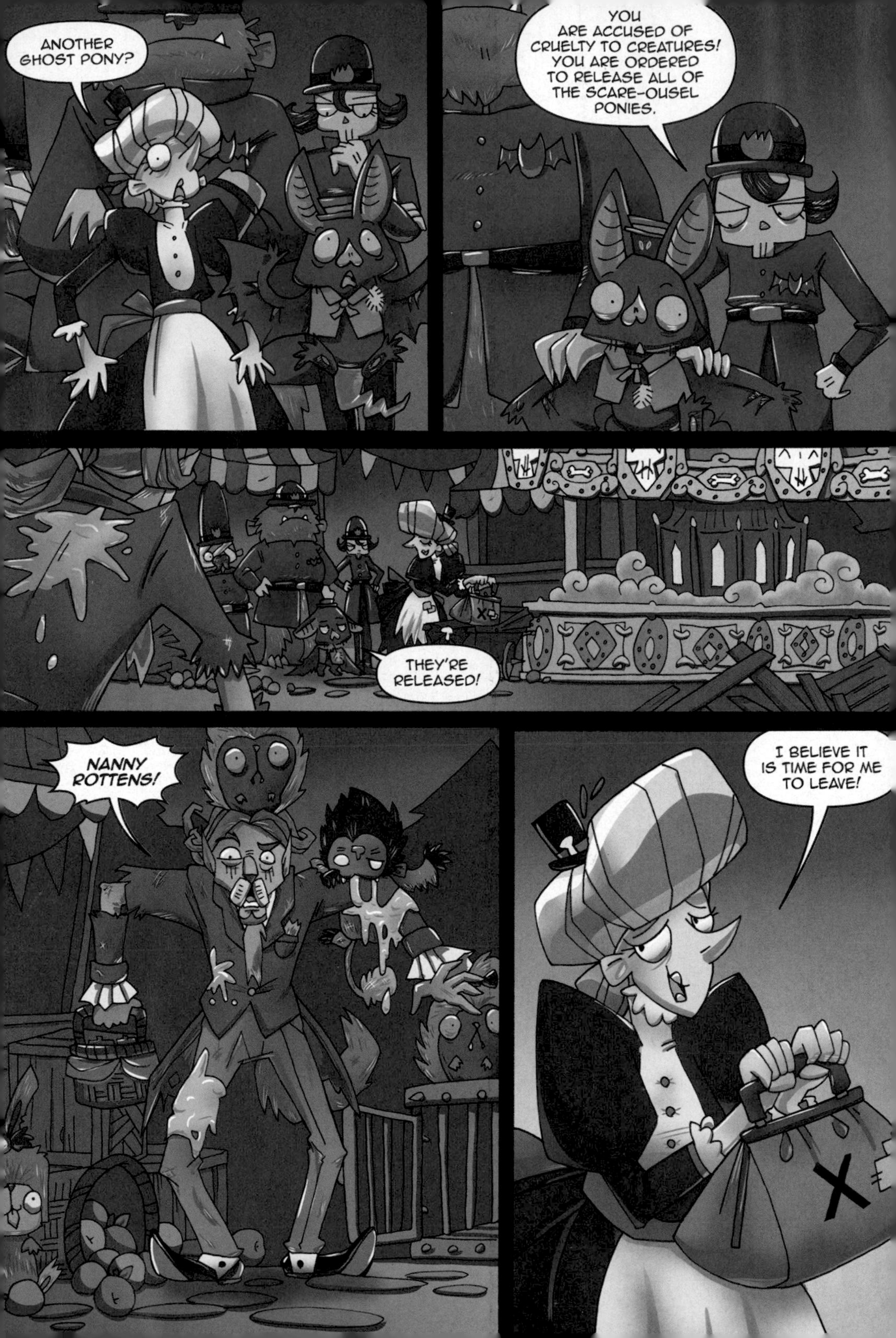
ANOTHER GHOST PONY?
YOU ARE ACCUSED OF CRUELTY TO CREATURES! YOU ARE ORDERED TO RELEASE ALL OF THE SCARE-OUSEL PONIES.
THEY'RE RELEASED!
NANNY ROTTENS!
I BELIEVE IT IS TIME FOR ME TO LEAVE!

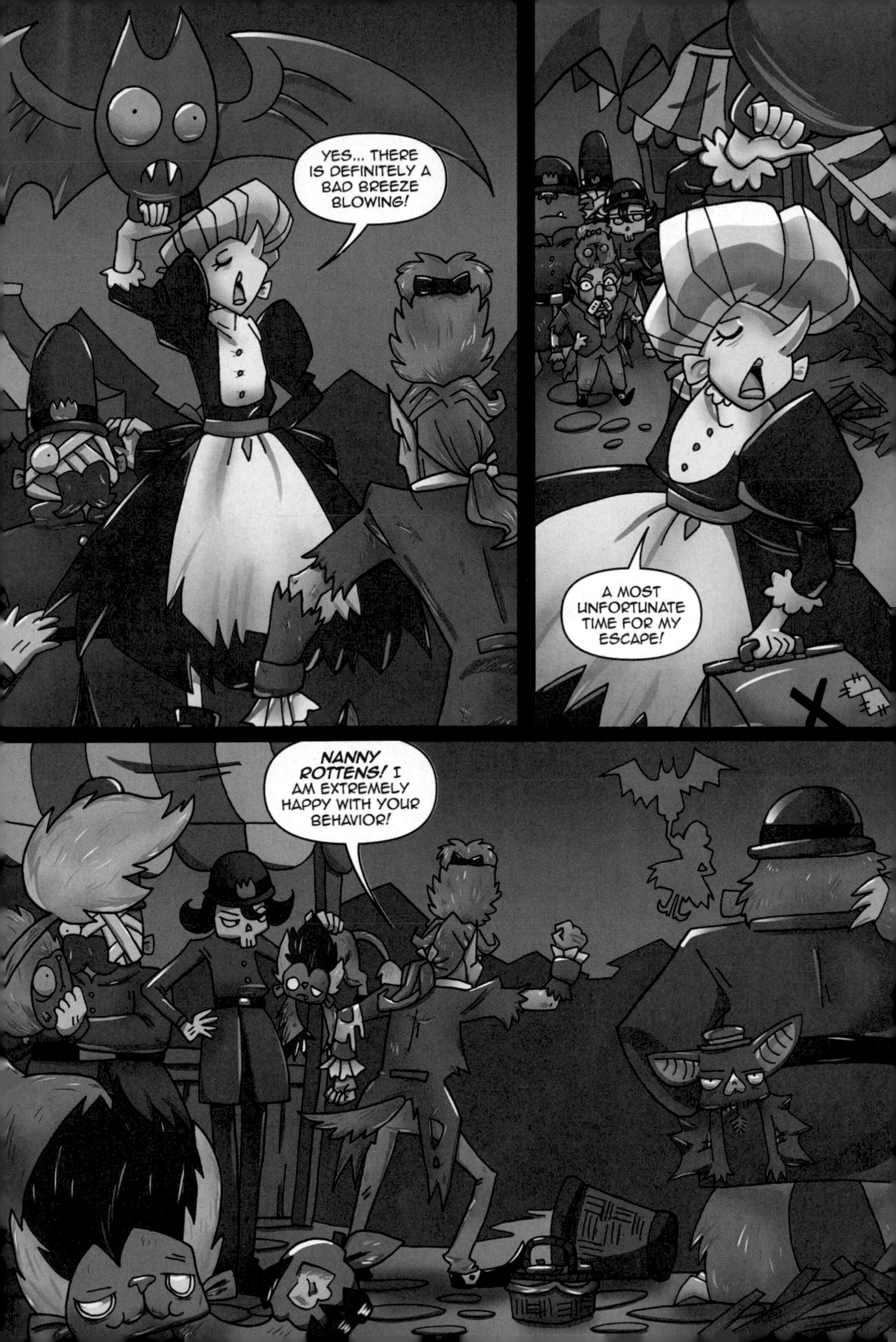
YES... THERE IS DEFINITELY A BAD BREEZE BLOWING!
A MOST UNFORTUNATE TIME FOR MY ESCAPE!
NANNY ROTTENS! I AM EXTREMELY HAPPY WITH YOUR BEHAVIOR!

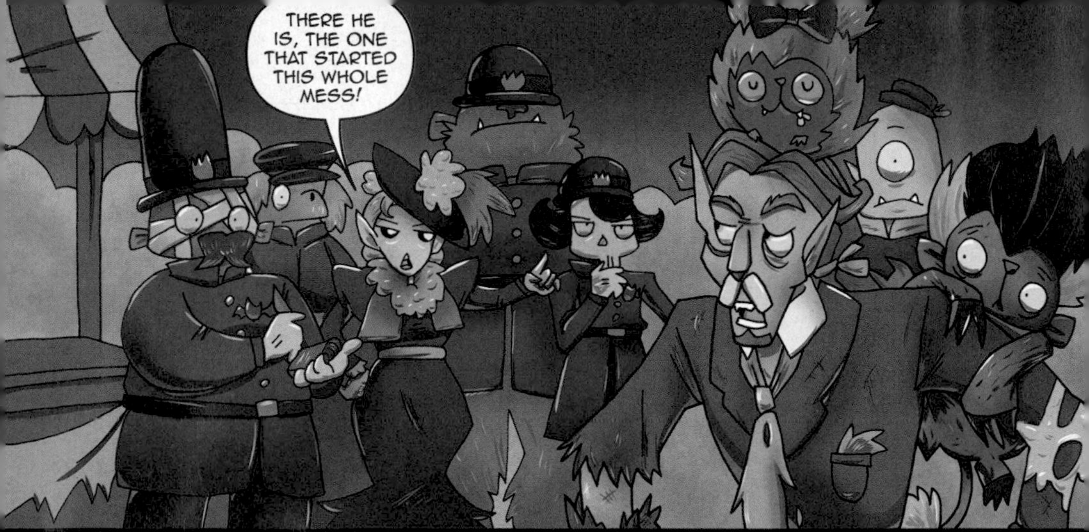
THERE HE IS, THE ONE THAT STARTED THIS WHOLE MESS!

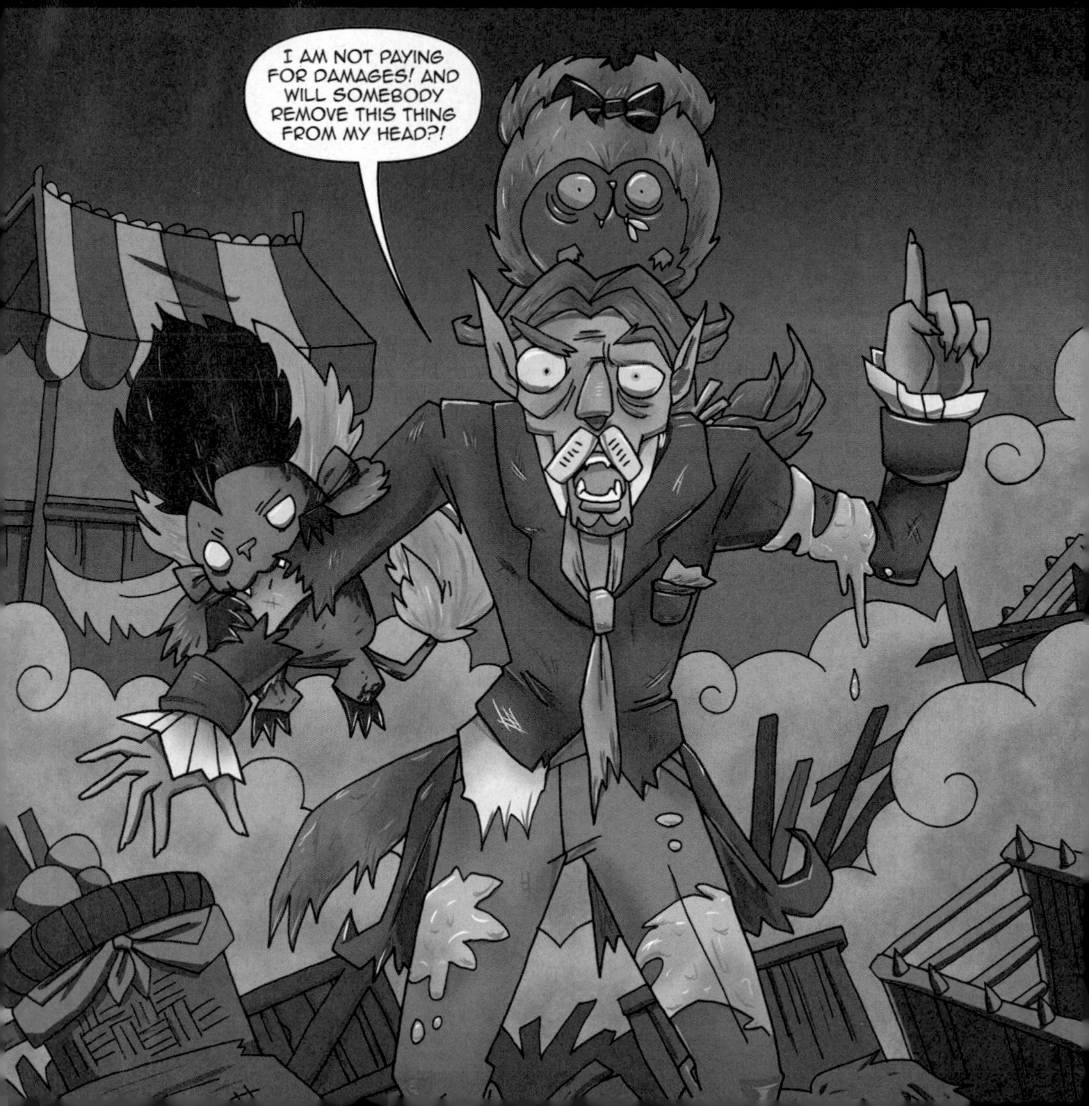
I AM NOT PAYING FOR DAMAGES! AND WILL SOMEBODY REMOVE THIS THING FROM MY HEAD?!

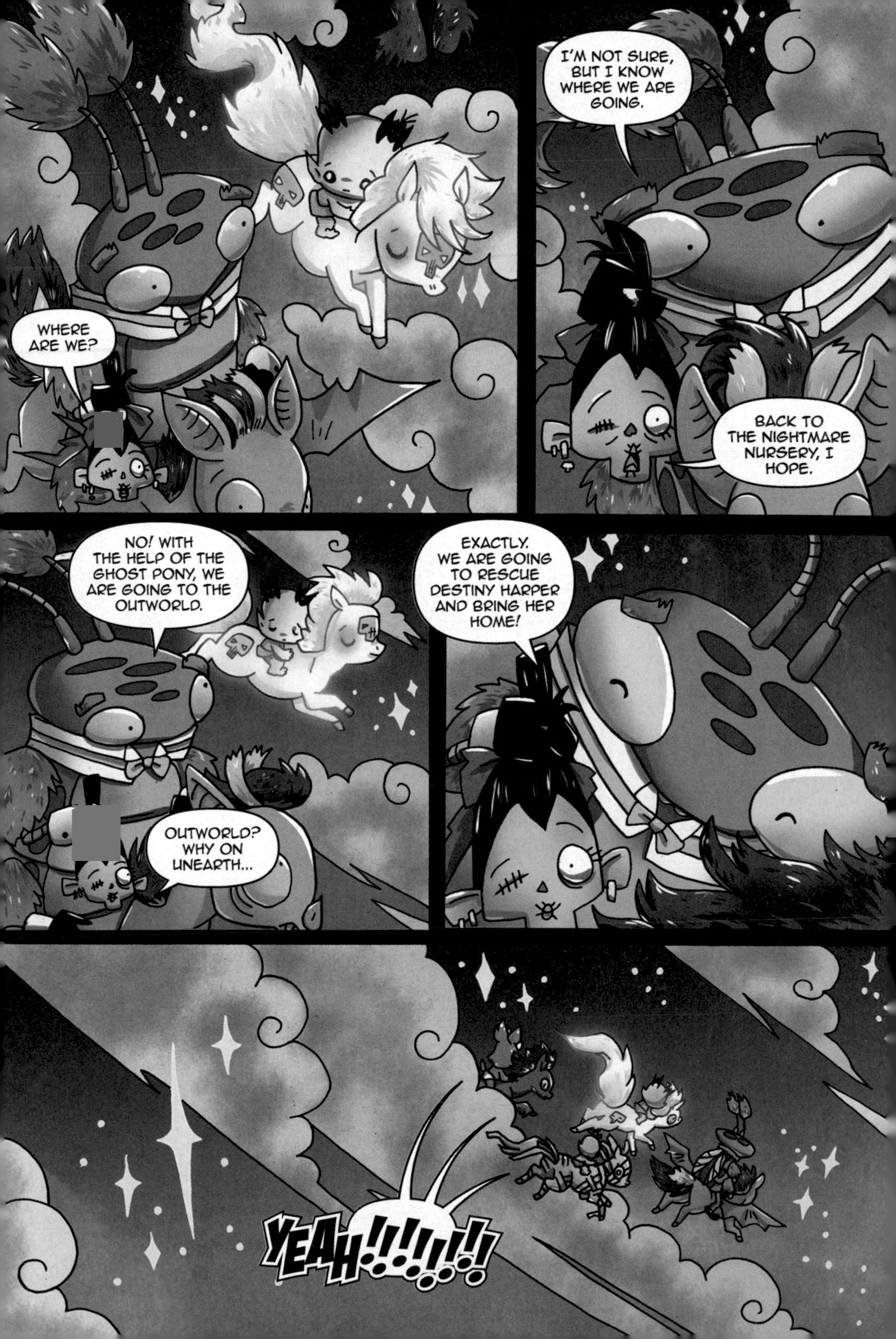
WHERE ARE WE?
I'M NOT SURE, BUT I KNOW WHERE WE ARE GOING.
BACK TO THE NIGHTMARE NURSERY, I HOPE.
NO! WITH THE HELP OF THE GHOST PONY, WE ARE GOING TO THE OUTWORLD.
OUTWORLD? WHY ON UNEARTH...
EXACTLY. WE ARE GOING TO RESCUE DESTINY HARPER AND BRING HER HOME!
YEAH!!!!!!!

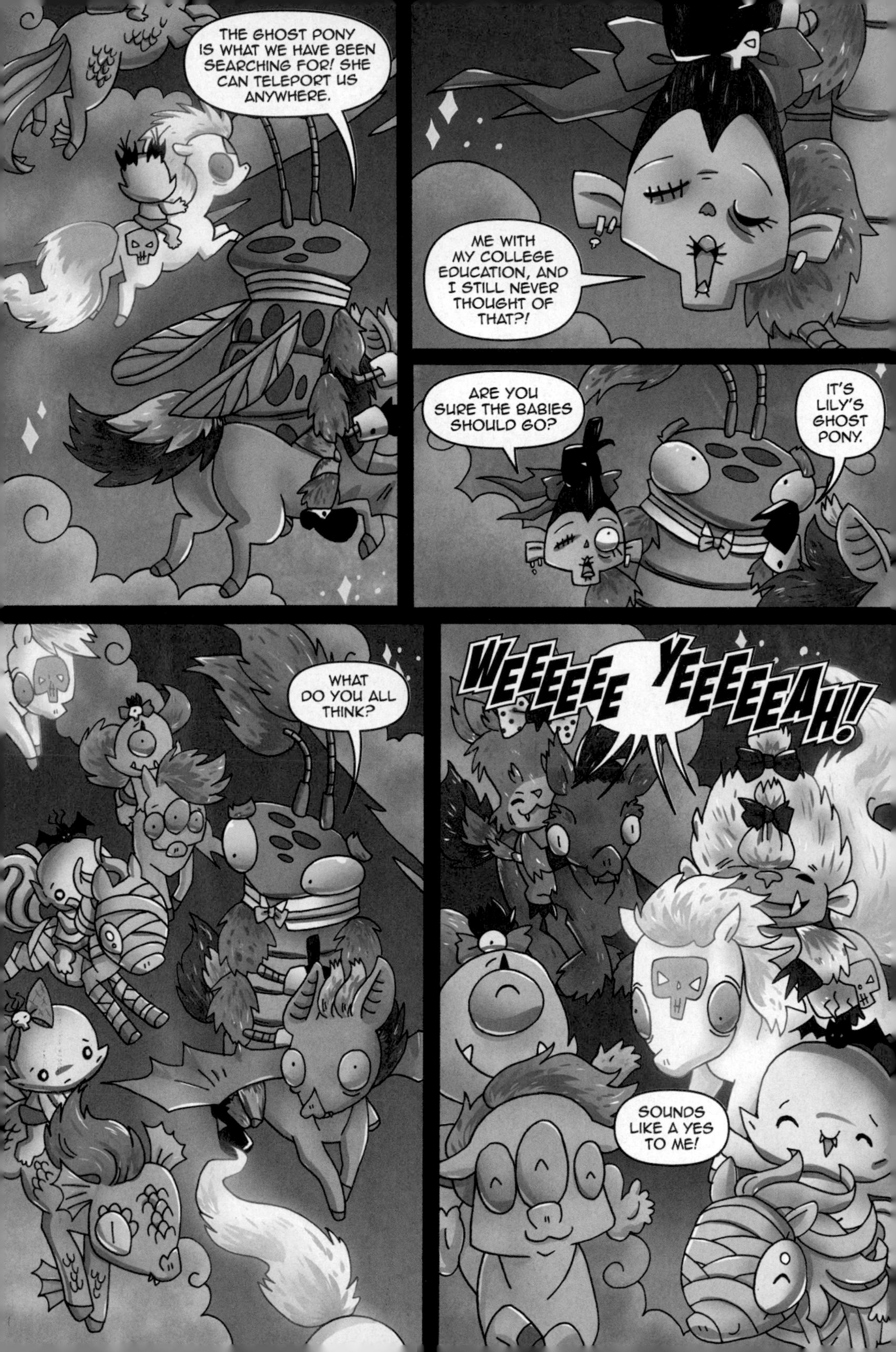
THE GHOST PONY IS WHAT WE HAVE BEEN SEARCHING FOR! SHE CAN TELEPORT US ANYWHERE.
ME WITH MY COLLEGE EDUCATION, AND I STILL NEVER THOUGHT OF THAT?!
ARE YOU SURE THE BABIES SHOULD GO?
IT'S LILY'S GHOST PONY.
WHAT DO YOU ALL THINK?
WEEEEEE YEEEEEAH!
SOUNDS LIKE A YES TO ME!

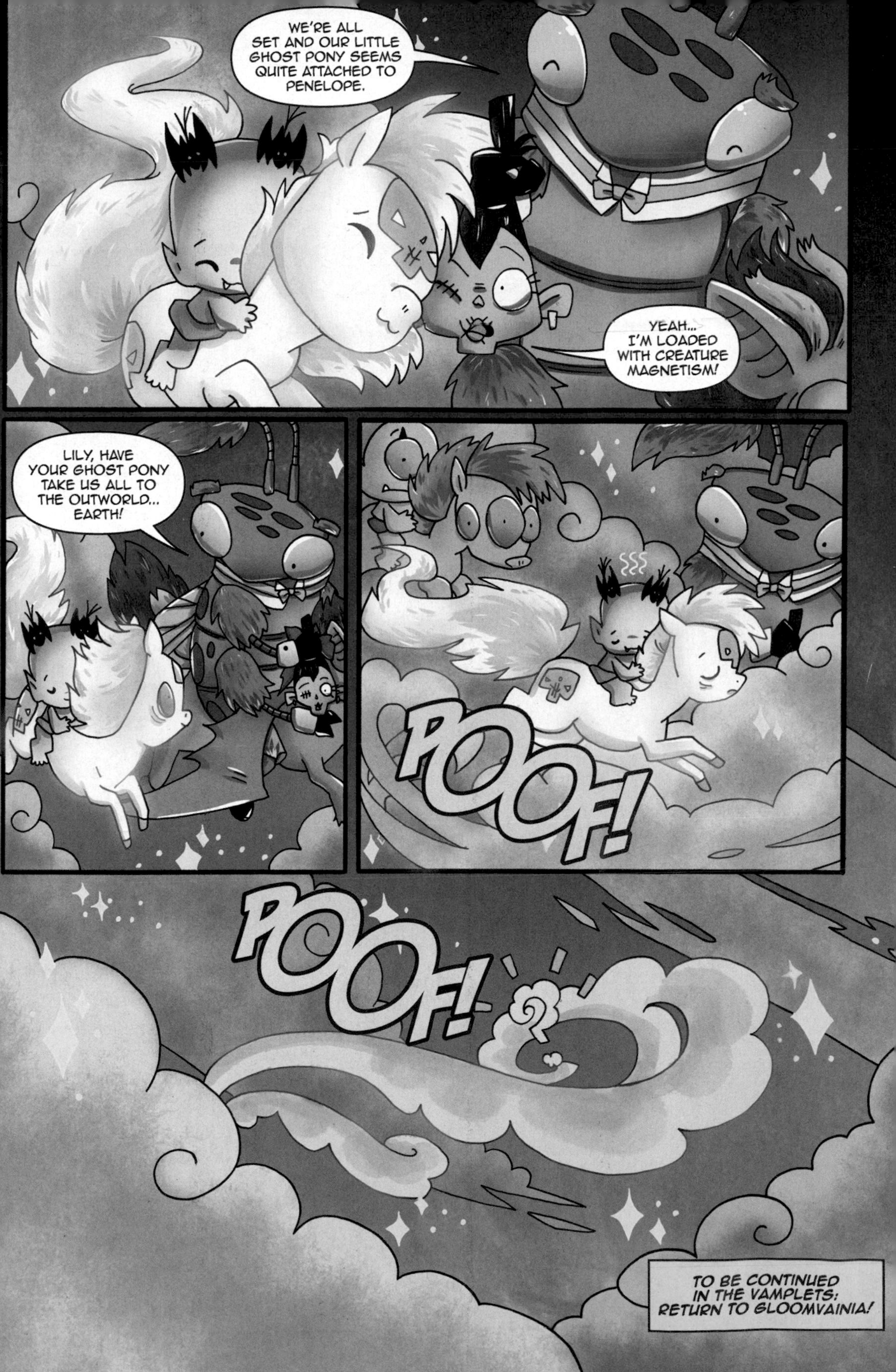
WE'RE ALL SET AND OUR LITTLE GHOST PONY SEEMS QUITE ATTACHED TO PENELOPE.
YEAH... I'M LOADED WITH CREATURE MAGNETISM!
LILY, HAVE YOUR GHOST PONY TAKE US ALL TO THE OUTWORLD... EARTH!
POOOF!
POOOF!
TO BE CONTINUED IN THE VAMPLETS: RETURN TO GLOOMVAINIA!

UNDEAD PET SOCIETY COVER GALLERY

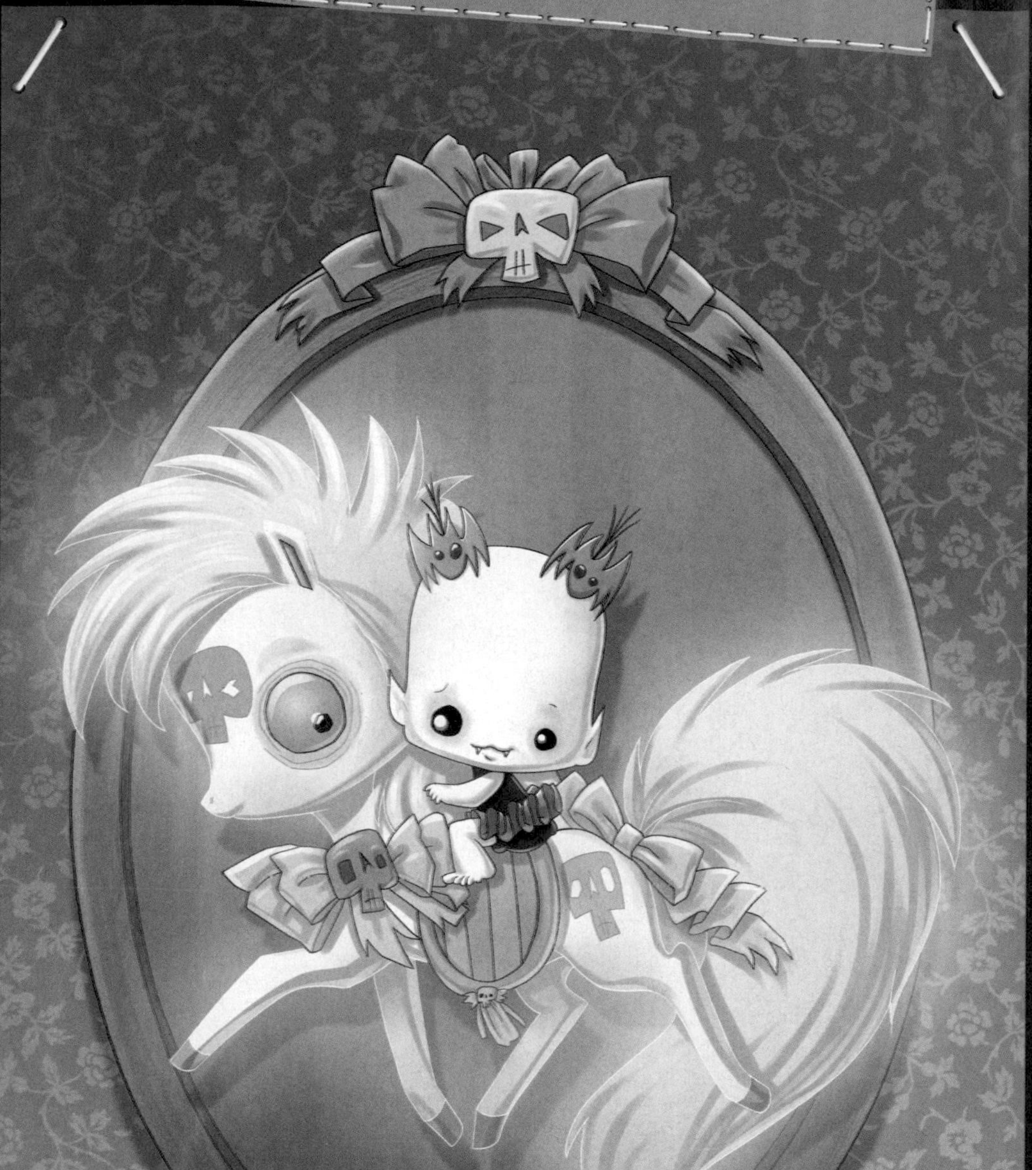

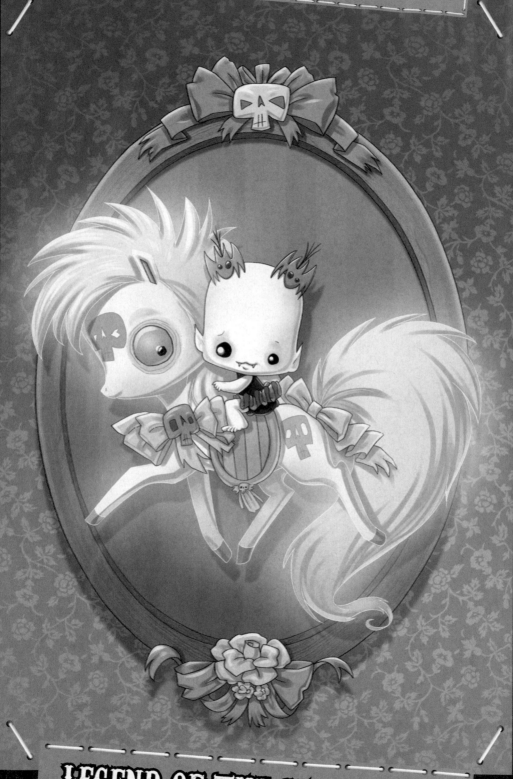

LEGEND OF THE GHOST PONY

UNDEAD PET SOCIETY COVER GALLERY

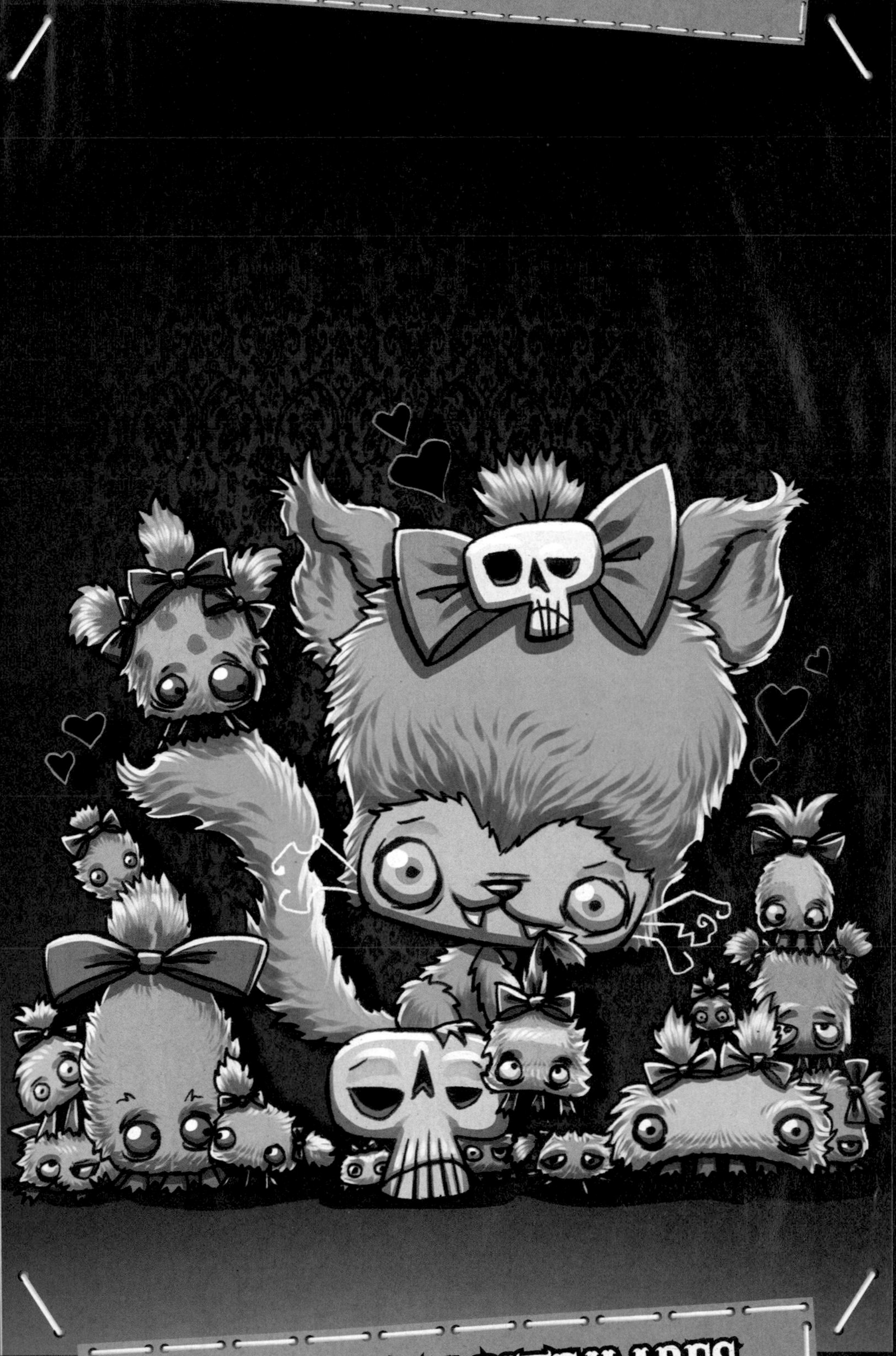

BEWARE THE BITEMARES

UNDEAD PET SOCIETY COVER GALLERY

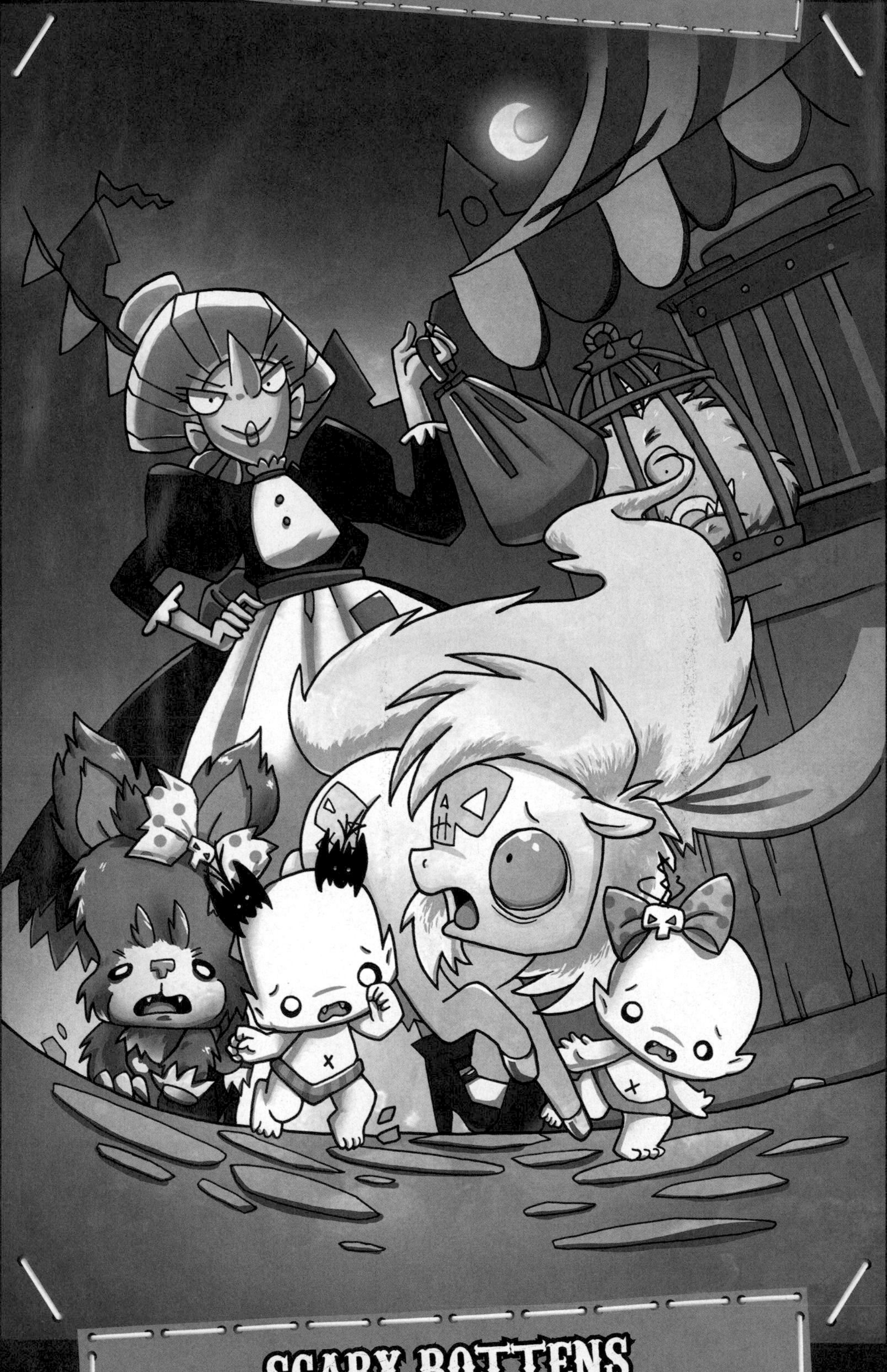

SCARY ROTTENS

UNDEAD PET SOCIETY COVER GALLERY

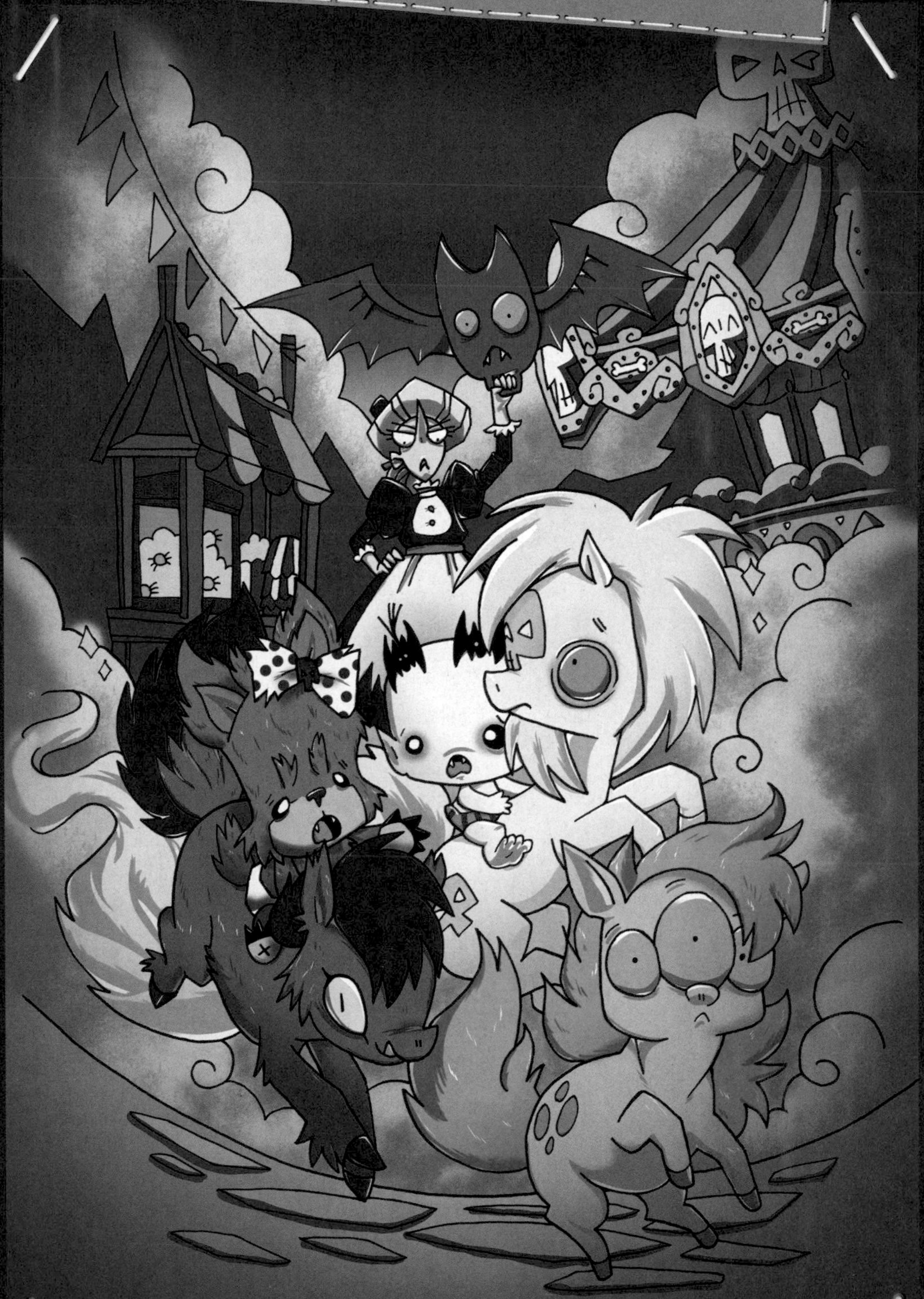

UNDEAD PET SOCIETY TPB

UNDEAD PET SOCIETY EXTRA COVERS

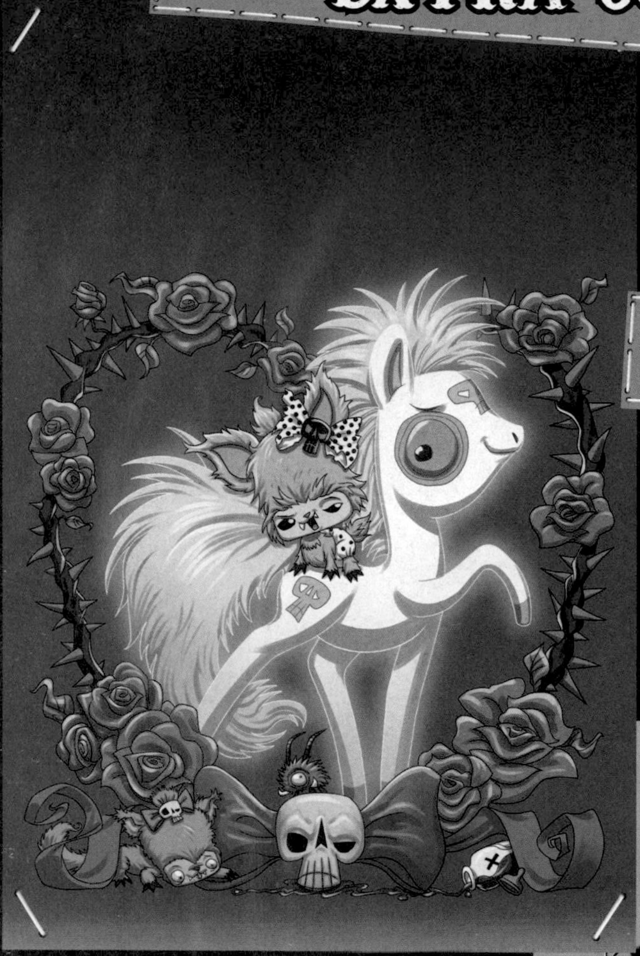

LEGEND OF THE GHOST PONY KICKSTARTER COVER

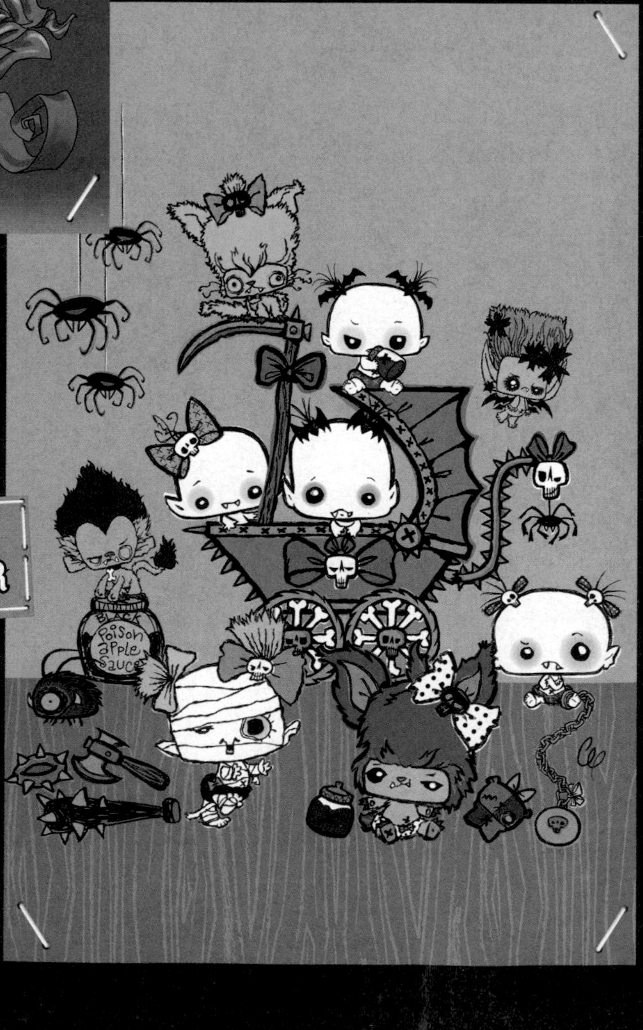
BLACK
Poison apple sauce

BEWARE THE BITEMARES SAN DIEGO COMIC-CON COVER